HAVE
Bassoon,
WILL TRAVEL

HAVE
Bassoon,
WILL TRAVEL

MEMOIR OF AN ADVENTUROUS
LIFE IN MUSIC

by George Zukerman

RONSDALE PRESS

HAVE BASSOON, WILL TRAVEL
Copyright © 2024 George Zukerman

RONSDALE PRESS
125A — 1030 Denman Street, Vancouver, B.C. Canada V6G 2M6
www.ronsdalepress.com

Book Design: Julie Cochrane
Cover Design: David Lester
Edited by Pille Bunnell & Audrey McClellan

Ronsdale Press wishes to thank the following for their support of its publishing program: the Canada Council for the Arts, the Government of Canada, the British Columbia Arts Council, and the Province of British Columbia through the British Columbia Book Publishing Tax Credit program.

Library and Archives Canada Cataloguing in Publication

Title: Have bassoon, will travel : George Zukerman's musical adventures / George Zukerman
Names: Zukerman, George, 1927-2023.
Identifiers: Canadiana (print) 20240323394 | Canadiana (ebook) 20240323408
  | ISBN 9781553807131 (softcover) | ISBN 9781553807148 (EPUB)
  | ISBN 9781553807155 (PDF)
Subjects: LCSH: Zukerman, George, 1927-2023. | LCSH: Bassoonists—Canada—
  Biography.
Classification: LCC ML419.Z94 A3 2024 | DDC 788.5/8092—dc23

At Ronsdale Press we are committed to protecting the environment. To this end we are working with Canopy and printers to phase out our use of paper produced from ancient forests. This book is one step towards that goal.

Printed in Canada

How should those who know of God meet and part?
The way an old musician greets his beloved instrument
And will take special care, as a great artist always does
To enhance the final note of each Performance.

—Hafiz, circa 1387

CONTENTS

Concerto for Two Hats

It would have been a lot easier if this book had been a biography. Then somebody else would be changing my hat or flicking a toggle switch between the two sides of my existence.

Instead, I have ended up with the task of describing a curious divide, spread evenly across most of my nine decades. On the one side I was a soloist, on the other a concert manager. When the switch was pressed a light shone, first on my world of performance, then on the business that made the music happen. Pressed again, I reverted to concert artist ... or was it a community organizer? Is it any wonder that I seldom knew whether to call myself virtuoso or impresario?

The answer, of course, is that I was both. The two roles in my life have always been inexorably intertwined. As far back as I can remember, I played concerts, appeared with ensembles or orchestras (kindly switch the toggle) and simultaneously planned tours, attended conferences and organized community audiences. Out of this pleasurable confusion poured a plethora of concert performances and a meteoric shower of logistical meetings. The result was vast tour plans for visiting artists, hundreds of concerts in unlikely places, and countless solo recitals and international tours. All of them gave me the opportunity to bring much music to Canada and, at the same time, take so much music from Canada to other shores.

If anyone had asked me, I doubt I would have been able to say precisely where the dividing line between the life of the virtuoso and the life of the impresario fell. It will forever remain unclear whether I was a soloist who managed and organized concerts on the side, or a concert manager who played solo recitals and chamber music in his spare time. I was never sure which hat or hats I would be wearing on any day.

Much of the action took place in Canada at a time when the nation was growing up musically. In the 1950s and 1960s, whatever one ventured was often being tried for the first time in the country's musical history. That was the wonder and miracle of music in Canada. Although I thought little about it at the time, it was also vitally important that, whether I was playing or organizing, I did things well, so that the next generation could build on what I, and my musical colleagues, had started.

By launching a solo career on my instrument, the bassoon, I did my best to free it from penal servitude in the back ranks of a symphony orchestra. My worldwide touring as a bassoon soloist cultivated audience awareness of this unusual instrument and its solo repertoire. I have been called "the high priest of the bassoon," "the Pablo Casals of the bassoon" and even "the Eddie Van Halen of the bassoon." Equally importantly, my performances kindled a fierce and enduring bassoon pride in the generation of young players who have followed me.

As impresario, I helped myriad Canadian communities develop self-supporting audiences for a vast spectrum of classical touring artists and ensembles. Then, just before the millennium, I launched Remote Tours Canada to bring instrumental groups to the smallest and most isolated communities in Canada's vast north. Those events in remote communities were far from traditional concerts. If anything, they served as a musical bridge between societies. Perhaps they could be described as a form of reconciliation through music, put into practice long before reconciliation became recognized as an essential national goal.

By organizing the tours, and sometimes playing in them, too, I often found myself wearing both hats simultaneously. This made it even more difficult to solve that ancient riddle: which came first, the Concert chicken or the Management egg? *Virtusario* or *Impresoso*? For the answer, we need to go back to where it all began.

I: INTRODUCTION

Finding Wings

England

If I glance at a faint scar on the palm of my right hand, memories flood back from a languid and sheltered childhood, growing up in England in the late 1920s. I recall a fall on a tiled patio with an oriental design pointing toward a flight of downward steps. At the bottom there is a beach. A distant wave rolls in across the foot of the sand, and a light drizzle is falling. As the sun tries to break through, somebody calls out, "Look, a rainbow!" I run over to see, and tumble down. There remains a child's irrational pain, a mother's loving grasp, a doctor's cooling hand, a tiny scar that has grown with me through eight decades.

The images come a little more frequently. I, perhaps less than three years old, am standing with my mother by a fence. Behind it is an airplane raging furiously, like a horse pawing the earth, its single propeller creating a blur of colour and noise, a shrieking sound, as if it were crying desperately to be allowed to take off. The pilot, its protector, stands by his cabin and waves heroically to us. Though he is hidden behind his helmet and shiny goggles, I wave back and suddenly discover that my hand is free. My mother is no longer there. I am lost! As the plane taxis away, I see that the pilot is still waving to me but I have nothing to cling to until another protector, with a tall policeman's hat, takes me on a tearful walk along the beachfront. Hand in hand with the local bobby, an hour later I am reunited with frantic parents.

Another summer holiday: a storm rolls in to a beachfront village. Rockets shoot up from the lifeboat rescue centre, and brave fishermen strike out to sea in tiny wave-tossed ships to reach a stranded freighter. My brother and

George and his brother, Joseph, with their mother, Frieda.

I watch in awe as a returning rocket strikes the thatched roof of a nearby village home. The flames are immense and dazzling, the house quickly engulfed. The rescue attention shifts from sea to land even as the rescue ships return, unable to reach the wreck. My mother takes us home before we see the misery of the house owners, the shame of the failed lifeboat rescue and the tragedy of daily life. Such things should not happen on a holiday.

Back in London: it is now October 1930. The pictures of the blazing wreckage and tangled steel framework of the airship R101 are on every newspaper front page. Images of falling, flying, burning and loss seem to encroach on all of those earliest childhood memories.

When George VI is crowned in 1937, we celebrate on the sports field below our school. I am trying to run but I cannot because one leg is tied to the leg of another boy of about my age. We are competing in the three-legged egg-and-spoon race. We are in the lead, our spoon extended. The finish line and victory lie immediately ahead of us, but as we reach for them, hobbling ever faster forward, the egg rolls off our spoon, and another couple of tied and giggling classmates crosses the line with their egg intact. What disaster!

There are also moments of playful conspiracy. My mother and I share a secret: she smokes, and I go to the shops to bring back her package of Player's. My role in the game is to insist on a shilling to buy four three-penny packets of three cigarettes each instead of the economical package of twelve for ten pence. In this way I collect four coveted cigarette cards instead of just one. While the manufacturers presumably bide their time for the day when we will buy their product for purposes of consumption, at this stage they are satisfied to prove their educational commitment to

George as a boy in the 1930s.

Britain's youth. What are they this week? Railway trains? Cricketers? Fish of the North Sea? Kings of England? Complete sets are prize currency to exchange for gleaming marbles on the school playground. Players indeed.

There is also the excitement of a journey to my journalist father's city office on Fleet Street, perhaps to watch a parade from his fourth-floor window overlooking that famous street of newspapers. The bus from Golders Green passes by Selfridges, Marble Arch, Wigmore Hall and Charing Cross Station. We walk past the citadels of the great newspapers of the day. Lingering in the air is the pungent smell of printers' ink and Linotype lead, and everywhere the rumbling roar of the presses. It is my earliest introduction to the thrill of printing and publications, the realization that words come to life through these massive machines.

As a child I collected autographs, although not very successfully. From my entire early time in London, only four pages of my book were filled. My father's name occupied the first page. (He is famous, at least in my childhood eyes.) A middle page was sanctified with the scrawled signature of cricketer Donald Bradman, obtained by crawling through a broken fence at Lord's Cricket Ground and boldly approaching the Australian team at tea time. Emma Goldman, anarchist and social activist, filled both pages three and four. Did I recognize her celebrity or grasp her link with my father's Jewish-socialist roots?

∼ BASSOON ENCOUNTER

Not surprisingly, the first time I saw a bassoon I had no idea what it was. At eleven and a half years of age, I was on the threshold of attending a well-known London "prep" school, the University College, on Frognal Lane in Hampstead. My brother, who had earlier gained a coveted scholarship, was proudly showing me around. We wandered past the windows of a basement chapel and glanced down to where an orchestra was rehearsing. A row of tall pipes seemed to reach for the ceiling. I could see and hear very little through the moss-covered stone walls and grimy opaque windows of the old school, and I wondered what on earth these strange-looking instruments were. My brother, already in Form IV, authority on much, including most musical matters, declared them to be bassoons, and the piece in rehearsal the annual *Messiah*. We walked on to explore my new school, and any awareness that I would spend my life playing that instrument would have been uncannily prescient. The bassoon remained buried deep among early memories.

There was music at Wessex Gardens Primary, but the choir, conducted by Miss Imogene Chillistone, engendered fear and dislike. How I dreaded those sessions! As I think back, I realize that she just wanted us to open our mouths wide and sing. "Sing, sing, like birds. Let your souls jump out!" she trilled. But the choir was too rigid; Miss Chillistone too chilly (does everyone fit their name so clearly?); the words of the songs too remote. "Begone, dull care! I prithee be gone from me!"—yes, I was prepared to go. There was more childhood confusion as we sang, "All we like sheep." Indeed, why shouldn't we like them?

My brother studied piano each week with an alluring Russian émigrée, Miss Movshovitz ("Miss Mov" for our anglicized simplicity). I was besotted with the mystery and faint perfume of this wraithlike woman from my mother's home village of Novye Dorogi in today's Belarus. The voluble post-lesson sounds of Russian thrilled me with the excitement of a foreign language. But the discussions between my socialist parents and the monarchist teacher were deeply political, often bitter. Nobody, at that time, explained to me the difference between communists and conservatives. They both began with the letter "C." Oblivious of political extremes, I insisted on piano lessons. At least they were neutral, and in any case, I was consumed with jealousy at my brother's proximity to Miss Mov.

Neither Miss Chillistone's choir nor Miss Mov's keyboard took serious musical root.

≈ OF FERRIES AND OCEAN LINERS

There is one last childhood memory that stands out. It is September 1939. We are on a beach in France, and there is talk of war, evacuation and a hasty return to England. We are caught up in the agony as well as the thrill of an escape. By bus, train, another bus and then a long, long walk along a pier to a waiting ferry, we move in snakelike columns made up of hundreds, all fleeing the same uncertain threat. We eventually board a vessel so crowded that we stand the entire way across the Channel, too adrenalin-filled to feel seasick from the usual rough crossing.

Prime Minister Neville Chamberlain speaks on the radio, declaring war. Thirty minutes later the sirens sound over London. There is a rushed and tearful evacuation to Littlehampton on the south coast. Hasty secrets are whispered among parents on weekends, and a decision is reached to go to America to join my mother's family in New York. Things move swiftly when they are so easily decided. A train to Southampton. Headlines of the sinking of a British ship, the SS *Athenia*. Trundling suitcases across railway tracks to shipside. The massive American flag emblazoned on the side of the SS *United States*. The lurching first swell of the sea as the ropes are cast off; the last view of the Isle of Wight; seasickness each morning. A bevy of slot machines requiring the mysterious American coin, the nickel, and then, just one day out of New York, a vast jackpot win of four hundred coins! A veritable fortune for our arrival at Pier 59.

While waiting for luggage and customs clearance at dockside, I play poker dice with a new-found cousin. The heady lessons of the slot machines were ill-learned, and the profit disappears even before we hurtle along the West Side Highway and Riverside Drive to our new home. From within the car—albeit apparently on the wrong side of the road—I am gripped by both the extraordinary sensation of speed and the remarkable first vision of New York's fabled skyscrapers.

We converge at an uptown apartment building where one of my mother's sisters lives. In the company of new aunts, uncles and cousins, my brother and I rapidly become denizens of a new neighbourhood. We become familiar with the streets, the shops, the trolleys, even the secretly foreboding entrance to the subway. It is a new land, a new way of life.

This, then, is my prelude to the next eighty years.

New York

The first challenge was to find a school. It was already October, and well into the term. In my mother's eyes, convenience prevailed over reason, and there was a school immediately adjacent to the avenue where we now lived. It was the newly founded High School of Music and Art. The school, launched just a few years earlier through a unique collaboration of New York's feisty and colourful mayor Fiorello La Guardia and conductor Arturo Toscanini, was the city's first specialized arts-related school. Entry standards, requiring some degree of musical or artistic accomplishment, were reputedly very high. Could I possibly qualify?

Perhaps those piano lessons with Miss Mov would now prove their value. I was marched down to apply at the austere building that housed the school. It had been built in faux Gothic style, and in the neighbourhood was whimsically known as the "Castle on the Hill." It didn't look like a castle, and there was no hill in sight.

By way of an audition, I played my one and only party piece (a simple Beethoven sonatina). To my surprise as much as anyone else's, I was admitted to the class of 1940! Dare I suspect that my acceptance had as much to do with short pants and an English accent as with any evident musical skill?

On the first day of school the entire first-year class of seventy youngsters was herded into a gym. Shelves surrounded the playing area, and although ropes descended from the ceiling and basketball nets hovered over the central space, there was no gym equipment anywhere in sight. Instead, there was an array of musical instruments on display.

"Boys and girls," announced principal Benjamin Steigman, poet, philosopher, author and passionate advocate for this unique school, "you are about to become an orchestra." He waved vaguely at us all, as if his very wish would turn us into instant virtuosi. He pointed to the shelves. "Take an instrument . . . any instrument of your choice . . ."

No British prep school could have readied me for such democratic and independent action, so I hesitated. On all sides of me, the pushy American kids ran furiously and grasped what they could most easily identify. The violins, clarinets, flutes, trumpets, cellos and drums disappeared into groping hands. When I finally reached the shelf, all that remained was an anonymous black box. I lifted it gently and carried it toward a teacher standing nearby. "Excuse me, Sir," I asked timidly, "but what is this?"

He looked down, and a broad smile covered his face. "Why, you are our bassoonist!" he declared. For a brief moment I recalled that *Messiah* rehearsal and the four mysterious pipes turned skyward. Hadn't my brother declared them bassoons? Was I now going to play such an instrument? Could one of those long pipes really fit in the black box I was holding? Worse yet, could my brother possibly have been wrong? Doubt must have suffused my face. The teacher put a consoling arm around my shoulder. "Yes," he repeated, "you really are our new bassoonist."

∼ THE RED BOOK

From the very first day at school, we were divided into predictable ensembles. The string players formed trios and quartets. The tuba player was given an opportunity to join a brass band. As a bassoonist, I was condemned to a woodwind quintet—that hybrid instrumental mix that combines the bass of the wind family with a flute, an oboe, a clarinet and a French horn.

As we were first learning to play our instruments, we also began, hesitantly, to read simple woodwind arrangements. Out came a dog-eared, tattered volume, a collection of varied classical transcriptions for wind quintet, known by generations of wind players as the "Red Book." First published in 1895, it was still in use in 1941, and for all I know it may still be around today.

As we played from it, it struck me that each instrument in the wind quintet was so individual that the ensemble would always be five soloists, vying for the most colourful leading part. The quintet boasted three prima donna sopranos, the flute, oboe, and clarinet, each forever seeking a melody. The bassoon, not satisfied to be consigned to the eternal bass line, longed to be a tenor whenever it could grab the spotlight. And the French horn, which was neither fish nor fowl in this ensemble, added colour and distinction, but—because of its brass origin—resisted blending with the others. Much as I enjoyed being part of an ensemble, I was not fond of either the woodwind quintet or the contents of the Red Book. Not until I heard and was utterly enchanted by Paul Hindemith's *Kleine Kammermusik für Bläserquintett.*

At the very top of the Castle on the Hill stood the "tower room"—a decorated turret, complete with an array of early twentieth-century gargoyles. The tower had been converted into a rehearsal hall. There were no elevators, so each day members of the school's senior orchestra trudged up six flights of stairs to rehearse. On special occasions they played there for distinguished visitors. Eminent conductors Arturo Toscanini, Leopold Stokowski, John Barbirolli had each come to the school in its early days.

When Paul Hindemith was the guest of honour, the finest wind players in the school were "sent to the tower" to play his quintet for him. The *Kleine Kammermusik* had a well-earned reputation for its difficulty. The invitation must have been both an honour and an occasion of profound trepidation for those who were called to play. Even as a listener I shared their fears. Will they get it right? How can they dare to second-guess a composer's intentions and meaning? What will he say? None of us need have worried. Even as they progressed through the work's five movements, we could tell that Hindemith was enjoying reliving his 1922 work and revelling in the youthful enthusiasm and vitality of the players.

Hindemith's success with the wind quintet was clear. Instead of lengthy melodic lines, he found unity in common rhythm. In the fourth movement, which is a brilliantly conceived cadenza, Hindemith allows each of the instruments a moment of glorious virtuosic display. The French horn sums up everything with five resounding notes, leading to a finale of fierce and determined rhythmic patterns.

The players at that performance were a remarkable group, each of whom later graduated to major positions in North American musical life. The horn player, who had the least to play, had the most to say. I can hear his nameless self, standing and innocently posing a question to the composer. "Mr. Hindemith," he said, "you gave everyone a wonderful cadenza, except for the horn. You left us just five notes. Is that fair?" Hindemith replied smoothly, in his heavily accented English, "Of course, my friend—only five notes. But ach! What five notes they are! Without them, there could be no finale."

⁓ RADIO AD HOC

In December 1941, my peaceful high school existence amidst bassoons, trumpets, flutes and violins was shattered by the American entry into the world war. Reality arrived for us with the unprecedented interruption of a Sunday afternoon broadcast of the New York Philharmonic to announce the attack on Pearl Harbor. The shock, the damage and the loss of life shook America out of isolationist lethargy. By the next day the nation was at war with Japan, and two days later, with Germany and Italy.

At school, Principal Benjamin Steigman wrote stirring words for a school song (set to Brahms's First Symphony): "Now upwards in wonder, our distant glance is turning, while brightly through ages, th'eternal light is burning ... our task unending, defending that realm above ..."

I suppose that this metaphysical suggestion was designed to turn us all toward the war effort, but somehow classes continued with a semblance of normalcy, and we found ourselves striving to move upward, not seeking eternal light but hoping instead to rise through the ranks of the school orchestras. There was one for each term of school, and the ultimate goal was the "senior" eighth-term orchestra.

By my third year I had made it comfortably to the seventh level and was on the threshold of moving into the exalted ranks of the seniors when we were told that we would be allowed to graduate six months early. Instead of a graduation ceremony, we were instructed to pick up our diplomas at the office.

Once on the outside, I joined with musical friends to found what we fondly named the New Chamber Music Society. What a pretentious title that was. For what little we knew, there may have been twelve other chamber music societies, new and old alike—but that didn't faze us! Besides, we reasoned, it was highly unlikely that anyone would ever hear us publicly!

One of us had found a copy of the Red Book, and we started with the little-loved woodwind quintet. It did not take us long to discover that there had been a heyday for woodwind compositions in the early nineteenth century. Franz Danzi and Anton Reicha, the one acquainted with Mozart, the latter a close friend of Beethoven, churned out an abundance of lengthy quintets. Not surprisingly, they comprised mainly a succession of alternating solo passages for the five virtuoso players. Each quintet became a shining opportunity for players of the day to show what their newly improved instruments could do in the hands of a master.

But we were not yet masters, and in any case, I was fervently jealous of the string players with their vast libraries of repertoire. I longed for the homogeneity of sound that they produced in their ensembles. We started sight-reading string quartets. There were obvious limitations. Flutes could not play pizzicato; oboes were limited in range; clarinets could not create harmonics; bassoons couldn't sustain double stops; and the French horn drowned out everyone else.

We met at each other's homes as frequently as we could to plough through whatever music we could lay our hands on. We were impulsive, musically reckless, with inexhaustible energy and curiosity. Our goals were boundless. We played Beethoven string quartets. We even tackled Heinrich Schütz's *Symphoniae sacrae* and Dieterich Buxtehude cantatas on our modern instruments, long before Early Music styles came into twentieth-century vogue.

In complete innocence, one of us approached the municipal radio station, WNYC, and proposed a weekly chamber music series. To our utter astonishment, the idea was accepted. For the next seventeen weeks, every Saturday morning we were invited to broadcast whatever repertoire we could assemble—winds, strings, voices, keyboard. WNYC seemed willing to accept whatever we produced. We were willing to try anything.

We soon realized why we had been offered such a glowing opportunity. It was easy to forget that this was wartime. Our ranks were constantly diminished by the irresistible call of the military draft board. From week to week, it was impossible to be certain who would still be there to play and who would be undergoing basic training at some distant military encampment.

Only two of us, clarinetist and composer Meyer Kupferman and myself, were underage for military service. I lived at the upper end of Manhattan. Meyer lived in Coney Island at the far reaches of Brooklyn. We each had to travel an hour by subway to reach the broadcast studio.

On the way each Saturday morning I would write a script, and Meyer would fill page after page of his music notebook with new compositions. At the broadcast, if necessary, we would fill the allotted time with his sketches, sight-read by whoever turned up at the studio. In reserve were always the three Beethoven duos for clarinet and bassoon, which Meyer and I had committed to memory in order to save time setting up music stands.

One Saturday morning we were planning to open the program with the great Mozart Divertimento for violin, viola and cello. We were anxiously waiting for the viola player to arrive. Instead, his sister turned up, clutching a trumpet case. "I came down to tell you that Jonathan has been called up. He left for Fort Dix early this morning. He didn't know how to reach you, so I offered to take the subway to let you know." Her instrument case was halfway open. "I could play, if you wanted," she added, both hesitantly and hopefully. The yellow studio warning light flashed. We had five minutes before going on the air with a violin, a clarinet, a cello, a bassoon—and now, a trumpet. The Mozart would have to be abandoned. We moved four music stands into a semicircle, and Meyer distributed his morning sketches, the ink still wet.

As we went on the air, I glibly announced that the New Chamber Music Society would begin with this new work. For twenty-two and a half minutes we valiantly sight-read from parts written originally for other instruments.

Parts of Meyer's work that morning were for a trio, so I rushed downstairs to the Municipal Music Library. There, by utter chance, I discovered the *Serenata*, written by Alfredo Casella in the late 1920s. I knew neither the work nor the composer, but it had won an international competition in Philadelphia, jointly with Béla Bartók's third string quartet when it was first written.

Fortunately, on each page of Meyer's Saturday morning compositions, he always took the precaution of writing a "coda" or closing section. As I re-entered the studio with the new work, he gave a signal to the ensemble, and even as his *Trio Sketch* came to a close, I arranged an additional music stand and chair and put out the music of the Casella. This time, each player received music actually written for his or her instrument.

I then took the microphone to introduce the *Serenata*. It seemed prudent to offer the listening audience—if, indeed, anyone was still listening—some explanation of what was happening in Studio 15 that morning.

"Good morning, ladies and gentlemen," I began. "As a unique experiment in broadcasting, we thought that listeners might be interested to eavesdrop on a public rehearsal of a brand-new work. This morning you will hear how a young ensemble rehearses a piece they have never before seen. We may stop and restart at any moment. We may have disagreements on how a certain passage should be played. This, we assure you, is all part of the excitement of discovery and rehearsal and will surely provide you with a valuable insight into how we go about learning and giving shape to new works in our repertoire."

With that, for the remaining thirty-three minutes of the program, we sight-read the Casella with stops and starts and discussions and arguments, exactly as promised. Since that hair-raising experience (both for us and for the audience), the work has become one of my all-time favourite pieces for ensemble concerts—subject to those rare occasions on which such an unusual instrumental combination can be assembled!

Eventually the municipal radio station determined, probably wisely, that Saturday morning listeners had heard enough of the *Sketches from the Composer's Notebook*, and even the Beethoven clarinet and bassoon duos. The replacement show was a thirty-minute newscast, followed by *Thirty Minutes to Read By*, which consisted of half an hour of absolute silence, and was appropriately sponsored by the New York Public Library.

By this time I had joined the musicians' union (the American Federation of Musicians of the United States and Canada), in fond hope that other playing (and paying) opportunities might arise. One day there was a phone call asking me to take part in a recording session of obscure twentieth-century American repertoire under the baton of an unknown young conductor—Leonard Bernstein.

In retrospect I realize that the contractor who engaged me for that job must have been close to panic as, one by one, he found that his regular bassoon players had been drafted for military service and sent to the foreboding staging post at Fort Dix. In desperation, he must have scrolled down the alphabetical list of union members. He had a long way to go to get to the letter "Z," where he was eventually rewarded with a live player, not yet recruited to the armed forces, apparently owning a bassoon and actually available for his engagement.

I do not recall a single note of that session, but six years later, Bernstein, by then widely acclaimed, invited me to join the Israel Philharmonic. I often wonder if he remembered that we had briefly crossed paths in a dingy 49th Street recording studio.

～ YOU MUST TAKE THE "A" TRAIN

Shortly before my seventeenth birthday, my father returned from England, where, during the early days of the war, he had maintained a European office for a consortium of three of the four New York Yiddish newspapers. Although they could no longer afford to keep him overseas, his employers still needed a regular flow of information from the chief of their former European bureau.

He promptly turned our apartment into his office. To meet his employers' needs, he would often prepare the same release from three different viewpoints: quasi-socialist for the *Jewish Daily Forward*; mildly business-oriented for *The Day*; and distinctly right-wing for the *Morning Journal*. Each newspaper ran parts of their news in Yiddish, and for a younger generation there were sections in English.

On a central desk my father had positioned both Yiddish and English typewriters. They could never be used simultaneously, since the carriage on the Yiddish keyboard travelled from left to right and would inevitably collide with the English machine travelling in the opposite direction. The machinery reflected the clash of cultures which every day filled the columns of all three newspapers.

My father was forever obsessed with deadlines and felt that he could not trust the once-reliable U.S. Postal Service to deliver his articles on time. Often I was asked to take those manuscripts to the main post office at Pennsylvania Station, or even all the way downtown to the various newspaper offices, which were located on the city's East Side.

New York was still a relatively safe city, and we thought nothing of travelling alone at night on the city's vast subway network. However, I lived in eternal fear of delivering the wrong envelope to the wrong newspaper.

To complete my postal missions, I would take the "A" express downtown. Duke Ellington's "Take the 'A' Train" was at the height of its popularity. Years later it crossed my mind that the Duke might have chosen to name his hit song after the "D" local to the Bronx or even the "F" express to Queens. Yet, somehow, the lyric "You must take the 'F' Train" would not have sounded quite right, either then or in our present century!

In order to gather and distribute information for his news service, my father eventually had a telex machine installed in the apartment. It was judiciously placed between the two typewriters. Having a telex was so unusual for a private residence that one evening at dinner, the apartment was raided by the local police gambling squad. A neighbour had blown the whistle, convinced that the endless chattering of the telex in Apartment 5A could only mean that our building had been turned into a gaming establishment. The police arrived with a warrant for that notorious bookie, William Zukerman. With a tip of a teenage hat, he was fondly renamed Willie the Zuk.

Shortly after our brush with the law, it became my turn to enlist. If I acted quickly I had a choice of service. Merchant Marine? Navy? At least I didn't have to wait for the postman to bring me the notice from the draft board. (Somehow, for that task the mail service remained as reliable as ever.) Manpower was in short supply, and in less than two weeks I was rapaciously accepted into the folds of the U.S. Navy. Willie the Zuk would have to manage without me for a while.

∾ WILLIE THE ZUK

An unlikely bookie, William Zukerman, Yiddishist, poet, writer, essayist, dreamer, pacifist, was a dedicated man who unfortunately never had much time to be a father to his two boys. Most of what I now recall of this extraordinarily mild and gentle man comes from faint memories of family life and lore, some tantalizing photographs from the time of World War I, and the 1931 memoirs of a grandfather I never met. Here's what I believe fashioned my father, William Zukerman.

As a boy of fifteen, in the year 1900, he travelled from near Vilna (now Vilnius)—one of those gloried seats of eastern European Jewry, part of the former Polish-Lithuanian empire—to join his father, Max, who had preceded the rest of the family to the United States. Pogroms were never far from their Lithuanian doorstep, and like so many families, they arranged to send one child at a time to safety in the new world. My father was the first to undertake the harrowing journey.

He crossed Europe by rail and recorded his impressions on scraps of paper that he hoarded as he travelled. At Rotterdam he boarded the SS *Darmstadt*. After less than a day at sea, he was accosted by a zealous group of older passengers who demanded to inspect his package of food. A self-appointed rabbinical court, they had taken it upon themselves to assure the purity of food consumed by all other Jewish passengers. It was an example of schoolyard bullying as much as an assertion of orthodoxy. His food was declared *trefe* (not kosher) and thrown overboard. For the rest of the sixteen-day journey he had to depend on the goodwill of other passengers to provide enough to eat. It left the young boy badly frightened and extremely hungry. But not so frightened that he could not record the shipboard events on those scraps of paper.

Not surprisingly, this single incident ignited in him a lifelong flame of hatred for orthodoxy.

His ship docked at Baltimore, and he sat for three days in an immigration centre, watching many of his fellow passengers swaying in ritual prayer. Even at age fifteen he had trouble reconciling the futility and frustration of the Orthodox practices that surrounded him with the hope and promise of the new land. He recorded these thoughts, too, on fresh scraps of paper.

Finally, on October 3, 1900, he was admitted to the new land. (The day and date are clear because exactly five years later he appeared before Circuit Judge Wilbur Ambrose in Cook County Courthouse, where he pledged his allegiance to the flag of the United States and became a citizen of the country.) With very little English at his command, and a tag around his neck showing that Chicago was his destination, he walked from the immigration centre onto the streets of Baltimore. "Where is Chicago?" he asked a friendly-looking peddler holding a mule at a nearby watering post. The peddler, whose own arrival had occurred less than two years earlier, replied in Yiddish, "A long way, kid, a long way!" "So how do I get there? Where is the train station?" the young man asked. "You need the HIAS," he told my father, and proceeded to lead the mule away into the heart of the city.

Now neither in Yiddish nor English, nor any other language for that matter, did HIAS mean very much to a hungry, lonely and apprehensive youngster from Eastern Europe, spending his first days in America on the streets of Baltimore looking for Chicago. But fortunately for him, and for many others, too, HIAS (Hebrew Immigrant Aid Society) was there looking for such arrivals. Within hours he had been found by a HIAS representative and fed his first decent meal in two weeks. They gave him some money, took him down to the railway station and put him on board the train to Chicago. Then they sent a telegram to the Chicago address that had been sewn to the inside of the youngster's jacket before he left home.

Telegrams worked in the new millennium, and William Zukerman was greeted at Chicago's Grand Central Station by his father and, more memorably, as recorded on one of the last scraps of paper, by the pervading stench of the Chicago stockyards.

William Zukerman, new immigrant to a new land, instantly started to blend into the vast melting pot that he was to come to love. Even within the framework of the Jewish society in which he would continue to live, he dedicated himself to assimilation into the life of the new country.

His first task was to go to school. He could not, would not, remain locked in a ghetto, even a free ghetto where Jews lived together by choice in this wondrous new land. Why recreate everything that he had escaped from? Why accept religious or ghetto orthodoxy in his new life?

His second need was to find a job. A boy of his age strolled down the street past the row of shabby brownstone houses, tossing the *Daily Forward* onto virtually every porch. If God had sent a plague that year to free the Chicago Israelites from oppression, he would have encountered no trouble identifying the Jewish homes. My father approached the delivery boy and they struck up a conversation. By the end of the day, Zukerman had reported to the newspaper and been assigned his own delivery route. He had a job.

His third task was to write home to his mother and siblings. With three cents from his first pay package, he purchased a stamp and wrote a letter full of all the impressions of his first days in the new land. Writing was a natural outlet for him. It was fitting that he now worked for a newspaper.

His father, meantime, was no longer peddling rags from a horse-drawn cart but had become a representative of an insurance company. With the glorious salary (before commissions) of fourteen dollars a week, one by one he brought William's mother, brothers and sisters from Lithuania to join the family in Chicago.

In his third year of delivering papers, now already fluent in English but still writing comfortably and idiomatically in Yiddish, my father approached the editors of the *Daily Forward* with a story he had written based on the notes of his trip. It ran on an inside page, and he received $1.50 for his first paid article. By this time he had already graduated from high school, was paying rent at home and was attending classes at the University of Chicago. At the age of nineteen, he became a full-fledged newspaper man, moving inside to become one of several night editors. That was the year of his American citizenship.

With America's entry into World War I in 1917, he enlisted in the army and was posted overseas, assigned to liaise with the Jewish Welfare Board. His military career was uneventful, and in 1918, still in uniform, he returned to New York. At thirty-three years of age he had to either find work in the burgeoning city or return to his family in Chicago. A colleague, fellow journalist and union activist Nathan S., put him in touch with the three flourishing New York Yiddish dailies, the *Daily Forward*, the *Morning Journal*, and *The Day*, and before long his Chicago newspaper experience had earned him a job at the city desk of the *Morning Journal*.

Nathan S. also introduced William to an intriguing young lady, and in an instant any lingering thoughts of returning to Chicago evaporated. Consumed with euphoria at the pending armistice that would end the war to end all wars, on August 31, 1918, William Zukerman and Becky Goodman were married. However, Becky was not destined to be my mother.

Enter Frieda Zeltzer. She had arrived in America to live with her aunt, Nathan S.'s wife. There she met the newly married couple. At first they were all good friends. Becky showed Frieda the town; William was a gallant chaperone for the glamorous twenty-six-year-old from the village near Minsk. But the inevitable happened. William became smitten for a second time in less than a year. A hasty divorce was agreed upon, and by November 1919, William and Frieda had sailed for Europe. Frieda, who eventually became my mother, was transformed from favourite niece to

Willie the Zuk at work.

outcast. So fierce the anger, so sharp the scandal, that from that day forward, not a single word was exchanged between aunt and niece.

The lovers lived in Paris, in Warsaw, in Danzig and eventually in Berlin, where they set up a bureau to gather and distribute news of Jewish affairs. William had also been given a sum of money by his family, which he was to deliver to relatives in Lithuania and Poland who were anxious to emigrate to America. This confluence of activity may have drawn unwanted attention to the young couple, and raised suspicions among various national authorities. William Zukerman was incarcerated by some unknown eastern European authority in some undesignated city with only the vaguest of charges, some relating to the money he was carrying, some to his violation of censorship regulations. It was never clear who the imprisoning authorities were, nor what were the charges.

The story varies. Sometimes it is in Warsaw, where he was jailed as a "Communist spy." Sometimes it is Danzig, where his crime was less foreboding but punished equally severely. Sometimes he is imprisoned for two weeks, sometimes the stories hint at six months. William only spoke of it once that I recall, dismissing it as a trivial "inconvenience."

Not so, according to the impassioned report of my grandfather. His son was being held incommunicado. The U.S. State Department issued calls for his release, but there was uncertainty about the jurisdiction of those holding him. One family story has a cousin in Warsaw taking him food every day. Another, far more appealing, is that Frieda, who fled her aunt's wrath to be in Europe with her lover, somehow succeeded in buying his freedom from less-than-dedicated guards.

Fast-forward to 1923. Frieda and William were in Berlin, still gathering news of Jewish affairs and writing with prescient foreboding about the clouds gathering over European Jewry, even while Germany enjoyed the socialist democracy of the Weimar Republic. But Frieda was now pregnant, and parents and family exhorted them to consider having the child in a "safe" country. By the end of that year they moved to London, where William Zukerman had accepted a position with his old New York employer, the *Morning Journal*. He became a foreign correspondent long before such a title assumed wartime significance.

In London, they bought a house on a suburban street with the bucolic name of Woodlands. There, Frieda gave birth to my brother, Joseph Wilfred, on April 3, 1924. Frieda and William were not married until March 17, 1925, and I arrived (legitimized by the time of my delivery) nearly two years later on February 22, 1927.

Here's what little else I remember about this enigmatic man. He lovingly nurtured Yiddish, no matter that so few were learning to read it. He also found solace in writing mystical essays, obscure short stories and poetry. He would work endlessly long hours, seldom trusting anyone to help him get the job done. His life was driven by deadlines.

He resigned from newspaper posts to challenge the Zionist establishment and struck out on his own to give voice to unpopular Jewish causes. All of his life he fought against bigotry and religious and political orthodoxy, and against nationalism whenever it trumped decency. For all that, he remained an introvert: shy, quiet, inward-looking, self-analytic, a closed book even to his direct family. Only in his writings did his personality emerge. His earliest book, *The Jew in Revolt*, published in 1937, presents a picture of his constant rebellion against conventional thought and popular opinion.

In post-war years he expressed that rebellion in his *Jewish Newsletter*, which he published from 1949 until his death in 1961. In the world of Jewish affairs it was a time of great euphoric hope and fervent belief in the humanitarian concept of a national state, a refuge for the remaining living victims of the Holocaust. It was decidedly unpopular to oppose the aspirations of a Jewish political state. But his greatest fear was the rise of nationalism, no matter whether Jewish or Gentile, and he gave voice to an opinion that in more recent years has perhaps found greater credence. When his *Jewish Newsletter* ceased publication after his death in 1961, a passionate voice of dissent was stilled.

He often recounted the biblical stories of Job and Jonah. I think he felt a parallel in his own life, of a suffering that he had no choice but to accept. As long as he could have his say (and meet those deadlines) he would endure whatever was inflicted on him. Like Job, he would castigate himself if he ever strayed from his convictions. Like Jonah, his "ship to Tarshish" led inevitably to repentance at Nineveh.

Interlude

Music dictated my military career. Shortly after I enlisted in the American naval service, my superiors discovered that I could distinguish musical pitch. With unerring military logic, I was assigned to a sonar-detecting program. The principle was simple: by listening to the Doppler effect of radio signals bouncing off any large object moving underwater, it was possible to report to tone-deaf senior officers the direction of travel of enemy submarines.

On board a naval vessel patrolling in the Channel, I proved to be a menace to my commanding officers. My first effort guided our attack destroyer to a pod of dolphins. On another occasion I completely forgot whether a rising pitch meant that the object was approaching us or escaping from the range of our depth charges. My superiors hurriedly removed me from this task. Nonetheless, as a simple reward for my musical skills, I had already been elevated in rank to an electronic technician's mate second-class. To the bureaucratic mind of our ship's executive officer, that seemed a good enough reason to find something associated with electronic communications to keep me occupied while I remained at sea. It was therefore ordained that I should repair radio antennae, located on the seventy-five-foot forward mast.

Below decks, where the sonar equipment resided and where we slept, I had been in a constant state of mild seasickness. On the main deck, motion against the horizon was far more noticeable, and on those occasions when I ventured out, I became extremely seasick. Given that the pitch of the vessel at deck level traverses a wider arc than below decks, imagine how wildly it sways across the horizon two-thirds of the way up the mast. Apart from the fact that I never succeeded in repairing whatever it was that ailed the antennae, my seasickness aloft became so severe that I was finally released from service at sea and deposited ashore at the U.S. naval base in Exeter, Devon, England. It was a return home for me. "At least you speak the language, Limey," was the executive officer's less than sympathetic parting comment.

I spent three relatively peaceful months in Exeter, speaking the language. Indeed, my English accent, which was much more pronounced in those youthful days, flourished in its home setting. My job there was to prepare news reports and scripts for the Armed Forces Radio Service, to be broadcast throughout Europe, wherever there were American troops stationed. However, hostilities in Europe were nearly over, and fear of imminent transfer to the Japanese theatre of operations was fuelled by endless rumours. We had, after all, enlisted, and might at some point be seriously expected to go to a more active war zone.

This time, my non-existent electronics background worked in my favour. There was a need for an electronic technician's mate second-class at the German naval base in Bremerhaven, and three days later, just ten days before the armistice in Europe, I found myself billeted in former German naval barracks on the Weser River. The base was situated on the edge of one of northern Germany's most bombed-out cities. From my window I could survey not only a city in ruins, but also a graveyard of seventy-eight discarded Kriegsmarine vessels. My task was to decommission their electronic equipment and change their radio frequencies to circuits of more use to the Allied occupation forces.

The chief executive officer of our base was an enlightened, patrician, New England reserve officer who preferred opera to operations. His mother, he proudly informed whoever would listen, had served on the board of the Boston Opera in the mid-1930s. He lamented (even to a mere enlisted man) that his deepest regret was to be posted in Germany where he had not yet been able to attend a single musical event—if, indeed, any were being held in those final weeks of the European war.

One day, shortly after the official declaration of the end of hostilities, I was summoned to the executive office. "With the signing of the armistice, there has been a lifting of restrictions on fraternization with the former enemy," explained my commanding officer. "We recently received a request from the municipal authorities for instrumentalists to play with the Bremen Opera Orchestra. In particular, they asked if by any chance we had a bassoonist." I did not know that he was aware of the avocations of every one of his ship's company, but obviously he had done his research and had discovered that I had brought my bassoon with me to the Bremerhaven posting.

"They are in the process of recreating their opera company, and I have initialled your assignment to play with the orchestra," he said. "Of course, you will continue your other duties here on the base, but a jeep will be available each day to take you to rehearsals." Then the commander revealed his full plan. "On performance nights, I will drive you there myself." As I saluted and turned to leave he added, "The Bremen Opera House has been badly damaged in the raids. I urge you to take a warm coat with you." Even then he would not let me depart so quickly. "Have you read all of the Grimms' fairy tales?" he asked. "Not recently, sir," I replied. "Well," he responded, "now at last you'll become one of the Town Musicians of Bremen." With that he returned my salute, and I rushed to my barracks to see if I could find a good reed.

I had never before played opera, and I soon discovered that the entire repertoire of this reconstituted company consisted of the operettas of Emmerich Kálmán, Hungarian fellow student of Bartók and Kodály, which were banned during the war years because Kálmán was Jewish. His works were all endlessly tuneful, wonderfully nostalgic and emotionally satisfying to an audience deprived of any relaxed entertainment during so many years of harsh warfare. Only later did I learn why we played this endless banquet of once-forbidden delicacies. In the shattered music library of the Bremen Opera House, the only intact orchestral scores and parts were of these Kálmán operettas. The scores of Mozart, Wagner, Weber, Rossini, Bellini and Donizetti operas had all been destroyed in the fire that gutted most of the opera house, but the Kálmán material had been discarded in some distant corner of the building, where, denied performance, it survived in hidden storage.

The orchestra rehearsed in bits and pieces for about forty-five minutes before the curtain rose, and after that it became a feast of sight-reading! Night after night we played Kálmán, Kálmán and more Kálmán in the unheated shell of what was once a magnificent 1,800-seat opera house.

We performed *Countess Maritza* sixteen times, *The Gay Hussars* on ten occasions, and *The Gypsy Princess* at least seven times.

I was not allowed to shed my uniform, and the astonished stares of the audience each night should have made me decidedly uncomfortable. What could be made of the spectacle of a young musician playing in Allied military uniform with an all-German orchestra, less than a month after the war's ending? Heaven knows what they would have thought if they suspected, on top of all else, that I might be Jewish. But I was young then and felt nothing more than the delight of sampling Kálmán for the first time.

The costumes had been rescued from some musty safe storage, where they had been mothballed since long before the war. The overpowering smell of camphor wafted downward into the pit, so that I shall always associate the delicious bassoon passages that accompany the tenor in so many Kálmán arias with the aroma of a dry-cleaning establishment. Indeed, tenor parts were often doubled by the bassoon, and since there was a desperate shortage of good tenors, each performance became a feast of glorious solo passages for me. Kálmán-in-Bremen in 1945 was a kind of bassoon-accompanied *Singspiel*.

The experiment with fraternization did not last long. The policy changed after five months of Kálmán immersion. My idyll ended as abruptly as it had started, and I was returned to my full-time naval duties. I learned later that the executive officer of the base had been transferred to Terceira in the Azores. His jeep no longer made its clandestine trips to the opera house, and presumably the tenors of the Bremen Opera Company had to make do with the second clarinetist covering the melody line on—what else—a tenor saxophone.

New York

⤳ FIGARO'S LURE

The war was finally over, and I was still working on decommissioning warships. Since I did not wish to remain in military service any longer than necessary, and the U.S. forces were as anxious to demobilize me as I was to retire from their care, I was very soon returned to North America, where I was granted an honorable discharge and left once more on my parents' doorstep with many choices to make.

One day I received a call from a former member of our erstwhile New Chamber Music Society, inviting me to take part in a production of Mozart's *Marriage of Figaro*. He was conducting and desperately needed a bassoonist. I was intrigued and anxious to experience some opera—any opera—other than Kálmán. However, there was one hitch. The production was at Queens College, one of New York's five public campuses, and in order to take part I had to be registered for a full course at the college. Well, why not? Like so much else, this was a decision that occurred by default. This time, college seemed to be the sensible route.

Mozart's *Figaro* is full of magnificent passages for the bassoon. To my inexperienced ears it seemed like a virtual operatic bassoon concerto. I was instantly hooked. Perhaps I could be forgiven for imagining that, like Kálmán, and now Mozart, all future orchestral and operatic playing was going to be equally fulfilling. Not surprisingly, at Queens College I remained deeply involved in musical activity.

∾ WHEELS AND A WALL STREET FORTUNE
(OR, A TRY AT WALL STREET)

In the same year that I signed up for my college courses, I purchased one of the first British cars imported to America following the war, a Hillman Minx. I had previously owned a 1936 Ford V6, but it met its ignominious demise when the transmission fell out on the West Side Highway. I urgently needed daily transport to the campus, which lay far out in the borough of Queens. From the moment when British cars were first advertised on the garish neon signs in Times Square, I was caught up in fond memories of my English upbringing. Who could not be enamoured of those turn indicators, which, like little illuminated wings, popped out and glowed orange as they pointed in the direction that the driver wished to head?

I was also absolutely certain that nobody could possibly fit a double bass into the back seat of a Hillman Minx. Why this concern? For months my old Ford had been the transport of choice for a fellow student who played the double bass but didn't own a car. We shared long morning drives to school during the week. The bass always came with us, snugly reposing on the rear seat. Aha, thought I. The Hillman Minx will fool him! No one could squash a full-size string bass into a small British car.

How wrong I was! Like an expert with a Rubik's cube, my friend studied the tiny car from all sides. Once he had visualized the spatial geometry of the vehicle, he made his move. Over the edge of the passenger seat, into the well between the driver's seat and the rear door, and then down across the section where the motor bulged into the body of the car. To my amazement, that double bass slid into the Hillman Minx as if the automobile had been designed, and especially lubricated, for that sole purpose. Transport of bulky musical instruments notwithstanding, we remained the best of friends.

One morning we noticed an intriguing advertisement: "Do you own a car?" it asked. "Earn upwards of $100 daily. Help us deliver New York's latest phone books." We were on a break in the school schedule, and my bass-playing colleague and I decided that we would try our luck. We removed the double bass to make room for a sufficient number of phone books, and then we reported to the depot, far north in the Bronx. Even as we arrived, we sensed that we were doomed. We were surrounded by large Dodges, Packards, Chryslers, a newfangled Chevrolet and even a Cadillac. The dispatcher shook his head warily when he saw two of us in the small British car. "You'll not be able to carry many," he warned. We did not tell him about the missing double bass.

We drew our assignments by lottery, and it seemed we were in luck. We picked an area in downtown New York, Wall Street—the financial district. It was a weekday. Businesses should be humming.

The arrangement was simple. We would receive ten cents for each directory we delivered, and five cents for each old one that we brought back. They suggested that if we delivered eight hundred books and brought back three hundred, we would earn close to a hundred dollars for the day.

We piled directories into the car until the springs literally sank to the level of the pavement, then set off cautiously toward our assigned district. As we headed downtown, we recognized that two factors would lead to rapid failure in the phone-book-delivery world. The New York telephone book consisted of two volumes. Both had to be delivered and picked up to qualify for the payment. Even more telling was the realization that it would take an hour and a half to drive down to Wall Street, so there would never be enough time to return for a second load of books.

I no longer remember where we found a parking space (perhaps we double-parked while we attempted delivery), but I do remember the ominous boldface, three-inch headlines on the morning papers: "ELEVATOR WORKERS COMMENCE STRIKE"—and the equally ominous silence in the lobby of the first building on our list. This was in the days before the existence of automatic elevators. Each lift had an operator whose task was to guide the machine to a smooth stop at the required floor. Here we were, in a building seventy-six storeys high, with no elevator service. Most of the office workers, at least those on upper floors, had already been sent home for the day. The phalanx of picketing operators had dissipated as more and more offices were locked.

But we were both young and healthy, and by noon we had delivered 520 volumes to the first twenty-one floors, carrying sacks of twenty at a time up ten sets of staircases, and distributing them to whichever offices we found open. We picked up only 125 old books. We reluctantly returned to the

Bronx headquarters and claimed our meagre pay for the day. We shared a pittance for our full day's labour. We had climbed 6,900 steps. It was a splendid cardiac stress test for both of us.

"ELEVATOR STRIKE UNRESOLVED," blared the evening headlines, just as large, just as boldfaced as those in the morning. Maybe the dispatcher didn't read the newspapers. He addressed us as if we were signing on for another attack on Wall Street's skyscrapers. "I can give you the same district tomorrow. Some outfit down there wants a hundred extras," he told us, glancing down at his desk where he had made a note. "Never heard of them, but it sounds like they're into telephoning in a big way. IBM. Don't forget them, they're a new outfit on the fifty-third floor."

We demurred, and our career as directory distributors was over. The springs in the Hillman Minx were allowed to return to normal. At the time, I wondered whether Rootes Motors would have wished to publish the following critical information in the Hillman Minx operating manual. It could have appeared under Recommended Weight Distribution: "Double basses may be harder to squeeze into the vehicle, but they are infinitely less strain on the suspension than double-volume New York telephone directories."

∼ A MISSED DOWNBEAT

Along with taking college courses, I had joined the National Orchestral Association, a training orchestra that rehearsed at Carnegie Hall three times a week under the baton of the distinguished Belgian conductor Léon Barzin. This was an invaluable opportunity to learn repertoire and become familiar with orchestral discipline. One of the goals of the National Orchestral Association was to reduce the dependence of North American orchestras on foreign-trained musicians. Founded in 1930, it already had an enviable record of placements of key instrumentalists in dozens of North American symphony orchestras. Membership was a clear route to future orchestral employment. In those early post-war years, the competition was intense. There were eighteen bassoonists accepted in my first season, along with twenty-seven flautists, fifteen oboists and thirty-five clarinetists!

Barzin's reputation of deliberate tyranny created an extraordinary atmosphere of terror at these rehearsals. We all arrived early and practised hard in the hope—and fear—that we would be selected to play principal parts.

One afternoon I found myself playing first bassoon in the ebullient Symphony no. 8 by Beethoven. I had never played the piece before, and I had also never played under such an imposing and demanding conductor. In the last movement there comes a splendid bassoon passage of repeated octave F's in a relatively snappy tempo. The orchestra stops playing, the conductor looks at the bassoonist and points, and the bassoonist (if he knows what is good for him) plays for eight beats, entirely alone, until the orchestra rejoins the fun.

I knew that I had to watch for the Maestro's cue, and the minute I saw his finger pointing at me, I began my octaves. But what I did not know was that I was also supposed to follow his beat, and that it might not be metronome-clear. Instead I happily sped up and found that I had finished the part long before the orchestra chose to come back in. In fact, on this occasion, the orchestra did not come in. Barzin had stopped conducting altogether.

A deadly silence ensued, and all I heard was the ominous tapping of the baton on the conductor's music stand. I realized that all of the other players were now looking at me and wondering what M. Barzin was going to say or do. Would he throw a tantrum? Would he smile and ask me to play it again? Would he point to another player and change, midstream? He had been known to do all of the above. Instead he looked at me with a beatific smile. In a very quiet voice he asked me, "Are you a part of this orchestra?" No answer. I was terrified beyond speech. A second question, "Do you think that you intend to become an orchestral player?" I nodded. My voice would still not make any coherent sound. "It is traditional," he continued, his voice rising in volume noticeably, "that orchestral players try, barely try would be quite enough, to follow this little piece of wood." He slammed the baton down on the podium and it splintered into pieces. His voice was now at full throttle. "If you intend to be a musician, and want to stay in this orchestra, or dare to stay in this room with Beethoven, you will watch this baton." (His assistant had presented him with a new one while he gave vent to his rage.) "You can leave now, or you have one more chance to get it right."

He turned to the orchestra. "Again from measure one hundred and sixty-five." The temper subsided, he raised the baton and we began on cue. When we came to that magic moment, I watched for his cue, then stayed glued to his baton and dutifully led the orchestra toward its next entrance.

After the rehearsal he came over to me. "You made the right choice. I'm pleased you stayed," he said. He was, of course, a born teacher; his tantrums were tools of his profession, and from that moment on in my orchestral playing, I seldom failed to stick like glue to the conductor's baton, no matter how erratic.

I soon realized that without formal training I would be limited to marginal musical activity, and I began to take lessons from the principal bassoon player of Toscanini's NBC Symphony Orchestra, Leonard Sharrow. He turned out to be a splendid teacher, not only of the bassoon but also of other important activities such as drinking beer and (not simultaneously) driving a car.

Some time later, when I played the Mozart Bassoon Concerto with the Queens College Orchestra (still conducted by my New Chamber Music Society friend and colleague), Leonard Sharrow turned up to hear me. "Wow, was that Toscanini's first bassoonist?" asked my fellow orchestra members. It was, and he pronounced me moderately ready for the next professional step forward.

⌣ COMMUNITY CONCERTS

Emboldened by my teacher's confidence, I accepted an offer to join the St. Louis Sinfonietta on a cross-country tour for the American concert service Community Concerts. It was my first steady professional engagement. I had not heard of the St. Louis Sinfonietta or of Community Concerts before. The conductor had once played in the second violin section of the St. Louis Symphony—hence the name of his travelling band of nomads.

Much truer to its name, Community Concerts was responsible for a network of over 1,200 "organized audiences" in countless small communities scattered across North America. From headquarters in New York they dispatched armies of touring artists to meet the insatiable need of this vast audience. We played for seventy-one of their concert societies in a coast-to-coast tour that lasted nineteen weeks. There was a concert almost every night, often with long travel distances between cities.

To secure the contract with Community Concerts, the conductor had invested in a battered highway bus that he drove himself. This tour occurred long before union regulations limited the travel permitted between engagements. The two women in the orchestra wisely admonished us never to drink too much water. There was seldom time for stops en route, and on many occasions our conductor drove us furiously through the night. In the great tradition of international long-distance drivers, he would flash headlights as a salute to every Greyhound bus and every articulated transport truck that he encountered on these nighttime journeys. When we finally arrived at our concert destination in the early hours of the morning, he would display a teamster's democratic egalitarianism. With a shared brotherhood of the road, he would dutifully salute milk delivery, garbage or city maintenance trucks out on their morning rounds. The unkindest among the players were overheard suggesting that between the driving wheel and the baton, our Maestro was a far better bus driver than conductor.

It was a first job for most of us, and although we may have grumbled at the long trips, we were all exhilarated by the touring opportunity, and we turned in some splendid performances. The conductor's demonic bus-driving determination, coupled with our unquenchable youthful musical enthusiasm, delivered a profound experience for the smaller cities we visited. In many instances they had never before welcomed an orchestra to their stages.

As the newest recruit to the orchestral ranks, I was paid the rock-bottom minimum allowed by the union, out of which I had to pay for my own hotel and meals. (Remember the Motel 6 chain? They really used to charge six dollars a night!) Still, it was a job. And to augment my salary, I offered to serve as press representative in each community that we visited. I had seen my father at work on enough press releases. With a ream of legal-size paper and a package of carbon paper at my disposal, I prepared and sent announcements of the concerts to the local newspapers. In the towns where we performed, I would try to organize interviews for the conductor, and after the concerts I made sure that the local committees forwarded copies of the write-ups both to the conductor and, provided the reviews were positive, to Community Concerts. In this way I obtained an inside look at the "organized audience" that was Community Concerts' remarkable method of galvanizing smaller centres for musical activity.

The schedule gave me plenty of time to think about how those concerts were organized, and how such extensive touring became possible by combining concerts in large centres with events in smaller towns that lay on the route. I soon realized that the success I was witnessing depended on a mix of professional excellence, audience appeal and touring stamina. I had no idea at the time that this plan would one day work so well in Canada.

Halfway through the tour we were in the midst of a nine-concert sequence that took us from California to Nevada to Utah to Wyoming and on to Nebraska. At Rock Springs in central Wyoming, a blizzard struck the town while we were performing. By the time the concert was over, the roads were impassable. Even the transcontinental train was snowed in. The hotels in town were hard-pressed to cater to hundreds of stranded visitors, including the nineteen musicians of the touring orchestra.

The refugees sat around the hotel, waiting for signs of the snowploughs. Clearly, the orchestra concert scheduled for Casper the following evening would have to be cancelled. "Well," muttered our conductor, "at least we should be able to get going and make the concert after that one, in Scottsbluff." However, luck was against us, and the roads remained closed for yet another day. In desperation, a call was placed to a fledgling airline based in nearby Laramie.

"Yes," they said, "we can probably get in there with a DC-3." We were instructed to abandon our bus and be prepared to fly out the next day. At the airport we waited until late afternoon, when the weather finally cleared sufficiently for a landing. The DC-3, from United Airlines, ever reliable for accessing short runways in mountainous terrain, dropped through the clouds and pulled up close to the terminal building. We hurriedly boarded the plane, abandoning the harp carrying case, which would not fit through the aircraft's doors. We didn't see the case again until six days later, when our tour bus caught up with us in central Iowa.

The plane fired up its two engines; we roared down the runway, rising above the snow, and landed one hour and fifteen minutes later, at 6:45 p.m., in Scottsbluff, Nebraska—in the midst of a raging sandstorm. "Get ready," shouted the conductor as the plane taxied to a gusty (and dusty) halt at the terminal. "There's a one-hour change of time, and the concert begins at 8. It's a forty-five-minute drive to town. We'll play the concert in plain clothes. I've called the governor. He's providing a state patrol escort." Sure enough, two state troopers on motorcycles greeted us, and they led us in our hastily rented school bus from the airport through the streets of Scottsbluff with sirens blaring and lights flashing. Violinists tuned up in the bus; oboists and bassoonists soaked their reeds; and we arrived at the school—which seemed strangely silent for a concert night.

Our fearless leader dashed inside, and we all followed, instruments and music stands at the ready. The hall was dark. A lonely janitor was sweeping the aisle of the auditorium. "We're here," gasped the conductor. "We almost didn't make it, but here we are. Tell them we're ready to start the concert whenever they want." The solitary employee looked at us as if we were all faintly mad. He continued his sweeping. "No concert tonight. You're due tomorrow. I'll let them know. They'll be glad to know you made it!"

We spent the next three hours driving through swirling clouds of dust and sand, looking for overnight accommodations. In the haste to get to Scottsbluff, nobody had bothered to check the hotel availability. The governor's motorcycle escort was nowhere to be seen.

The tour had started just before the end of my final school year at Queens, so at its conclusion I found myself once again deprived of a formal graduation ceremony. I returned home, buoyed by the experience of a rugged one-night-stand tour. My college diploma had arrived in the mail while I was away. Which would have the greater influence as my life moved forward?

~ WHERE IS VANCOUVER?

On weekends during my college years I had often found myself playing with a network of small orchestras within driving distance of the city: the Scranton Philharmonic, the Wilkes-Barre Symphony, the Orange Orchestral Society and the Vermont State Symphony Orchestra. These all depended on the student freelance corps to augment resident semi-professionals.

From the more experienced players on these engagements I had begun to hear about that essential musical rite of passage: the audition. I had never auditioned for anyone. I had always fallen into my musical activities by default, and as if to prove the point, one early November day I received a call from the conductor of the orchestra in Scranton, where I had played on previous weekends. He was conducting some concerts in Vancouver, Canada, and his first bassoonist was in hospital having her appendix removed. Could I fill in?

I was not entirely sure where Vancouver was, so I rushed to our copy of the *Encyclopedia Britannica* and read the brief article about Canada's west coast port. There was even a glamorous picture of the 1934-era Marine Building. The city certainly seemed bigger than Rutland, Vermont, and less covered with coal dust than Wilkes-Barre, Pennsylvania, so I told the Maestro that I would be pleased to play for him once again.

A telegram from the orchestra arrived the next day. "Will you play four or six weeks with the Vancouver Symphony?" it read, and then proceeded to list various terms. I assumed that the uncertain duration was because they could not predict exactly how long their regular player might require for a complete recovery. The salary, on a weekly basis, sounded acceptable. I wired back my enthusiastic assent.

My father by this time was no longer working for the Yiddish press but instead operated a subscription news service for Jewish publications in smaller North American cities. Usually when I told him about concert engagements, he was bemused. Music had never seemed like proper employment to him. But this time, when I mentioned Vancouver, he was reminded that he had a subscriber in the city who hadn't paid the account for several months. "Would you like to drop in to meet him and perhaps collect what he owes us?" Things were looking up. I now had a commission as well as a playing job.

An airline ticket arrived by registered mail, and I set out to fly to Vancouver with Trans-Canada Air Lines. The flight from Toronto to Vancouver was an unforgettable eleven-stop journey with a DC-3. I remember the stops with great clarity because since then I have visited every one of the towns on the route: Toronto, North Bay, Kapuskasing, Sault Ste. Marie, Fort William, Winnipeg, Saskatoon, Regina, Calgary, Lethbridge, Cranbrook, Kelowna, Vancouver. Although we left at 10 a.m. and were flying west, we did not arrive in Vancouver until 11:30 at night, sixteen-and-a-half hours later. The terminal (the current South Terminal at YVR) was virtually deserted at that hour. A talkative taxi driver took me downtown. "What brings you to Vancouver?" he asked. "I've been invited to play with the Symphony," I replied. "Hmmm . . . ," he said. "I didn't know we had one." With that he dropped me at the Hotel Vancouver. Fortunately, a room was reserved in my name, and there was even a message at the desk. There was a rehearsal the next morning at 9 a.m. The Vancouver Symphony really existed.

My first performance with the orchestra took place later that week, in the old Georgia Auditorium on Denman Street, near where the Westin Bayshore sits today. At the close of the concert, I asked about the rehearsal schedule for the following week. "Goodness, no," I was told, "there's no rehearsal next week. We're off until two weeks from now."

I reread the terms of my engagement. The words were glued in familiar yellow strips onto a standard Western Union form. *We offer you four or six weeks engagement with the Vancouver Symphony.* The text had not changed.

Clutching the telegram, I went to see the manager. "But my dear friend," he said, "you agreed so wholeheartedly to our proposal, we sent you a telegram." "Precisely," I replied and produced the message with a flourish of triumph. He read it several times, and then exclaimed, "Oh my dear fellow, how very unfortunate. What a silly mistake. Our message read 'four *of* six weeks.' They must have inadvertently changed the 'f' to an 'r' when it was dictated over the phone to Western Union. We would never have offered consecutive weeks of employment. We always have gaps between our concerts."

Long deliberations ensued, and the Symphony accepted partial responsibility and offered to pay me for the blank weeks at half of the agreed salary. I had no choice, but it also meant that I had a great deal of unexpected time on my hands in the city of Vancouver.

At least I would have no problem fulfilling my father's commission. One morning I called on the publisher of the *Jewish Western Bulletin*. As I was heading up a set of steep, narrow stairs in the Jewish Community Centre, I collided with a young woman, who most apologetically helped me up, dusted me off and quickly introduced herself. "I'm Netta Ksienski," she said. "I am the social worker here for the centre. Must run. Are you visiting Vancouver for a few days?" She had left before I could respond.

∽ FIRST MARRIAGE

Abe Arnold, editor-publisher of the *Jewish Western Bulletin*, was most affable, and I quickly concluded my father's business affairs. The afternoon seemed to evaporate as we exchanged stories of common interest (or was he interviewing me for the *Bulletin*?), and just as I was about to leave, Netta Ksienski reappeared. As I left Abe's office, she asked, "Since I knocked you down so unceremoniously, would you care to come tomorrow for Friday night dinner at our house? We always have room for a guest on Shabbat." I was intrigued by her English accent, and little as I fancied the idea of sitting through a formal Friday evening dinner, the invitation seemed very warm and genuine. I accepted and dutifully presented myself at the family home on Friday evening. I was introduced to Netta's mother, who was busy in the kitchen making potato pancakes. We chatted casually, and as fast as she turned out the latkes, I managed to devour them. I think that I determined then and there that I would probably end up marrying Netta. Recalling our meeting on the staircase, one could say that I had been bowled over.

The remaining four weeks passed quickly. Abe Arnold of the *Bulletin*, the ever-willing facilitator, let me borrow his car, an Austin Mini. Here I was in Vancouver, and I had wheels! By the time my six weeks with the Symphony were up, and on the very evening of the final concert, I proposed, and Netta accepted. Her father objected vehemently. It was clear I was not an observant Jew and had no visible means of supporting their daughter. Netta's mother, on the other hand, seemed to approve of me and came down to the registry office, where Abe and his wife, Bertha, acted as witnesses. The morning after that final concert, we left for New York.

My father was busy at his desk when I arrived to introduce my wife. "Dad," I interrupted, "this is Netta." Type, type, type, carriage return, zing, type, type, zing, zing. He looked up briefly from his article. "Hello. Excuse me, I must finish this off. Mustn't miss the post tonight!" Type, type, type, zing, zing . . . type, type, type.

It wasn't indifference or even embarrassment. It was that old devil, deadline.

On my second day back in New York, the St. Louis Sinfonietta called with an offer of another three-month tour. I declined. Newly married, I determined to stay close to New York. However, the telephone remained ominously silent.

I returned to the National Orchestral Association and, recalling the advice of my Sinfonietta colleagues, began to prepare myself for the audition treadmill. Each year, around March or April, orchestra managers from across the country came to New York to seek out young players for their forthcoming seasons. New Orleans, San Antonio, Cincinnati, Oklahoma City, Kansas City, San Jose and a myriad of other smaller city orchestras were always seeking new players. They advertised in ruthless competition in *International Musician*, published by the musicians' union, which covered both the United States and Canada. I studied the magazine and determined to try the roulette wheel of the audition circuit. I began an arduous routine of daily practice.

Meantime, to earn some much-needed income, I secured a part-time job writing advertising copy. "Public relations" was the new buzzword. Ad agencies were the meccas of promotional writing. I sold an immensely successful limerick advertisement to the agency that handled the advertising for Ballantine beer. They paid me for it and then apologetically declined to send it to their client because it suggested a link between alcohol and the devil. Just what the temperance people were looking for:

> *When Paganini fiddled away*
> *Some thought they heard the devil play*
> *But others knew it all the time*
> *That Nick was fond of Ballantine*
> *So fiddlers one and fiddlers all*
> *Discard your bows and heed this call:*
> *Like Paganini pluck a chord*
> *For a tasty drink all can afford*

Little assignments like this allowed me to stay focused on the audition season.

⁓ FIRST AUDITION

My father's news service was flourishing. As a fine journalist he understood which stories were likely to be of interest to the outlying Jewish communities in smaller cities across the continent. One such story crossed his desk. It was 1950, and the newly minted Israel Philharmonic Orchestra was due in New York to celebrate the emergence of the new state. He recognized that this event had singular interest to his younger son, who seemed to be teetering between careers in music and journalism. What better combination of the two career paths?

"Why don't you go down to Idlewild and meet the musicians?" he suggested, handing me an invitation from the press office of the fledgling orchestra.

Idlewild Airport (later renamed JFK) was New York's newest aviation jewel. The city's air travel needs could no longer be contained at LaGuardia Field, and the new airport, clearly a prescient recognition that the aircraft of the future would require longer runways, was located far out on Long Island.

Air travel was still glamorous, and the arrival of a flight from every distant overseas point merited an announcement in the daily newspaper under "arrivals and departures." Although I no longer have any recollection of how I found my way to Long Island on that day, I knew where to find the temporary home of the new Israeli airline, EL AL (poetically named "To the above"), at the equally temporary Quonset hut terminal of Trans World Airlines.

It is hard now to imagine an aviation world in which security did not exist. I vividly recall that I walked through the terminal and straight onto the tarmac, where the plane was just arriving. I stood behind a simple metal barrier, placed there solely to protect visitors from the whirling propellers of the DC-7. The orchestra disembarked, two by two, with familiar instrument cases.

I took the mandatory photographs (long lost), met the publicity secretary and accepted the glowing press release about the orchestra, its conductor Leonard Bernstein (ah! Yes . . . I once played a recording session for him) and its recent transformation from the Palestine Orchestra. Lacking paparazzi training or experience, I barely caught a view of Bernstein as he was whisked away in a limousine. Little did I know that I was to meet him less than a week later.

I introduced myself to Mordechai Rechtman, the orchestra's principal

George with Leonard Bernstein (white coat).

bassoonist, and as he boarded the bus to the city, he suggested that I drop by and visit him at the hotel. I did not immediately guess the reason for his invitation. But when, in the midst of our visit, Mordechai suddenly asked me if I would be interested in joining the orchestra, I don't think I was terribly surprised.

The orchestra needed musicians. For many of the current members, the move from the Diaspora to the new Jewish homeland had been a simple case of survival. Others were drawn to Israel by a commitment to "áliyah"— the homecoming of the exiles. The result was a mix of talents and abilities. Even under its former name, the Palestine Orchestra, the ensemble was re-nowned as a virtuoso orchestra of concertmasters. Leading violinists from every major European city had found their way to the new land. Mordechai, originally from Berlin, was one of a small group of young musicians who had enjoyed serious professional training before emigrating to Palestine. For the most part, however, the woodwind and brass playing still reflected the military-band traditions of the British army of the Palestinian Mandate. To strengthen and maintain its ranks, the orchestra needed musical skill and ambition as well as Zionist commitment.

What a confluence of opportunity! At one level, here was a working opportunity to participate in the dream of the newly established nation. My wife of only six months had been brought up in England in the socialist-Zionist Habonim movement, and although I shared no such political goals, a move to Israel would be a dream fulfilled for her. At the same time, it was a superb orchestra that would compel me to strive upward to share their international goals. Here was a practical way to meet divergent needs and interests. The possibility even came with a sort of blessing from my non-Zionist father. He had, after all, turned me loose to meet the orchestra.

"If you are interested," Mordechai told me, "there will be a vacancy next season . . . you will have to audition for Lenny."

I barely hesitated before giving my reply, at which point I was whisked to another room to meet the manager, then to meet the chairman of the orchestra committee. One by one, they all said the same thing: "You'll have to play for Lenny."

Was I in good enough shape? Could I handle a major orchestra audition? I really didn't know. I had never before auditioned for a professional orchestra, let alone a major international one. Yet within half an hour I left the hotel with instructions to be in the Green Room, backstage at Carnegie Hall, at ten the next morning. The mantra was loud and clear: "You'll have to play for Lenny." I rushed home to tell Netta. The expected jubilation prevailed. We indulged in an extravagant dinner, which we could ill afford. Nonetheless, even as we toasted the occasion, she reminded me of the harsh reality: "But you have to audition for Lenny."

I found myself slipping into the orchestra world just before the time when rigid protocols for auditions were established (and accepted) by most orchestras. Today, orchestral auditions are usually held behind curtains. The material that each candidate is expected to play is prescribed in advance, down to the precise orchestral excerpt. Such tests of instrumental proficiency, often judged more for virtuoso technique than for sensitivity to the music, or adaptability to stress, reveal some aspects of a musician's capability but tend to conceal the personality and the individuality of the player. Indeed, stories abound of auditions held according to all the current rules where the juries select a completely unexpected candidate who, alas, turns out to be unpractised and inexperienced, unable to deal with the daily demands and high pressure of a major orchestral post.

Was the alternative any better, when a martinet musical director listened, judged and arbitrarily selected? The affirmative action of the current method was an inevitable result of the numerous injustices of the earlier one.

Ah, but there was a third kind of audition, neither autocratic nor blindly meritocratic, and it involved "playing for Lenny." Such was the one and only occasion when, with my skills on the line, my career and future rested on a single knock on the Green Room door at Carnegie Hall.

I arrived at the fabled backstage room at 9:15 a.m., determined to warm up and be comfortably ready for my perceived moment of terror. The stage doorman showed me the way and wished me luck; he had probably witnessed generations of aspiring young players turning up at the Green Room for such auditions over the years.

I found a good-sounding reed. Alone in the room I played and played. I went through every orchestral excerpt that I could remember, from the opening of Tchaikovsky's Sixth Symphony to *The Sorcerer's Apprentice*, from *Peter and the Wolf* to the most terrifying of all, the *Sacre de printemps*. And then I included *Boléro*, *España*, *El Salón México*, and Beethoven's Fourth Symphony. For good measure, I added *Scheherazade* and the opening bars of *Boris Godunov*. I even played the cadenza of Shostakovich's newly composed Ninth Symphony, which had just been banned in the Soviet Union for its "flippancy." I played Donizetti arias and Bach cello suites. I played and played and played, and finally, feeling reasonably ready for whatever was to come, I sat and waited. Only then did I look at my watch. It was already 10:30.

I began to worry. What was the procedure? Would the manager come for me to invite me on stage before Mr. Bernstein and key members of the orchestra? Had they expected me to present myself somewhere on the dot of 10 a.m.? I listened for sounds in the hallway outside. There was an ominous silence. So I played some more excerpts. By 10:45 I concluded that the job must already have been filled. Or perhaps, in my exuberant acceptance of the invitation, I had arrived a day early for the audition? I put my good reed away (would it ever sound so well again?). Reluctantly, I pulled my instrument to pieces and began to clean it out, and just as I was about to close the case, there came a gentle knock at the door. Was it the stage doorman coming to tell me that the room was needed for somebody auditioning for second trombone? Was it the cleaning staff anxious to vacuum the carpets?

I went to the door and opened it . . . to Leonard Bernstein, standing there with a puckish smile on his face. "Hmm," he said. "I've been listening to you for the last forty-five minutes. You have the job."

I was stunned. "Then you heard all those stops and starts? I was just warming up!" I stuttered.

"Yes," he replied, "good stuff. I only thought the passage in the *Jupiter* Symphony should have been a little snappier, perhaps like this." And he sang the bassoon part quite differently from the way I had just played it.

At that point, I remember thinking, "By Jupiter! [what else?] I've just succeeded in the first and only audition in my young professional life! I wonder where this will lead?"

Interlude

The invitation to join the Israel Philharmonic led to frantic preparations to move to Israel in time for the start of the new season. Since the orchestra offered to pay only a single airfare to Tel Aviv, I was in urgent need of paid employment to cover my wife's expenses.

Economic salvation came from an unexpected source. Along with several other younger (and equally unemployed) wind players, I was regularly invited to the elegant home of patrician Carleton Sprague Smith. He was chief of the Music Division of the New York Public Library, where he had held court since 1931. His mansion on East 70th, a few doors down from the Frick Collection, reflected both the musical and social worlds in which he was so deeply embedded.

He was also a brilliant amateur flautist and had accumulated a vast collection of woodwind chamber music. We gathered each Thursday evening, before a small and exclusive audience, to plough relentlessly (and valiantly) through as much of this obscure repertoire as our sight-reading ability and our collective embouchures would permit.

When our host finally acknowledged that even he could play no more, we dined with some of New York's musical elite. Over pâté and cognac we mingled with composers, performers, critics and historians. Léon Barzin, conductor of the National Orchestral Association, where I still rehearsed regularly, was among the distinguished guests.

At one such evening I met the curator of Special Collections at the New York Public Library. He was apparently aware of my plan to join the Israel Philharmonic, and when he learned of my financial needs, he invited me to the depths of the library's basement, where for the next three months I helped edit previously unpublished works by early American composers. It was tedious troglodyte work, but it made the journey possible. What I did not know then was that it had all been splendidly orchestrated by Carleton Sprague Smith and Léon Barzin.

Léon Barzin's influence was also at work as we started our overseas odyssey. The National Orchestral Association had offered me an unprecedented interest-free loan to purchase a new instrument from the celebrated Heckel factory in Wiesbaden, Germany. Heckel instruments are recognized as the Stradivarii of bassoons.

We had been advised to take a car with us to Israel, and since our route now required a stop in Germany, we decided to pick up a vehicle in Paris. The popular guidebook at the time was entitled *Europe on 5 Dollars a Day*, and that suited our frugal planning perfectly. We had very little disposable money, but I owned one of the first Hillman Minx sedans in New York, and it was easy to arrange to trade it in for a similar model in Paris.

Like a Catherine wheel, we made three circuits of Place Vendôme in the centre of Paris and, as if by centrifugal force, spun outward toward Wiesbaden. It lay directly on the route to Naples, where I had booked space—with the car—to travel by sea to Haifa. My wife, Netta, would fly from Rome, and I would pick her up at Lod Airport in the newly formed land of Israel.

Wilhelm Heckel, patriarch of the distinguished family of instrument makers, met us at the door of his workshop in Wiesbaden. He greeted us with courtly old-world dignity, but I suspect that at that moment we were being examined to ensure our suitability for the precious right of ownership of a Heckel bassoon. We must have passed the test. Before long we were invited into the inner workshop, where lathes were still operated by treadle, and single unshaded electric bulbs hung loosely next to abandoned gaslight fixtures. It was all faintly and wonderfully musty, as if we had been transported to the 1830s, when the Heckel family first began to manufacture their memorable instruments.

Trees for Heckel's bassoons were selected as carefully as those for Stradivarius's violins, two and a half centuries earlier. In the workshop, artisan craftsmen were already at work on a maple tree that had been felled in the Black Forest, not far from Freudenstadt, in October 1929. Normally, eight or ten years of aging and drying would have sufficed. However, the war had intervened, and this particular tree had remained in a storage shed for ten years longer than usual. Those extra years of aging may have given my future instrument an extraordinarily mellow tone.

Heckel bassoons were numbered chronologically. By 1951 the pace of modern times was beginning to resonate even in the world of bassoons. Their total production over 125 years was approaching ten thousand! Two cartons of cigarettes sealed the contract for bassoon #9174. It would be shipped to Tel Aviv in six months.

Tel Aviv

~ PROTEKZIA!

From Naples, I sailed on the *Kedmah* (Hebrew for "forward"), a former World War II Liberty ship. The passengers were a mixed lot. Some were former Palestinians heading home for the first time as citizens of their own land. Some were survivors, displaced persons, at last admitted to a haven after years of terror in the camps. Some were dedicated youngsters on áliyah, emigrating from the Diaspora to the land of their forefathers. Yet others were tourists, anxious to visit the new country, offering economic and moral support. Some, like me, were on contract to the new land for a specific job.

On board the *Kedmah* were an Italian chef and a Rumanian maître d'. Their daunting task was to maintain a kosher kitchen. Within moments of the vessel casting off, a magnificent buffet appeared, replete with artificial shrimp that would have withstood the most severe rabbinical scrutiny. "Eat well," warned the old-timers. "Austerity is around the corner in Israel." It was good advice, but they forgot to add that the *Kedmah* had no stabilizers. The crossing was rough and, along with most of the passengers, after that first night I never again managed to enjoy the opulent nightly buffet.

In various degrees of seasickness, we sailed past islands of antiquity—Capri, Sicily, Lampedusa, Malta, Rhodes and Cyprus. The *Kedmah*, at its maximum speed of eleven knots, reached Haifa three days later on a Friday evening, where we disembarked to modest chaos.

The nation was so new that immigration officers did not yet have uniforms. The line of passengers wound past trestle tables that served for immigration and customs inspection. A plainclothes inspector silently scrutinized every page of my passport and contract. Then, without a word, he took my documents and made his way toward a glass booth at the end of the dock. Some of the other passengers, who had been hoping to share a ride with me to Tel Aviv, looked helplessly in my direction. They shrugged their shoulders sympathetically and moved ahead in the line.

I stood there, bereft of passport, and had visions of a turbulent return journey on the *Kedmah*. Minutes later the inspector returned with an older gentleman at his side. "I am the director of immigration," the newcomer announced in precise and cultivated English. "Please come with me."

We entered the glass booth. The director moved to his desk and invited me to sit down. He then removed a bottle from one of the drawers, and two small glasses. "Would you care for a schnapps?" he asked. A broad smile crossed his face as he thumbed through my passport. "I understand you have come to play with the Tismoret, the Philharmonic."

"Yes, yes," I said, and hastily pointed to the crumpled contract. "They expect me at rehearsal on Sunday!"

"Of course they do," he replied. "You shall be there! Drink up. It is Shabbat, the start of the Sabbath!" I sipped, still mystified. Did immigration authorities greet each new arrival with such cordiality?

My interlocutor leaned toward me, and this time he spoke as if he feared that his words might be overheard. "The orchestra will be playing in Haifa next Thursday," he whispered. "It is sold out." There was a pregnant pause. "Do you think you could arrange tickets for me?" He slipped a calling card across the desk, and in the same motion stamped my passport with a multi-coloured entry visa. Now, in full voice, "Welcome to Israel. I look forward to hearing from you!" At last I understood the intent of the choreography. In my first hour on Israeli soil I had learned the essential meaning of *protekzia*. Clearly, in 1951, it was a good thing to be known as a member of the Israel Philharmonic, even though I had not yet played a single note with the orchestra!

Back at the customs hall I claimed my luggage and wandered over to the Hillman Minx, where it had been unloaded from the *Kedmah* along with two other cars. Before the trip from Naples, the fuel tanks had been drained to avoid a fire hazard. There was perhaps half a litre left in the tank. "Where can I get some gas?" I asked the shipping company representatives.

They shook their heads sadly. "It's Shabbat. Everything is closed." Someone interjected, "You might be able to get petrol at the bus station." The other vehicles had already disappeared. Their drivers had apparently been forewarned and had each brought a spare jerry can of fuel.

The *Kedmah* sounded a plaintive foghorn lament, and the steady cloud of smoke that had accompanied the excitement of arrival and disembarking was reduced to a lonely puff from the ship's single funnel. Stevedores started to dismantle the trestle tables. The shipping company representatives checked their manifests one last time, then strode off into the darkness. The lights on the dock dimmed. A lone patrolman on night watch came over and informed me that overnight parking was not allowed. He pointed the way to the bus station, and I cautiously drove up a long hill, hoping that the half litre of fuel would be enough to take me to a friendly gas pump.

At the bus station, a suitable wad of Italian 10,000 lira notes helped fill the tank. Onward to Tel Aviv. There was no map. The north of Israel at that time was a narrow strip of land. To the right, as one headed south, was the Mediterranean. To the left was gentle sloping farmland, but a hostile border lay only a few miles inland. As I drove through the night, there was a sprinkling of lights to the east, but it was impossible to know where the border lay. Every time the highway veered away from the ocean I stopped to make sure that I had not inadvertently taken a wrong turn. I had enjoyed enough nocturnal passport inspection for one day!

I passed through Hadera, Netanya and Herzliya. Just before midnight on that subdued Shabbat evening I finally found myself in Tel Aviv, at a blinking traffic light on the corner of Allenby Street and Rothschild Boulevard. I reread my instructions from the Philharmonic and headed to the hotel that had been booked for me for the weekend. I wearily unloaded my belongings and stretched out on the bed. On Sunday morning I would attend my first rehearsal of the Israel Philharmonic.

⌇ THE HOUSE OF THE PHILHARMONIC

As I arrived for rehearsal, I could not escape teenage memories of the first day of a new school term. In place of returning students and a new headmaster, I was introduced to my colleagues and to the all-powerful "inspector," who was responsible for whatever orchestral discipline prevailed. I can tell you now, it was not much! Yiddish, Polish, German, Hungarian, Czech, English and French competed with each other to interpret a Beethoven symphony. It is a cliché, but I wondered, "Isn't the common language of music supposed to overcome linguistic barriers?"

Apparently not always. As the rehearsal ended, somebody addressed me in Hungarian. With the help of an Austrian cellist and a Polish clarinetist, I discovered that the orchestra administrators were asking me to drive the guest conductor and some of the foreign musicians to their residence. "By the way," they added, "it's the Bet Tismoret—the House of the Philharmonic. That's where you will be living."

From that moment I was appointed the unofficial chauffeur for guest soloists and conductors and, space permitting, for as many fellow residents of the Bet Tismoret—along with their instruments—as could be squashed into a Hillman Minx.

On that first trip, the conductor, three musicians, my bassoon and luggage were all piled into the car for the drive across the city. I did not yet know the way, so I was at the mercy of back-seat (and front-seat) drivers. "Turn left!" "Straight ahead!" "Stop and ask directions!" each in a different language. I would have to learn quickly how to survive in polyglot surroundings. Without a single word of Hebrew being spoken, we finally arrived at the House of the Philharmonic.

"The House" actually consisted of two Italian prefabricated buildings acquired by the orchestra for the use of their foreign guest musicians. They had been planted on a hillside at the outer edge of metropolitan Tel Aviv, between an abandoned lemon orchard and the busy two-lane highway to Haifa. The upper residence was a comfortable four-room bungalow and was designed to accommodate conductors and guest soloists in modest luxury. The lower house was for the orchestral musicians. It was not particularly comfortable and it certainly was not luxurious. It was located two hundred metres down the hill, close to the Haifa highway, and was a motel-style structure with four sparsely furnished rooms on each side of a central corridor. Shared kitchen and bathroom facilities flanked the entranceway.

The conductors and visiting soloists were entrusted to the care of a Rumanian couple who had emigrated to Palestine in 1948. A celebrated chess grandmaster, the husband proudly proclaimed that his wife, too, was a champion. However, because of a pronounced lisp, it was never quite clear whether he had said "Champion chess" or "Champion chef." The orchestra administration chose to believe the latter and bestowed a mantle of culinary virtuosity on the lady of the house. Nobody ever found out if she also played chess, but it turned out that she was as fine a chef as he was a chess player, and guests at the upper bungalow, in austerity-racked Israel in 1950 and 1951, were often seen licking their lips in anticipation of fabled cuisine at the upper residence of the Bet Tismoret.

The occupants of the other house were expected to take care of themselves.

On my second day in Israel I headed to the airport to meet Netta's flight from Rome. I had already experienced the prestige and respect garnered by the mere mention of the Philharmonic, so it did not surprise me that a brass band was waiting on the tarmac. A red carpet was rolled out to await the incoming DC-7, and a small military honour guard was standing by. I reminded myself to thank the orchestra administration for such a thoughtful greeting.

It was a short-lived dream. When the aircraft door opened, the Italian prime minister stepped out on his first state visit. His entourage followed. The band played. The honour guard was inspected and the red carpet rolled up in preparation for the next diplomatic arrival. Only then were ordinary passengers permitted to disembark.

One hour later my wife was introduced to ordinary life at the Bet Tismoret. Our fellow residents included a Belgian horn player with his Parisienne wife who, it turned out, was a recent Cordon Bleu graduate; an Israeli-Austrian double bass player who had broken his ankle and could not navigate the steps at his own house, and whose wife came each day, mainly, it seemed, to scrub and rescrub the kitchen countertops; a Swedish viola player whose wife believed that a smorgasbord should stretch from one end of the kitchen to the other; and an American trombonist, first sighted eating baked beans directly from the can heated over a one-ring electric burner in his room at the far end of the corridor.

As might be imagined, cooking coordination became a nightmare. Counter space in the communal kitchen was limited. Apart from food shortages, there were not enough pots, pans or utensils. One person's soup would spill over the next person's salad. Electricity was also rationed, available for only a few hours each day. Nobody knew when the oven would be working. The kitchen became a battleground between cooking cultures.

It did not take long for us to discover that our existence in Israel would be divided between two grand imperatives: rehearsals and concerts on the one hand, and the eternal search for food on the other. Austerity and shortages dictated a clear division of labour. Years later, an aunt in the Soviet Union reminded me of the inescapable truth of an old Russian proverb. "The women do all the work," she said. "The men do the rest."

So it was that year in Tel Aviv. While the men played in the orchestra, our wives were the involuntary front-line troops in the battle for survival. That daily hunt for dinner involved standing in endless lines for food, and sometimes coming home empty handed. We all had ration cards for modest shares of essential foodstuffs such as butter, eggs, meat and sugar, but there was never a guarantee that the rationed item would be available.

⌁ THE SIDEWALK OMELETTE AND THE SCHNITZEL POLICE

One morning, word circulated that there were eggs available at a small grocery shop near the rehearsal hall. We pooled our ration cards, and my wife headed with us to the city with the glorious prospect of a dozen eggs! By the time we arrived, the line at the grocery shop already wound around the block. Three hours later, we stepped out from rehearsal into the sweltering noon sun just as our victorious shopper emerged from the store. As if to tell us of her success, she raised the shopping bag over her head. For a brief moment it hovered in triumph. Then, with one rending tear, the flimsy paper bag split open, and twelve eggs tumbled to the concrete pavement. The shells, from poorly nourished Israeli chickens, were fragile. There was little distinction between yolk and albumen. As the eggs shattered on the sidewalk, the contents sizzled into an instant omelette. An army of stray dogs and cats descended on the feast. A cry of despair rose from sympathetic passersby.

Among the distressed onlookers was a local policeman, who took us aside and pointed down the street to a nearby alleyway. "Ask for Habibah," he told us. "She will probably have eggs." He cast one last forlorn look at the sidewalk omelette and returned to his beat.

Habibah sat in her alley, attired in traditional black Yemenite garb despite the heat of the day. At our request, she silently raised the first of several petticoats. There was a stick of butter, apparently refrigerated by the black material. Beneath petticoat number two lay a solitary pear. Finally, beneath petticoat number three we found eggs to replace our loss. They were placed safely on the velvet lining of a trombone case, and as we drove home an improvised *Fanfare for a Dozen Eggs* echoed down the entire length of Jabotinsky Street.

Which came first, the chicken or the egg? At last, an answer for this recurrent question. In this case, the dozen eggs came first, from beneath Habibah's petticoat. The chicken came later. On weekends, our resident American trombonist (having retrieved his egg-carrying case) often played on nearby kibbutz settlements with a Dixieland band comprised of other Philharmonic musicians who shared his love of jazz. From these events, he would come home with fresh produce. A fee for a bar mitzvah was generally a bagful of onions, peppers or cucumbers. Weddings were better. After one such late-night kibbutz ceremony, he returned with a live chicken. Nobody at the Bet Tismoret knew where to find a *shochet*—a ritual slaughterer. A friendly Arab neighbour performed the grisly task. Somebody plucked the bird. What remained was scrawny, flea-ridden, emaciated, but still, a chicken! Lovingly boiled, it became stock for soup and a feast for the residents until the next kibbutz wedding.

Sometimes we ventured out for meals. Although food was desperately short, great restaurant traditions thrived in 1951 Tel Aviv. Tables were elegantly set with an extravagant panoply of dishes, cutlery, glassware. A count of the knives, forks and plates suggested far greater culinary opulence than the kitchen would ever be able to provide.

With a flourish that would do justice to a circus ringmaster, a maître d' would present an elaborately printed dinner menu. If earlier that week a shipload of frozen cod from Iceland had reached Israel's shores, then cod would be conspicuously present on each page. Garlic-crusted, herb-coated, lemon-baked, oven-fried, beer-battered or tomato-crowned, all previously frozen, and all from diplomatically friendly Iceland.

There might be a hint of variety farther down the menu. Swedish Salad (ignoring the niceties of Scandinavian distinctions) turned out to be the same previously frozen cod on a bed of homegrown lettuce. Poor Man's Lobster, while a tantalizing and mouth-watering alternative in print, was none other than baked cod, similarly frozen and dependably Icelandic.

If one had a taste for more substantial fare, it was rumoured that a certain barely legal establishment in the village of Herzliya offered a black-market menu with pork schnitzels challenging both civil and religious law. "Guaranteed, they'll have schnitzel," a colleague promised us when we first set out to visit the establishment. "Expensive, but delicious," he added. The room was stark, the tables unadorned, the service unpolished. Waiters poured from the kitchen carrying overloaded plates of schnitzel to bare wooden tables. Clearly this was the right place, the promised land within the Promised Land.

But we were like uninvited guests who had crashed a private party. When, after a long wait, a menu was grudgingly provided, it looked familiar. Swedish Salad topped the printed offerings. Behind us the kitchen doors repeatedly swung open, revealing more tantalizing meat dishes on their way to surrounding tables. Our colleague successfully caught a waiter's eye. "Schnitzel?" he asked. "All gone" was the curt reply, while plate after plate continued to pour from the kitchen. We had no choice but to order the daily special from the menu and watch the happy diners at the other tables attacking their schnitzels and savouring succulent mouthfuls.

Suddenly there was a furious hammering at the door. Waiters rushed out, seized plates from under diners' noses and carried them relentlessly out of sight. Some diners hid their plates on their knees below the table. Others departed by a barely concealed rear door, their half-consumed meals left behind as congealing evidence of gastronomical crime.

Four young men in trench coats and flashing identity badges took up positions in the corners of the dining room and started yelling instructions in voluble Hebrew. Wherever they found a diner close to the remnant of a schnitzel, they busied themselves writing tickets for the mandatory fines. Our table remained undisturbed. The manager, who seemed to be on the best of terms with the invading police contingent, pointed us out. Presumably somebody wrote in a notebook that the restaurant also conducted legitimate dining business. Icelandic cod never tasted better!

In the weeks ahead we returned three more times before the owners decided that we were not police informers. By the fifth visit we were "regulars," and even though we had memorized the route to the secret rear exit, we miraculously survived a year without a citation from the "Schnitzel Police."

～ OHEL SHEM

Rehearsals and concerts took place in the Ohel Shem, an old converted military Quonset hut. The ambience was inhospitable, and the acoustics wildly resonant. No surprise that the English-speaking players referred to it as "Hell of a Shame." Its original curved roof was still in place, solid, corroded tin. On either side of the hall stood four-storey concrete apartment blocks. On the third floor in one of these adjacent buildings lived an immigrant family recently arrived from Romania. Their child of eighteen months suffered terribly from infant colic and cried endlessly and inconsolably.

One morning, in the middle of rehearsal, the child began his interminable howl. His mother could stand it no longer. She did what any apartment dweller does when the neighbours make too much noise. She reached out of the window of her bedroom, and with a large hammer began banging on the tin roof of the Ohel Shem. Downstairs in the rehearsal hall the din was amplified a dozen times. The conductor had no choice but to call an intermission. The orchestra inspector hastened upstairs to inspect.

From the solitary pay phone in the lobby of the hall, a frantic call went out to the prime minister's office. Mr. Ben-Gurion was busy, but within half an hour Yitzhak-Meir Levin, minister of welfare in the newly formed government, turned up in his official self-drive Volkswagen Beetle. Mr. Levin was accompanied by Ze'ev Sherf, the cabinet secretary. Clearly the prime minister took the matter seriously.

The representatives of the Government of Israel, the orchestra committee and the mother with her yowling baby gathered on stage. Space was created between the tympani and the brass section. There they entered into high-level negotiations.

Even King Solomon would not have found an immediate solution. Neither baby nor orchestra could be cut in half. Finally, Minister Levin asked if anyone had small change for another phone call. Somebody produced a coin, and the minister called a colleague in the housing department. Within twenty minutes the family from Romania had a new apartment, three blocks away from the Ohel Shem. Mother and baby were mollified. The hammer lay unused. The brass players returned to their seats, the orchestra resumed rehearsal and, summoned by no less an authority than the cabinet secretary, a large moving truck appeared on the scene to help reinstate musical peace at the Ohel Shem.

~ THE CHESS MASTER'S APPRENTICE

When we weren't worrying about the next meal, we were rehearsing and performing. There could be no doubt that this was a superb orchestra. As a young player on my first serious professional engagement, I had the remarkable fortune to be surrounded by some of the finest players from a dozen of Europe's greatest orchestras, who had escaped the Nazi scourge to join the embryonic Palestine Orchestra under Bronisław Huberman and Arturo Toscanini.

Now reborn as the Israel Philharmonic, the orchestra had no permanent musical director. It was led by a parade of guest conductors, and as a result had not yet acquired a style of its own. String players altered bowings at whim. Some of the woodwinds played in warm German style, others struggled to overcome their military-band background. The brass, a number of whom were new immigrants from France and Belgium, played with a completely different, characteristically Gallic sound. Guest conductors seldom had sufficient time to blend the various sections.

Artistic decisions were made by an elected committee. With ex-concertmasters and principal players from Berlin, Warsaw, Budapest, Prague, Leipzig, Dresden, Vienna, Bucharest and Sofia, it was an orchestra of determined musical individualists. Chaotic rehearsals were conducted in any one of six languages, so it was no surprise that it was difficult to maintain any sort of musical discipline.

Players failed to turn up if they disliked a particular conductor. Others played deliberate wrong notes to see if the conductors noticed anything. A conductor with an indecisive baton would be ignored, and the players would watch the bow of the first violinist. In ultimate indignity, one of the five alternating concertmasters was known to switch places with his identical twin brother, who played the tympani. The conductor's downbeat would elicit a ferocious drum roll, a cacophony of non-musical violin squeaks and unkind laughter from some of the less sensitive musicians. The Israel Philharmonic in 1951 was an orchestra that was always on the edge of its extraordinary potential.

In spite of this, concerts were overwhelmingly successful. The orchestra was wildly adulated by the general public. It was said that members of the Israel Philharmonic Orchestra (along with the prime minister and taxi drivers) were the most revered people in the new nation. Musically, the combined experience of so many fine players, and the added brilliance of many great conductors and soloists, was exactly what the audience wanted. Each concert was performed nine times in Tel Aviv, three in Haifa and four in Jerusalem. The orchestra was eternally busy, and I could not have experienced a more valuable apprenticeship to the international musical world.

And what an apprenticeship it was! Principal bassoonist Mordechai Rechtman, who became my Israeli mentor, was only two years older than I, but he had already held the post of principal bassoonist of the orchestra for five years. He was not only a superb player but also an international chess master. At rehearsals he would often be engrossed in seven or eight simultaneous chess matches with competitors around the world. On a second music stand, he carefully laid out the postcards for the next moves, ready to be mailed at intermission—this one to New York, that one to London, this one to Moscow, another to Prague.

My job in the orchestra was officially that of second bassoon, a critically important musical position in the woodwind section. The glamorous solo bassoon passages, with their associated psychological pressure, were the realm of the principal player. But he would often be engrossed by a tricky move in one or another of his chess matches. From my first rehearsal I discovered that apart from being ready for my own entrances, I was also expected to keep a wary eye on my colleague's music and to make sure that he was warned just before each important solo passage. Better he played Beethoven than the risky Nimzowitsch Queen Pawn Defense. Although it never became necessary, I had to be ready to play all of the principal's parts as well as my own. What finer introduction to orchestral life could I have hoped for? He seldom lost a match, and never, as far as I recall, did he miss an entrance.

Halfway through the season, my new Heckel bassoon arrived from Wiesbaden. Miraculously (or was it protekzia again?) it cleared customs and was delivered directly to the Bet Tismoret. I opened the case and stared lovingly at the instrument. Did I know that it was going to remain my companion for a lengthy international career? I tried a few tentative notes—it sounded well enough—and then, in an act of incredible recklessness (bassoonists, and other musicians, are always advised to break a new instrument in slowly, getting to know its personality and capabilities before playing in public), I left my old instrument behind and took the new bassoon with me to rehearsal.

There I was met by the orchestra inspector with a worried look on his face. "Your colleague is ill. You will have to play principal today."

On the program was Ravel's *Boléro*, with one of the most daunting bassoon solos in our repertoire. There are only two melodies in the entire work, and it is the bassoon that announces the second of these two themes, starting in its very highest register and sinuously working its way down to the warm middle range of the instrument. I had no time to panic, no possibility to escape. The *Boléro* was first on the rehearsal schedule. The conductor pointed at me, and the instrument rose gloriously to its task. Perhaps some deity of the bassoon world recognized that reputations of instrument maker and player alike were on the line. Perhaps the additional ten years' aging and drying of the wood was already showing in the instrument's resplendent sound and easy response. My woodwind colleagues shuffled their feet in muted appreciation of the solo, and the *Boléro* continued to its orgiastic climax.

In the entire seventy years that I played on that instrument, I never again worried that it would let me down in the high register.

～ A SOLOIST IS BORN

When the orchestra management recruited me to act as Bet Tismoret chauffeur, they did not know what they were unleashing. As I drove conductors and soloists to and from rehearsals and concerts, I would overhear their post-rehearsal frustrations and pre-concert fears, and would often share their late-night post-concert euphoria. It was a strangely intimate and easygoing time—even in the frenzy of Tel Aviv traffic jams.

One morning, the guest conductor from Argentina surprised me as we sat in traffic on the way to rehearsal. "Do you know this piece?" he asked me, brandishing a miniature score. The red light changed before I could look. "It's a bassoon concerto by the Italian, Wolf-Ferrari." I nodded and drove on, unwilling to admit that I knew more about Ferrari as an automobile than Wolf-Ferrari as a composer. Two trucks crossed in front of us, travelling in opposite directions, and stopped in the middle of the intersection. The drivers rolled down their windows and started a spirited conversation. The clamour of fifty automobile horns filled the air. The trucks didn't move. Oblivious to the noise around him, the conductor leafed through the score.

"You should learn it," he said. "We would like you to play it next week at a youth concert." I could hardly believe what I was hearing. I was a junior member of the orchestra to which I had belonged for less than six months. I had absolutely no experience as a soloist. As well, this was an unknown work, by a relatively unknown composer. I would be playing on a new instrument. Furthermore, I knew that the bassoon was rarely thought of as a concerto soloist. The risks were enormous, as much for the orchestra as for me.

In addition, solos were usually the prerogative of the principal player. I had sense enough to ask if my colleague might object. "Not at all," replied my passenger. "It was his idea." I needed no further encouragement. Three traffic lights and fifty automobile horns had turned me from second bassoon into incipient soloist.

Once we reached the rehearsal hall, I had a chance to look more closely at the score. It was a fascinating work, but it soon became clear that if I really wanted to play the piece, I would have to copy out a full set of parts for the orchestra. I set to work that evening—and learned an important lesson that proofreading is just as important in music copying as it is in the editorial room of a newspaper. Half the ensuing rehearsal was spent correcting errors in my frantic nighttime copying. In spite of that, my solo debut occurred later that week before a thousand bemused high school students. For them, it was a chance to hear a musical rarity, a bassoon concerto. For me, it was the beginning of a soloist's dream.

Next morning I returned to my more modest role of apprentice and woodwind section player. Mordechai was engrossed in a match with Istanbul, but between two moves of the Trompowsky Attack he nodded his critical approval of my concerto performance. I made sure to return the favour, counting carefully and giving him suitable advance warning before his next important solo entrance. Only afterward did the significance of the occasion strike home: we were rehearsing *The Sorcerer's Apprentice* by Paul Dukas.

My solo debut at least had the benefit of *some* rehearsal time. Other performances were not so lucky. The third horn player of the orchestra was a former Berlin wrestling champion who had emigrated to Israel in the mid-1930s. At that time, possibly because there were few others who played the instrument, he had been the principal horn player of the early Palestine Orchestra. By 1951, with the arrival of many younger players, he had moved over to the less-taxing position of third horn, which meant that he had much more free time on his hands.

When he invited me to play woodwind quintets at outlying kibbutzim, of course I was excited. "When do we rehearse?" I asked, guilelessly. "Brother," was the bellowed reply from the depths of his wrestler's gut, "we don't rehearse. All we want is the money!" Fees for woodwind quintets, I discovered, were not quite up to the Dixieland band chicken level, but there was the pleasure of playing for country audiences, and we would always go home with plenty of green peppers and onions for the perpetual soup.

∽ CHANGED DIRECTION: BULLETS AND BELIEFS

Pianist Artur Rubinstein was playing a Brahms piano concerto with the New York Philharmonic on the day the Japanese Navy Air Service attacked the U.S. naval base at Pearl Harbor in Honolulu in 1941. As a teenager I was listening to that concert on the radio and heard the incredulous and tremulous voice of the announcer interrupting Rubinstein and conductor Rodziński to tell the listening public of the attack.

Almost exactly ten years later, Rubinstein played that same concerto with the Israel Philharmonic. After the concert I drove him back to the Bet Tismoret, and we shared our common recollection of that momentous afternoon in 1941. In New York, at the very moment the concerto finished, a manager had rushed on stage to break the news to a stunned audience. Instead of the anticipated ovation, tears and gasps of disbelief greeted the artists. Ten years later, Israel was bathed in a euphoria of optimism that could not be dampened even by the prevailing austerity. At the close of that same Brahms concerto there was thunderous rhythmic applause and a standing ovation that brought the soloist and conductor back to the stage five times. The music surely reflected a nation's unbridled hope for the future.

The orchestra also occasionally played at some of the larger, more established kibbutzim. One evening, in an outdoor amphitheatre that lay in the shadow of the Golan Heights, the opening movement of Robert Schumann's *Spring* Symphony was filling the nighttime air when sporadic gunfire broke out. A stray bullet struck the power generator and the entire village was plunged into darkness. The orchestra played on; even without light, most of the musicians managed to complete the opening movement. By then the gunfire had receded, but darkness and an eerie silence prevailed. The audience remained in their seats, spellbound. The conductor, well known as a viola soloist, reached down and borrowed an instrument from one of the musicians, and for twenty-two magical minutes, until the generator was repaired, he played unaccompanied Bach. When the lights came on, the orchestra resumed at exactly the point where it had stopped.

We understood then how music could overcome both danger and fear.

Neither danger nor fear entered into Netta's and my decision to leave Israel at the end of the year. Rather, it was a combination of circumstances and changing attitudes. For my wife, who had grown up in England deeply committed to the Habonim pioneer youth movement, Israel should have been the consummation of her Zionist dream. Instead, she was overwhelmed by the hardships of daily life. Austerity and political statehood blocked fulfillment of those ardent socialist ideals. She couldn't wait to rejoin her family.

For me, it was the opposite. I had arrived in Israel without Zionist inclination or intent, certainly never holding any sort of fervent belief that I was destined to return from the Diaspora to Israel. Yet it was hard not to succumb to the temptation of a musical career with one of the world's great symphony orchestras. "Member of the Tismoret" was an intoxicating sobriquet, a heady position with respect, recognition and privilege. The orchestra was musically stimulating and promised unlimited opportunity.

There was one nagging factor. I had tasted the nectar of the soloist's cup. The lure of that elusive world of musical liberation beyond the ranks of the orchestra, coupled with my wife's desire to escape from austerity, tipped the balance, and we determined to leave at the end of the season.

Our odyssey shifted into reverse. The coveted Hillman Minx went to a non-governmental agency that was in urgent need of wheels. Our ration cards, good for the balance of the year, went to our friends who stayed behind in the Bet Tismoret. Since clothing, like food and electricity, was severely rationed, my tail suit, which I had acquired in a dingy second-hand store on West 49th Street, went to the second oboist of the orchestra.

Years later, when the Israel Philharmonic toured North America in 1969, they played in Seattle and I drove down from Vancouver to hear them and to meet some of my former colleagues. The oboist was still there, now promoted to principal of his section. We met for coffee before the concert. "Still wearing your suit," he told me, as with a practised thumb (his grandfather had been a tailor in Vitebsk in pre-war years) he felt the cloth. "Good material! As durable as it comes." That wasn't the only thing that was durable and unchanged. Mordechai was still playing chess during rehearsals. But when I met him, he complained bitterly that his second-desk partner constantly missed cues. "It's not the same," he told me. "I have to count for myself!"

The changes were all on our side. *Tikkun olam* is a Hebrew phrase that, loosely translated, means "mending the world." Sadly, I don't think our year of discovery in Israel contributed very much to any of the needed repairs. We had failed to fit in with the New Society. Maybe back in North America, in more familiar settings, we would be able to achieve new goals.

Interlude

⌣ SALAMI CASINGS

I returned from Israel to New York with a new bassoon and a certainty that with my Israel Philharmonic background I would find a place in the "Big Apple." But the city was full of returning veterans, resuming their places in a disrupted concert world, and I was still remarkably inexperienced. The playing opportunities of my dreams never materialized.

The frenetic Belgian Léon Barzin continued to terrify aspiring young musicians at the National Orchestral Association. The loan for my new instrument was now repaid, and I was pleased to show them the product of their generosity, but there was still no honorarium for the thrice-weekly rehearsals. The orchestras of Scranton, Wilkes-Barre, Orange, Vermont and New Hampshire were also still there. They paid their musicians a pittance. It hardly constituted a musical livelihood. This was not the mainstream of New York musical life that I had visualized and hoped for. It was certainly not the soloist's life, which, once sampled, now needed fulfillment. Somehow, I needed to diversify.

My father helped me secure an evening job writing publicity for the United Jewish Appeal. Night after night I attended fundraising banquets, organized on an industry-wide basis. The manufacturers of aluminum storefronts, swimsuits, leather gloves and even salami casings were gathered together for the public blackmail known as "reading of the cards." Exposed before their competitors, each participant had to announce an annual donation, which not only displayed loyalty to the cause of the United Jewish Appeal (how they each vied to assert their fervency!) but also revealed the state of their finances. After each banquet, my task was to write up the results as a news story, which was submitted, night after night after night, to the editorial desk of the *New York Times*. Every now and then a 250-word press release was reduced to a twenty-three-word entry in the business news: "Last night the salami casings industry gathering of 37 New York-based manufacturers raised a total of $135,750 towards the United Jewish Appeal." I received a seven-cent raise from the basic hourly rate for every item that appeared in the columns of the *Times*.

It was midsummer, and New York was experiencing a monumental heat wave. The owner of our apartment building was anxious to tear down the old brownstone and develop a high-rise on the site. To encourage his few remaining tenants to leave voluntarily, he turned the furnace on full blast.

Sweltering from both external and internal heat, there was little choice but to pack up our sparse belongings and escape. Perhaps my musical aspirations could be better met elsewhere, and Netta's desire to rejoin her family could also be fulfilled. Somebody else could keep the *New York Times* apprised of the nightly successes of the United Jewish Appeal. The National Orchestral Association would carry on with at least eighteen other young bassoonists, and nobody at Scranton, Pennsylvania; Montpelier, Vermont; or Orange, New Jersey, would ever really miss me. We headed west to Vancouver. Sadly, my marriage to Netta did not survive the move. Shortly after our return, we agreed to a divorce.

II: EXPOSITION

Divided Highway

Vancouver

~ THE QUIET CITY

To a young man born in London and educated in New York, western Canada seemed a fine compromise between the hectic pace of America and the ingrained memory of childhood England.

Since my first visit a few years earlier, the copper roof of the Hotel Vancouver had turned a slightly darker shade of green. The massive oversize clock atop the Birks Building still hovered over Granville Street. The gracious old Sylvia Hotel still presided at English Bay. Of all Vancouver's iconic edifices, none reached higher than the twenty-two floors of the art deco Marine Building, which from its position at the heart of the downtown core dominated Burrard Inlet and the city's busy harbour. The Georgia Auditorium stood on the edge of Coal Harbour—close to collapse but nonetheless available to rent for events ranging from wrestling to symphony concerts. The Woodward's Building, with its massive letter "W," and the long-vacated Sun Building marked the decaying former city centre at Victory Square (commemorating victory in World War I, that is). Further uptown, the Showboat still rose every summer at Kitsilano Beach. Oak Street had extended south toward Marpole, opening up many new suburbs. The city was growing.

I wondered what, if anything, had grown musically and what opportunities there would be for me in Vancouver's orchestral world.

~ UNION RULES AND THE FOUR-MINUTE MILE

The Vancouver Symphony season still lasted only twenty-three weeks. The CBC Radio Orchestra was the jewel in the city's musical crown, broadcasting thirty-nine hour-long concerts each year under the baton of pioneer pianist and conductor John Avison. I had no contract with either, but in 1953 Vancouver it was reasonable to believe that both orchestras would welcome a modestly experienced bassoonist.

I had not counted on George Leach, one of the only other bassoonists in Vancouver at that time. He was also secretary of the musicians' union. I called on him to "deposit my transfer"—the formal process of moving from one city to another within the jurisdiction of the union.

"So you play the bassoon, laddie?" he asked me, belligerence bursting from every syllable. He insisted on calling me "laddie" to emphasize his Scottish working-man's roots. "You've been invited up here by the symphony, have you?"

I assured him that was not the case. I explained that my wife's family was here, and we had made the determined move to a smaller city. "Better to be a large fish in a small pond than a tiny sardine in an ocean of barracudas," I quipped.

He didn't take kindly to my humour. "You aren't planning to teach, are you, laddie?" I was taken aback by this new attack, for I surely expected that if there were any potential students not yet spoken for, I might well undertake some teaching. I told him so. "I wouldn't do that, laddie," he intoned. "You would be creating your own competition!"

He returned to his original theme. "You've come here to play in the symphony, haven't you?"

"Of course I would hope to," I replied.

That was sufficient to condemn me. "So it's as I thought!" he thundered. "You've been imported to take the symphony job! That's all you'll be allowed to do, laddie."

As much as I denied it, he insisted: I was an "imported" player, and according to his whim, he accepted my union transfer but limited me for two years to playing only with the Vancouver Symphony Orchestra. He knew as well as I did that the season was not sufficient on its own to keep anyone in Vancouver.

At least in one respect, my life in Vancouver was not going to prove much different from life in New York. Performance alone was not going to provide a livelihood. Calling on my experience with the United Jewish

Appeal, I accepted work writing publicity for the United Fund, but this was seasonal activity, so eventually I had to look further afield.

In July and August 1954, Vancouver hosted the British Empire and Commonwealth Games (forerunner of the Commonwealth Games), and through my United Fund connections I found myself performing odd jobs for the Games administration. The first assignment involved the CBC. I was asked to interview athletes as they arrived in town for the Games. To compensate for the vast time differences between Vancouver and the southern hemisphere, interviews with Australian, Fijian and New Zealand athletes had to be taped and rebroadcast at sensible hours. The CBC provided me with a portable wire recorder.

Re-enter George Leach. I was summoned to the union office. "There is a contract in place with the CBC," he intoned. "Recording is not permitted without the local's permission," and he pointed to the clause in the master agreement with the musicians' union.

"But I'm not recording music!" I argued.

"No matter, laddie. It clearly states in the union regulations: 'no recording shall be permitted without approval of the Secretary,' and I am not giving my approval, laddie."

In front of me, he then phoned the regional director of the CBC. Whatever union action he threatened, it was apparently quite sufficient to compel the network to cancel my ongoing employment. An apologetic producer stopped by that evening and picked up the wire recorder. Suitably admonished, I turned to more mundane work for the Games, including driving athletes to and from events (an activity thankfully not covered by any arcane union regulations).

I remain eternally grateful for this turn of events. One of the athletes committed to my care was the late Dr. Roger Bannister. One of the highlights of the 1954 Games was the "Miracle Mile," when Bannister and John Landy both ran the mile in under four minutes in the same race (Bannister had run the first sub-four-minute mile only three months earlier).

Roger Bannister was a physician as well as an athlete, and in the course of our several trips from hotel to stadium and back we spoke about breathing, the common currency of sprinters and wind players. I learned a profound lesson from this physician, one that served me well during my entire playing career. In blowing a bassoon, as in running, the challenge is not how to fill your lungs, but how to expel the stale air before taking in new breath. We also shared an unexpected common understanding of what Bannister called the "exquisite pain" of our respective accomplishments.

How often, when playing, have I taken pleasure in using breath to the very last moment of possible endurance? It happens when you hold a particularly poignant high note for its full duration. Every part of you—embouchure, lungs, diaphragm—concentrates on sustaining the full intensity and sonority of that single tone. Then you start a steady diminuendo, without sacrificing any of the resonance or vibrato. At the very last moment, when your lungs might seem ready to burst, you hold the note yet a second longer. At that point, you may experience ecstasy or "exquisite pain" in a moment of achieved beauty. It's the wind players' version of the four-minute mile.

∼ REFLECTIONS ON THE SILVER SCREEN

Despite the union-imposed restrictions, I accepted the symphony contract for the coming season and took my seat in the Vancouver Symphony. This was an orchestra on the threshold of excellence. Of the thirty-five players on contract, only a small nucleus had played in professional orchestras elsewhere. Many of the others had non-symphonic musical backgrounds. The trumpet and trombone came from the glamorous world of the big bands. The principal flute and clarinet were refugees from the Pacific and Orient ocean liners, where (between bouts of seasickness) they had entertained thousands of passengers en route to Japan, the Philippines, Hong Kong and Australasia.

There were two high school teachers, one medical practitioner and a dental surgeon who reputedly performed root canal treatments on fellow musicians while testing their knowledge of the themes of Beethoven symphonies. There were women who had resumed playing after raising their families. There were young players in the orchestra, just returned from overseas study. There was also a shoe salesman, two real estate agents and a friendly insurance broker whose business thrived splendidly from congenial contact with his fellow players.

With so many members involved in other daytime activities, we could only rehearse on evenings and weekends. Because the orchestra had no permanent home, we converged at the Lions Club hall, the Scottish Auditorium or the old Lord Byng High School gym. On Sundays, with the grudging permission of the Lord's Day Alliance, we were allowed to rehearse and then perform in the Orpheum Theatre.

We were proud to be able to show the audience that the orchestra was coming of age. But our greatest concern at those Sunday afternoon concerts was entirely non-musical. At that time the Orpheum was an acoustically lively movie house, and management was eternally petrified that one of us might accidentally scratch the giant silver screen behind us. As far as I know it was never damaged by a passing tuba, or by any other musical instrument for that matter, but our presence, however well protected the screen, and however benign the musical content of the afternoon, was a permanent irritant to the theatre owners. They argued that if the Lord permitted a musical entertainment on Sunday, why should He not equally allow a movie? Certainly 2,800 Sunday movie-goers would contribute far more to the operator's bottom line than the meagre community-rate rental that they were cajoled into charging the symphony! These skirmishes continued until 1959, when big industry prevailed and the orchestra was tossed out of the Orpheum. But more on that later.

Overture to a Lifetime Comedy

~ RULE COLUMBIA

For some inexplicable reason the union did not choose to interfere with chamber music, so to help fill some of the open time in the symphony schedule, I formed a woodwind quintet with other principal musicians from the orchestra. We called the ensemble the Cassenti Players.

Nobody was ever quite clear where the name "Cassenti" came from. It might have been the name of a lesser-known Italian composer—so obscure that nobody knew any work that he or she had ever written. More likely the name derived from a melding of two popular eighteenth-century musical forms, cassations and divertimenti. Both forms were commonly used by both Haydn and Mozart, and over the course of our existence we played enough of each to justify the choice of name.

We met each week and rehearsed assiduously. We felt the glowing satisfaction and the comradeship of ensemble playing. When we finally had cobbled together a half-decent program, we looked at each other over the top of our music stands and wondered where on earth we could perform our freshly learned repertoire. Our group therapy needed an audience.

A senior executive of Columbia Artists—arguably North America's largest and most prestigious concert agency—was visiting Vancouver, and I had the good fortune to meet him at a post-concert symphony reception. I blithely offered him the exclusive availability of our newly formed ensemble.

"We are the principal players of the Vancouver Symphony," I told him, adding hastily, "The group is also very inexpensive."

There was a lengthy silence. Then he laughed, unkindly. "We have all the wind quintets we want," he told me. "Our clients need artists and groups from New York, maybe Los Angeles or, perhaps, from overseas." He paused to catch his breath. "Vancouver musicians? You must be kidding."

I wasn't kidding, but at that moment I realized why, in 1954, unknown Canadian soloists and ensembles could not depend on an American agency for their future careers. Columbia not only offered its clients a choice of many well-known celebrities. It also maintained a vast list of its own un-known American artists. There would be no immediate Columbia tour for the Cassenti Players.

During my nineteen-week tour with the St. Louis Sinfonietta in the mid-1940s, I had learned how Community Concerts successfully organ-ized their thriving network of small communities for regular concerts. Financially, it was foolproof. It didn't matter how large or small the town. Money for concerts was raised by advance subscription, and no contracts were signed until the cash was available. More community members meant a larger budget for more expensive artists, or for additional concerts. It was a plan in which there could be no failure—only varying levels of success.

Of course, the American idea of a "small town" included Buffalo, Green Bay, Joplin, Reno and San Jose, all cities over 100,000 population. But Community Concerts had also approached many smaller centres, including several Canadian border towns. For artists already on tour in Washington, Idaho and Montana, for example, British Columbia represented a new opportunity. To those cities that signed up, Community Concerts sent a stream of unknown young American artists and ensembles, who happily extended their tours beyond the northern states, treating Canada as part of a regular American touring circuit.

The audiences were flattered that New York actually deigned to pay them any attention at all and, indeed, there were many wonderful artists and groups among these touring pioneers.

So if Columbia didn't want the Cassenti Players to play for them, I de-cided I would offer my services as a field representative. Would they be in-terested in sending me out on the road in British Columbia to organize new towns for their Community Concerts circuit? I spread out a map on which I had circled, in red, a number of British Columbia communities that I thought might be ready for an organized concert program.

The answer was an echo of the earlier response. "We really have all the Canadian towns we want," he drawled. "There just aren't any more that could support our kind of series."

He was terribly wrong, of course, and that was the moment I decided I would go out and do it myself. Canada was coming of age, and Canadian communities were ready to make their own concert plans and to welcome Canadian groups and soloists, even if at the time they were equally unknown. Within a decade, *Maclean's* magazine would write that I had successfully outsmarted the Americans at their own game.

⮑ PLEASE ADVISE NEXT MOVE

If, in 1955, I had turned left instead of right at Keremeos on the Hope–Princeton Highway, I might never have launched the Canadian version of the "organized audience."

I had set out that morning to find the city of Vernon, which I had been told might be interested in a concert by the Cassenti Players. Confronted by massive road construction, I followed a detour and discovered instead the eternally beautiful city of Nelson, "Queen City of the Kootenays." There, by chance more than design, I persuaded a group of enthusiastic volunteers to consider not just a *single* concert but an entire *series*. Nelson was a good place for a start. It had not yet succumbed to the allure of the "Big Apple." It still has not!

I strolled up and down Baker Street and spoke with a myriad of interested citizens. I visited the library, city hall, the newspaper offices, attended a choir rehearsal, dropped by a piano studio. "We aren't ready for this," somebody warned me. "Nobody around here would pay two dollars for a concert even if Mozart himself turned up."

I persisted, and others were more receptive. With the help of a public health nurse, a librarian, a choir conductor and the wife of the high school principal, I called a meeting. Twenty-one music enthusiasts turned up!

I no longer remember exactly what I told them, but I must have been persuasive that evening. Three weeks later I received a cryptic telegram:

NELSON CONCERTS
SUCCESSFULLY COMPLETED MEMBERSHIP DRIVE
217 SUBSCRIBERS STOP
HAVE AVAILABLE $1850 STOP
PLEASE ADVISE NEXT MOVE

Next move? I was equally in the dark, not entirely sure what had to be done next. However, I knew that, somewhere, somehow, I had to find at least three artists or groups willing to perform in a city approximately seven hundred kilometres from Vancouver.

I had colleagues on the burgeoning Vancouver concert scene, and even a few contacts in Toronto and New York. The phone lines were busy (this was years before e-mail), and before the week was out I had lined up an opening series: a pianist (Help! Do they have a decent piano?), a violinist and a male vocal quartet.

The Nelson experiment hinted at the beginning of something new and exciting, and I chose the name "Overture" to suggest that there was considerably more to follow!

Indeed, there was. I was reminded of the red circles that I had marked on the map for Columbia. Over the course of the next six months, I became familiar with the schools, libraries, town halls, churches, newspaper offices and main streets of dozens of small communities in the British Columbia interior.

By the following season I had successfully organized seven more concert societies. I had created a network of small towns, not one of which had a population at that time in excess of 3,500 people.

⁓ MUSIC AND MAGIC

In preparation for one such trip to the interior of British Columbia I phoned ahead to a rural party line (number 276, ring 4). My contact was apparently not interested, and I was about to hang up when the local operator interrupted. "Ring 3 would like to talk to you. I'll connect you to Myrtle." Not every word on Myrtle's phone line was entirely clear, but before long I had an invitation to visit the community and meet with a committee.

Delayed once more by highway construction, I realized that I would be very late. From a pay phone I called again. This time the line constantly cut in and out as we spoke. As best I could, I told Myrtle at ring 3 about some of the stellar musicians who were willing, even anxious, to give concerts in their town. Ring 3 was joined by ring 2, and they assured me that they would be waiting for my arrival.

Tired and dusty, I finally sat down with the group. As I spoke, I had a strange feeling of disconnection. It seemed there was absolutely no interest in anything that I proposed. Piano, voice, violin, chorus, orchestra, chamber music—nothing seemed to register. All around me I encountered blank faces. I was completely confounded until a woman interrupted, as gently as she could. "Mr. Zukerman," she said, "you know that both times you called we had a terrible phone connection. We now realize that you must have been talking about *musicians*, but we all thought you said *magicians*."

Looking at it many years later, is there really so much of a difference? Music is its own form of sublime magic, and a musician is a kind of magician. A few seasons later, that community successfully organized their concert society.

In common with all our groups, it was a subscription series. Membership was open to anyone at any time, but single tickets were not available for the individual concerts. On the last day of the membership drive, a young lady came into the headquarters where I was busy with the committee, signing up new subscribers. She was in tears. "I want to join, please, but they won't let me," she lamented. I tried to reassure her that we would welcome her as a member. "Everyone can join," I consoled. "You can become a member at any time. What made you think you couldn't join?" Between tears the young lady explained. "Your poster says 'no single admissions' and I'm not getting married until December." The young lady joined. Five years later she was chairperson of the committee, proudly telling her unmarried friends that there were definitely no single admissions.

∼ HUROK OF THE HAMLETS

As early as 1958, Overture Concerts had expanded eastward to the prairies, and in that year alone the number of affiliated communities more than doubled to seventeen. One year later there were thirty-three affiliated concert societies. Despite Canada's relatively small population and far-flung geography, it seemed there was no limit to the number of communities—at least in the west—that were ready to present live classical music on a guaranteed, risk-free basis.

Up until that time, most North American concert touring had been organized from the United States on a north-south basis. Driven by the needs of large cities, a tour might extend from San Francisco, Portland and Seattle to include Vancouver and Victoria. Salt Lake City and Denver were the links for tours to Edmonton and Calgary. Minneapolis served Winnipeg. A tour that played Duluth might add on Port Arthur or Fort William. In the east, with larger populations, it was less obvious, but Boston, New York and Chicago were respectively the anchors for tours that might include Halifax, Montreal and Toronto.

Now, with the Overture Concerts network, for the first time tours were being created across Canada. The towns and cities along the Canada–U.S. border no longer needed to be treated as the end of the American touring line. Saskatchewan was not condemned to the status of a musical suburb of North Dakota. A new west-east touring route across Canada was taking shape.

I tracked reports in the business section of the newspaper, seeking new towns that were springing up, fuelled by the nation's economic growth. Concert societies emerged in the same year as the first barrel of oil was pumped from a new field, the first tree felled under a newly acquired timber license, the first ore extracted from a new mine, the first aluminum flowed from a new smelter.

We deliberately avoided the large cities. Overture Concerts was a phenomenon of Canada's small centres, where the real drive stemmed from an absolute belief in the "organized audience" concept. We applied "the method" as fervently as any actor would swear by Stanislavsky.

The proliferation of new Overture Concert Associations created an insatiable demand for touring artists. If I had trouble finding performers for three concerts for a single city, how was I to locate people for dozens of concerts in the new towns? It didn't take long to exhaust my few contacts, and still I needed many more artists and ensembles who would be willing to explore the territory.

It would have been easy to depend on the established links with American managers, but it became increasingly apparent that there was a need—and an opportunity—to encourage Canadian soloists and ensembles to take advantage of the new touring possibilities. We were all new at the process. I was a novice impresario. My staff were novice organizers. Most of the communities were new to the touring world. Canadian artists and ensembles had yet to discover touring as a way of life, with its remarkable opportunity to perform outside home cities. Artist management agencies sprang up to assist them in their tour planning and, ultimately, in their career development. Funding programs were launched nationally and provincially to stimulate touring and to strengthen the newly formed cross-Canada links.

I decided to attend a booking conference. There were none yet held in Canada, but I had somehow learned of a major gathering of concert organizers that took place each year in New York. It would be an occasion to find out about the world of touring artists, and at the same time it would provide an opportunity to visit my parents.

I registered for the event, which was to take place at the distinguished vintage Sherry-Netherland Hotel in the heart of fashionable New York. I discovered that the conference was organized by the great American impresario Sol Hurok, renowned for bringing to worldwide stages glittering attractions from the Soviet Union. Did I really imagine the Bolshoi Ballet dancing at Williams Lake? The Red Army Chorus on stage at Gibson's Landing?

My father, for whom writing was the most normal human expression, could never quite visualize a musician's life. "What do you really do for a living?" he once asked me. I told him that I was one of eight professionally trained and experienced musicians who played in a small-city symphony orchestra. I also told him that in my extensive spare time I had started organizing concert series in smaller centres in the hinterland of the province that I now called home. None of this struck him as a serious endeavour. However, when I told him that I planned to attend Sol Hurok's management conference, his eyes lit up. He had long been on Hurok's mailing list for event invitations. He quickly arranged an interview for me.

I arrived at Sol Hurok's intimidating offices on Sixth Avenue. The meeting was short and to the point

"Zukerman?"

"Yes."

"Father wrote for the *Morning Journal*?"

"Yes."

"I remember him. Didn't like the ballet. Never came to my openings. Why don't you write too?"

"I prefer concerts."

"Meshuge" (Crazy).

In the heyday of his concert empire, Hurok regularly invited his colleagues, whether arch-rivals or novice beginners, to his annual banquet, which concluded the conference.

Among the guests at the first of those glorious gatherings that I ever attended were Artur Rubinstein (he remembered me from Israel), Isaac Stern, Marian Anderson, Jascha Heifetz, William Warfield. "Not bad, my stable, a few good people here and there," muttered Mr. Hurok as he wandered around the massive dining room, stopping momentarily at each table.

I sat at the farthest table from the dais with several other managers from distant corners of the Americas. Not one of us at table #17 could afford a single artist or group from Mr. Hurok's distinguished list. But we basked in the presence of the great array of internationally renowned performers and the lustre of the Hurok hospitality.

What does a great impresario provide for entertainment at his once-a-year banquet for the trade? Would he ask Anderson to sing? Rubinstein to tickle the ivories? Heifetz or Stern to fiddle? Obviously he would not want to justify such a choice to any one of them. Instead, he sallied out on West 47th Street, not far from his suite of offices, and engaged the services of the seediest magician plying his skills for weddings, bar mitzvahs, parties and meetings. Rabbits were extracted from Heifetz's violin case, Marian Anderson discovered that a chicken had laid an egg in her handbag, and Rubinstein, in the midst of recounting a hilarious anecdote in Russian to Igor Stravinsky, discovered that his copy of Beethoven's Opus 110 had been changed into a stream of red, green and blue ribbons.

That trip to New York did not result in any of Mr. Hurok's artists appearing for my embryonic network of small western Canadian centres. It would be a number of years before Isaac Stern played in Lethbridge, Alexander

Brailowsky in Brandon and Victoria de los Ángeles in West Vancouver. In the meantime, I would have to hunt elsewhere for artists to appear in smaller and more isolated communities in distant corners of Canada. Hurok would probably have still said, "Meshuge," but Jack Wasserman, well-known and well-loved columnist for the *Vancouver Sun*, understood the significance for Canada when he later dubbed me "the Hurok of the Hamlets."

∼ TO THE NORTH POLE AND BEYOND

On return from the New York conference, I realized it was time to let the music world know that Overture Concerts existed and would welcome artists who were willing to tour an unfamiliar territory.

Musical America was the trade magazine of the North American classical concert industry. It was a particularly staid and sober publication. The advertisements were traditional and unwaveringly conventional. Management agencies published their rosters and announced their artists with glamorous photographs, panegyric press quotations and glowing lists of major concert appearances. The formula never varied. No touch of levity crept into their stolidly institutional messages.

Overture had nothing to sell, but for seven consecutive seasons the imagination ran wild with a series of lighthearted cartoon advertisements in *Musical America*. The concert world had never seen anything like this before!

In the first one, which ran in 1960, Overture Concerts declared it was prepared to hold concerts at the North Pole. Nobody should have been surprised that it was followed by announcements of plans for concerts on the moon, in outer space, in Shangri-La, in Atlantis. In Heaven, they had trouble finding concert managers. Another of the advertisements took readers to prehistoric times, where a crazed percussionist played xylophone on the skeleton of Tyrannosaurus rex. "It's one of those avant-garde pieces in the 12-bone style."

Over their seven-year run, the advertisements told of the growth of the Canadian organized audience. Red Deer, Medicine Hat, Swift Current, Flin Flon, Wawa and Uranium City were part of a tantalizing new touring circuit of Canadian towns that many of *Musical America*'s readers had probably never heard of. At its peak, nearly four hundred Overture concerts were reported in seventy-two communities across Canada.

∼ JOHN AVISON

As Overture Concerts got off the ground, I continued to play with the Vancouver Symphony. In 1957, the union finally relented and I was allowed to play with the CBC Radio Orchestra.

Nearly seventy years have passed since I first met the conductor, John Avison. To young professional musicians just arriving in Vancouver, as well as to those who were returning to their home city after study abroad in the early post-war years, his presence was proof that we were in the right

George in action, performing with the Vancouver Opera orchestra.

place at the right time—that serious music was going to thrive in western Canada. In those heady years of the city's remarkable musical escalation, John Avison was everywhere on the music-scape.

As pianist, he accompanied most visiting artists who came to the city, as well as many local performers. As composer, he wrote background music for countless radio dramas. And after he founded what was originally known as the CBC Vancouver Chamber Orchestra in 1938, he remained its conductor until his retirement in 1980. His thirty-two-piece orchestra presented a seemingly endless stream of daring repertoire from a makeshift studio in a former clothing store on Howe Street, racking up national (if not world) records for performance of Canadian and other contemporary music.

Union rules in 1956 still prohibited taping, so all broadcasts were un-edited "live to air." Those three-hour pressure-cooker sessions were never dull. The orchestra premiered hundreds of works by Canadian composers, along with a glorious array of symphonies by Mozart and Haydn. Guest soloists from around the world were given a platform in the traditional manner of prestigious European radio orchestras.

Rehearsals continued until the last possible minute before the "On the Air" light flashed. Everyone's breath was held momentarily as the studio fell silent. The broadcasts were produced with stopwatch accuracy by composer Robert Turner, and later a succession of distinguished CBC executives, including playwright Peter Garvie, novelist Norman Newton, historian Gerald Newman, impresario George Laverock and music producers Karen Wilson and Denise Ball. Today, no producer would dare record with so little preparation.

John Avison was not the greatest pianist or the most skilled conductor. On the podium, he often became enraged at his own frustration, struggling with the complex rhythms of contemporary works beyond his conducting skills. In spite of that, he was loved and admired because he showed us just how far we could go. He was willing to plunge in and try his hand at every-thing because of his abiding belief that somebody had to get things moving!

When I first arrived in Vancouver, John Avison told somebody that I was a "brash young upstart." It was probably true. But *he* must have been Vancouver's brash young upstart of the 1930s and '40s. Along with many other newcomers in the second half of the twentieth century, I was only carrying the ball that John Avison had thrown in our direction.

The CBC Radio Orchestra was the last remaining radio orchestra in North America when in 2009, in an inexplicable act of musical destruction, it was shut down by Canada's national broadcaster.

∽ THE EIGHT-DAY WEEK

With weekly broadcasts now added to my schedule, my dwindling free time was filling up. The Beatles may have sung about it, but I had little success promulgating my idea of an eight-day week.

I soon realized that it would be impossible to carry on all the activities of Overture Concerts from my dining room table. I needed office space and I needed help, both in the office and on the road. In this I was extremely lucky to collaborate with a stellar "cast" of people with various links to the world of music and performance.

At a barely furnished office on Richards Street, Delia Visscher, a former dancer from New York, who had been a member of the celebrated Radio City Music Hall's corps de ballet, turned up one day and stayed for twenty-eight years. In those pre-computer days, she was an amazing general factotum, single-handedly establishing control of our burgeoning concert activity. She seemed to know every artist, every manager, every community, each chair of each committee. Over the years she successfully dragged our reluctant organization into modern times with a telephone answering system, a fax machine . . . and—far ahead of the times—one of the first electric typewriters.

In contrast, Karl Norman conducted his entire seventeen-year management career with me on a badly battered Remington typewriter. He became my invaluable associate, in charge of our touring world during my playing absences, and taking particular care of our finances with a steady and eternally reliable hand. A popular tenor, Karl sang leading roles in early Vancouver Opera productions. I suspect that his greatest administrative problem was finding replacement ribbons for his ancient typewriter.

I firmly believe that Susan Kessler, who was in charge of travel arrangements for Overture's artists and ensembles, was the only person in the world who could have successfully organized travel from Kapuskasing, Ontario, to Swift Current, Saskatchewan, in a single day to allow for consecutive night concerts. (Travelling west, it *can* be done!) Susan acquired her travel skills in pre-war days in her home city of Budapest. Her harrowing post-war route to Canada took her through Austria, Portugal and England, where she met and married Jack Kessler, who later became concertmaster of John Avison's CBC Radio Orchestra. (What a world of small circles we inhabit!) Susan glittered, a constant presence at every exciting concert on the blossoming Vancouver music scene, and she lived to the glorious age of 107.

Across Canada, new towns were springing up at mines, mills, smelters and oil and gas exploration sites, so while I was touring, I was constantly on the lookout for communities that might be ready for a new concert series. Baritone, and later journalist, Kenneth Asch joined me and rapidly became the "miracle" organizer of the century. On one spectacular occasion he established five new concert societies in a single week. When, between us, we booked seemingly impossible schedules for our artists, Ken would rent trucks and buses and drive maniacally through the night to make sure that the performers turned up at the right town on the right day.

Stephanie Conroy, another ex-dancer, divided her time between the office and the road. When not shuttling string quartets around the country in her motorhome, she assisted concert committees with their advance promotion. Born in Ocean Falls, B.C., Stephanie felt a kinship with each of the small towns to which she mailed her well-wrapped packages of publicity material.

Helen Hove, former secretary of the Grand Forks concert society, also found it easy to convince other small-town residents that the "organized audience" could work for them. And Lynn Harlton dazzled us all when, on a journey to organize small northern Ontario communities, she decided to take a weekend break in Newfoundland and negotiated our first-ever $100,000 contract, sending a troupe of Chinese acrobats to the St. John's Arts and Culture Centre.

With both a staff and an office, I thought I would be able to turn my attention to the playing side of my existence. In fact, I found my playing even more closely tied to my organizational activity. This became clear when we realized that one of the most pressing needs of our network was for touring ensembles.

Cassenti Capers

⌣ GHOST OF RED BOOKS PAST

I often recall my earliest ensemble playing. As soon as I could sound the first notes on my first high school bassoon, I knew that music would always be a group activity for me. It started with the Red Book—yes, that tattered volume of classical transcriptions for wind quintet that turned up in those early school days. From the very first common chord on the first page of the Red Book, I was helplessly caught up in transcendental awe at the miracle and wonder of ensemble playing. It was a passion that would last a lifetime.

For many years beyond those school days, my ensemble playing was haunted by the spectral presence of the Red Book. Its familiarity for generations of wind players lay in the simple arrangements that made everyone perfectly content just to sight-read them. The Red Book was musical comfort food.

It turned up at WNYC, where its familiar contents required little rehearsal for our weekly chamber music series. It was waiting on our music stands in Israel when we arrived to sight-read at kibbutz concerts. And it turned up again in Vancouver when we formed the first Cassenti Players woodwind quintet.

I thought at first that the content of the Red Book would work for the quintet's many new audiences, but with its limited repertoire it proved to be no more saleable to Overture audiences than it would have been to Community Concerts. We needed more variety, and I finally found the courage to abandon the Red Book.

This was a musical epiphany. No longer limited to woodwinds, I turned to a pair of colleagues, the violinist Arthur Polson and pianist Harold Brown. With them, the Cassenti Players took on an unusual and flexible nature, built around the trio of violin, bassoon and keyboard. I added other instruments, depending on the repertoire we wanted to perform. We could be as small as a trio, or as large as twenty varied instruments on stage.

In a curious way, it was a recreation of my music-making in wartime New York. Then, with the New Chamber Music Society, there had been no choice. Different ensembles gathered each week depending on who happened to be available on a given Saturday morning.

In Vancouver, the decision to mix winds, strings and keyboard was deliberate. It allowed us to explore a vast repertoire that lay beyond the limits of the Red Book.

∼ HOW MOZART AND HAYDN CAME TO THE PRAIRIES

If you branch off Highway 16 between Wynyard and Foam Lake, you will find the hamlet of Mozart, Saskatchewan, founded by hardy German settlers in 1903. The sign at the highway intersection reads "Mozart 2 km." How close to genius can one get?

Harold Brown, our Cassenti Players pianist, was born in Wynyard. Among his earliest musical discoveries must have been the streets of nearby Mozart, which included Liszt Street, Schubert Street and Haydn Street. Originally a four-elevator town and a thriving railway stop on the grain circuit, by 2016 Mozart enjoyed a diminished resident population of 25.

The village lacked sufficient population for a Cassenti Players concert, but we found ourselves (now recipients of one of the earliest Canada Council touring grants) en route to another Saskatchewan community with a musical resonance to its name: the potash-mining town of Esterhazy. This conjured up visions of Franz Josef Haydn, who for much of his life had enjoyed the patronage of the Esterhazy family. We dreamed of this town basking in its glory as a vibrant and vital musical centre.

The Cassenti Players arrived, in decidedly ominous weather, with only a few minutes to spare before concert time. A decidedly ancient upright piano awaited us on stage, but Harold's initial distress was tempered by the sight of a card, thumbtacked to the edge of the instrument. It suggested a recent tuning. Harold bent over to scrutinize the message, but as he removed it from its pinhole, the paper began disintegrating between his fingers. Under the dust of many years, we could just barely make out the spindly writing, which stated, "This piano was tuned on Sept. 29, 1931."

Somehow we managed to play the concert, with much transposition, detuning of strings, switching of instruments and improvised programming. The Esterhazy family would have expected no less from Franz Joseph.

Outside the hall the snow was beginning to pile up at the start of a fierce winter storm. We had planned to leave early the next morning to catch a flight north from the nearby airport at Dauphin, Manitoba, but we decided, instead, to make the drive at night before the snow blocked the highway completely. It was Saturday evening, and there might not be any snowploughs at work on the roads early on Sunday. Fortified with many sandwiches, we headed off into the night. Above the drifting snow we could see the starlit sky. But what we could not see was the black ice forming beneath our tires as we hurtled toward our destination.

About halfway there, somewhere between the towns of Russell and Roblin, we found ourselves sliding gently off the road, coming to rest in a shallow ditch with the headlights beaming high into the sky. The time was shortly after midnight. For over two hours not a vehicle passed on that desolate stretch of road, although our headlights might have suggested that we were advertising an important movie premiere.

Finally, a solitary transport truck slithered to a stop half a kilometre away. After a long trek through the snow, the driver promised to summon a tow truck from the next village. It was a busy night for tow trucks, but finally, at 6 a.m. we were pulled out of the ditch and pointed in the right direction. Albeit under-slept, we were still comfortably ahead of our plane departure time. As we reached the outskirts of town, the snow subsided and the road became moderately passable. We had thirty minutes to spare.

Overhead, we heard the engines of the plane making its approach. We dashed into the terminal and arrived breathlessly at the check-in counter. The aircraft engines continued overhead, then suddenly increased in power and pitch, and we realized that the plane would not be landing. Along with the flight, our concert plans for the night had just been aborted.

What does one do at 8:45 on a Sunday morning with an unexpected free day in a strange town? I changed hats. Somewhere on a file card I had the name of the editor of the local newspaper. I had approached him once about the possibility of organizing concerts for his community. I found his name in the phone book and took a chance calling on a Sunday morning. "Would the community be interested in having a concert tonight?" I enquired.

What followed then was a miracle of community organization. The editor spoke to his son, who spoke to his friends at the high school, who spoke to the principal, who spoke to the mayor, who spoke to the librarian, who happened to be married to the town's hospital administrator, whose daughter also attended the high school ... and from this exchange came an extraordinary plan to hold a concert that night, for which the high school music club would be responsible.

We would enjoy the entire proceeds of the gate, less the organizers' expenses. Throughout the day the young people of the music club laboured valiantly. A church was booked, the local radio station made announcements. A printer was roused from his Sabbath to prepare a program. The editor's wife and I walked the streets of the community, knocking at doors and inviting her friends and neighbours to come to the concert.

And so we made our way to the church, music stands at the ready, and prepared for our 7:30 p.m. concert. At 7 p.m. there were three people present. At 7:15 the crowd had swelled to eleven. By concert time there were eighteen present. We delayed the non-existent curtain for ten minutes and were rewarded with seven more paying guests.

After the concert we sat with our student entrepreneurs and paid the bills, then divided the earnings for the night. Each of us pocketed the grand sum of $7.48! What a splendid day's work.

∼ THE STUFFED CASSENTI QUAIL

Some of the Cassenti Players' engagements took place in nearby American states. Columbia Artists may not have wanted to tour an unknown Canadian ensemble, but their Community Concerts division suddenly found it useful, and inexpensive, to have Canadian attractions available for their vast network of towns. On one such tour, we found ourselves in the city of P____.

Beneath swirling clouds from a dozen factory smokestacks, a haze of yellowish mist hung over the entire downtown. I have encountered few places that smelled so indelibly putrid. The sole industry, employing virtually everyone in town, was a gigantic fertilizer plant. Depending on the direction of the wind, malodorous traces of this bustling community could be detected miles from the city centre. Nonetheless, its 56,827 residents cheerfully abided the miasma that blanketed their town. It carried with it the aroma of prosperity.

Shoppers, store clerks, office workers, taxi drivers, municipal and federal employees all claimed to be inured to the smell. "You kind of get used to it after a few weeks," a gas station attendant insisted. Hotel guests and other visitors were less generous with their dismissal of the prevalent odour. A few hours in the heart of the city left eyes tearing, throats sore and nasal passages clogged with rich agricultural fragrance.

Visitors—especially the important ones, which included politicians in campaign mode, and touring concert artists—were taken on a guided tour of the plant. Everyone in town was proud of their fertilizer, and the idea was not only to smell it, but to learn a little about how it was produced. On our tour we were introduced to the scientists who determined the potency of the product as well as the technicians who controlled the volume of production. We also met the chief gatekeeper of the loading dock, the head of the stenographic pool, one of the many forklift operators, the chief electrician.

In common with most small American cities, "downtown" consisted of a cluster of shops, offices, hotels, schools, a post office and other government buildings. Adjacent to a central square was a stately and serene municipal garden, where the flora benefitted from an overabundance of free nitrogenous fertilizer. At the centre of the downtown core stood an ornate opera house, built in Chautauqua days and repurposed first for vaudeville, more recently for movies. On Sundays and on other dark days for movie attendance, the old opera house was rented to local community organizations for concerts, graduation ceremonies and political rallies.

Our concert took place in the opera house, just across the street from our hotel. There, at intermission, Madame Chair of the Community Concert committee swooped down on us in our dressing rooms. "You will join us at a dinner and reception at our house on The Terrace after the concert," she pronounced. "A real dinner," she added, "none of those tiddly sandwiches. My husband will pick you up. Watch at the stage door for a white Cadillac."

It was hard to tell whether it was an invitation or a command, but in either case we played the second half of the concert extremely well, salivating happily at the thought of a rare post-concert sit-down meal. After suitable applause and backstage small talk, we packed our instruments and headed to the exit. As promised, there was a large white Cadillac, a cigar-smoking fertilizer executive at the wheel. "Pile in, gents," he exclaimed genially, and he drove us rapidly out of the fog, up the hill, into the fresh air of The Terrace, a splendid street of elegant mansions built high above the city's smell-line. The houses were as brilliantly illuminated as the ceiling of stars above us. Downtown it was still a hazy cloud-filled evening. On The Terrace there was no haze, no foggy blanket, no stink.

We were guided into a home, and in a large drawing room stood forty or fifty guests, sipping martinis and manhattans, breaking into applause when we entered. For a few moments we were allowed to mingle with guests, continuing the usual post-concert small talk: "Where are you from?" "Where is your next concert?" "Did you like our theatre?" "Did you notice the smell?"

Before we could answer, we were whisked from the living room to a large private dining salon where we were served a splendid five-course meal. Was it a liveried butler who poured the soup, or was it the gatekeeper from the plant? A neatly attired waitress served the main course (or was she the young woman from the stenography pool?). Finally, our jovial host and Cadillac driver poured cognac and offered his prized Cuban cigars. We were relaxed, well-fed, contented.

Suddenly there was a furious hammering at the front door. Into the dining room stormed an enraged fury. Addressing nobody in particular, she shouted, "You stole my guests!" and proceeded to haul our pianist toward the front door. (Harold had the misfortune of being closest to the invading force.) "It's the wrong house ... the wrong house. We are across the street! Our guests are waiting." At that moment we recognized the lady in distress. She was the one who had come to our dressing room and invited us to dinner. Simultaneously, it dawned on us that in the house where we had just dined so extravagantly, we had not even met our hostess, only her cigar-toting, Cadillac-driving husband.

Sheepishly we extinguished our cigars, drained the last drop of cognac. Before we could thank anyone for such glowing hospitality, we were dragged across the street to another equally opulent illuminated mansion. There, another fifty-three guests were milling around the drawing room. They were already on their third or fourth martini or manhattan.

One, slightly more sober than the others, explained. The two hostesses, each married to a senior vice-president of the company, were eternal rivals, alternating chairpersons of the concert society and in fierce competition for the hosting rights to visiting artists. A glance out the window confirmed our worst fear. In the driveway of this house there also stood an impressive white Cadillac.

Without any chance to mingle with guests, we were led to a dining salon and seated around a heavily laden table, where the same five-course dinner service began all over again. Soup, pâté, two vintage wines, individually stuffed quail, a lemon pie. The liveried butler this time was the forklift operator from loading dock number three. The wine steward was none other than the electrician from the power plant. Our new host poured cognac and offered cigars as we answered the same questions, "Where are you from?" "Where is your next concert?" "Did you like our theatre?" "Did you notice the smell?" Thus the evening drew to a fattening close.

The drive down the hill, back into the miasmic blanket of fertilizer effluent, was almost a relief. I counted at least five more brightly illuminated mansions along The Terrace, and two of them sported white Cadillacs in their respective driveways. Midnight buffet, anyone?

∼ THE BAIL BOND BASSOONIST

Back in Canada, my bassoon and I once spent the night behind bars.

Well, not quite the entire night, and not really behind bars. We were only incarcerated for a few hilarious hours, and while in detention the only barrier to the front street was an unlocked wooden gate. It wasn't much of a prison, either. It was a friendly neighbourhood community police station. No truncheons, no sleep deprivation. But we were arrested, and we were charged. And it required the services of a solicitor, roused from his family hearthside on a snowy Sunday evening, to organize our release.

In its eighth successful season, the Nelson society had invited the

Cassenti Players to appear in its thriving series. The engagement fell between a CBC broadcast and the start of a biweekly symphony rehearsal schedule. To avoid conflict, we needed to fly to Castlegar, the airport that serves the city of Nelson.

Even with instrument approach, Castlegar (locally referred to as "Cancelgar") is one of the more challenging commercial airports in North America. With ominous mountains surrounding the single short runway, there is no possibility of a circular approach. Pilots need a high ceiling and decent visibility.

Neither was in place on the day of our departure. All flights to Castlegar were cancelled.

The concert was scheduled for 3 p.m. It would take ten hours to drive to Nelson, even if all the mountain passes were open. Clearly that option was out of the question. The weather front had not yet closed in on American airspace to the south. We could drive to Bellingham and catch a commuter airline connection to Spokane. There we would rent a car and drive the 225 kilometres to Nelson. It was just barely possible, and since we had no alternative we piled into our car and headed to Bellingham airport.

Luck was with us. There was no delay at the U.S. border. At Bellingham there was a spot in the airport parking lot directly in front of the terminal building, and the flight had space available—even an extra seat for the cello. The weather was fine as we took off on schedule at 9:15 a.m., heading over the Cascades to the heart of the Inland Empire.

Spokane, however, was now experiencing the same weather system that had reduced Castlegar to whiteout conditions. Our flight skidded to a hair-raising stop at the Spokane terminal. The snow was thick and heavy. But at least we were on the ground. Within half an hour we were driving north through increasingly hazardous road conditions. We had been warned that the ploughs would not attempt to clear the roads until the blizzard had exhausted its fury. At the Canadian border we encountered our next hurdle. As Canadians, we learned, we could not take a U.S. rental vehicle across the border without explicit permission from the owners. We had neglected to obtain the permit.

I produced a copy of the *Nelson Daily News*, which the previous week had emblazoned our picture across the front page of the entertainment section. The border guards were not impressed, although one admitted that his wife and children were in Nelson that afternoon, planning to attend the concert. After a frantic call to the Spokane rental agency, we somehow persuaded Canada customs that we were not planning to sell the rental car in Canada and were allowed to proceed. Nonetheless, the authorities at the border placed a call to the RCMP detachment in Nelson to make sure that we returned the American vehicle to Spokane the next day.

It was 2 p.m. and we had ninety-five kilometres to go. We phoned the committee and told them that we were well on the way. We would play in our street clothes, but we would be there by 3:30. The concert could start just thirty minutes later than scheduled. They promised to have some sandwiches ready for us backstage, and, "Oh yes... don't forget there's a reception after the concert. Plenty of time to unwind after your long drive." Life was looking up!

We reached the outskirts of Nelson at exactly 3 p.m. Highway 6 descends to the city through a series of hairpin bends, and on the last of these S-curves there is a junction leading to the municipal ski slope. Since it was a perfect afternoon for skiing, the parking area was full, and vehicles were lined up along the edge of the access road. One station wagon protruded onto the highway. We came slowly around the last S-curve, and it was impossible to stop. I was driving and I struck the vehicle, causing the kind of minor damage that keeps autobody companies happily profitable through the winter.

We had fifteen minutes to go before we hoped to be on stage. On a piece of music paper hastily extracted from the cello case, I scribbled a note with our licence number, advising that we were heading into town where we would be on stage at the Capitol Theatre. I placed the soggy note under the wipers of the injured car.

Still shaking from the incident, we drove past a community police station. I thought it prudent to stop for another minute and report the accident. The duty office made a note of our licence number, checked my driver's licence, inspected the minimal damage to our rental vehicle and said he would notify his superiors. We carried on to the hall where, after devouring all the sandwiches within sight, we finally arrived on stage. The concert began at 3:38 p.m. that snowy Sunday afternoon.

It ended with a rousing encore. As my colleagues strode off stage, I phoned the hotel from a pay phone in the wings. They were expecting us. We had not yet checked in, and I wanted to make sure that the dining room would stay open for a late-night dinner for five hungry overnight guests.

My bassoon and I were the last to leave the stage, and we walked into the waiting arms of two uniformed RCMP officers. "Are you George Zukerman?" I acknowledged my identity. "Are you the driver of the green Dodge, Washington State licence number KT178GV?" I acknowledged that too. "We have been advised that the vehicle is illegally in Canada and that you may try to leave it in Nelson," one of them said.

I must have gasped, but I retained enough composure to assure the officers that we had spoken to the rental company and were committed to returning the vehicle to Spokane the next day.

Undeterred, they delivered their *coup de grâce*. "In any case," said the senior of the two officers, "we have a warrant for your arrest." He paused for effect, then continued. "Hit and run at 3:06 p.m." He snapped shut his notebook and smiled in triumph.

By now we were surrounded by my colleagues and by several members of the committee, who had come backstage to guide us to the reception. It was obvious that they knew the officers personally. The chairwoman of the concert society spoke up, maternally, "But of course, Charlie, Mr. Zukerman announced the accident to all of us here at the concert." That gave me the opportunity to produce my winning card. "You will find it on file at the Baker Street police station," I stated, "that I reported the incident to the local police at 3:26 p.m. this afternoon. I may have hit, but I certainly didn't run." I didn't have a notebook, but I figuratively snapped one shut.

"That may be," replied the senior officer, "but the incident occurred outside city limits. That is not the jurisdiction of the local police. The offence was on our territory, and we are merely doing our duty."

It was useless to argue. My bassoon and I were taken into custody and driven in a police cruiser to the holding facility, which turned out to be none other than the local community police station where I had reported the accident in the first place. The same officer was still on duty. "Didn't you report the incident?" I asked. "Sure I did," he replied. "We followed proper protocol and turned the matter over to the RCMP."

Without hesitation, the local committee decided to hold the post-concert reception at the police station. Even as I was brought into the jail, an array of sandwiches, cold cuts, fruits and cheeses, accompanied by a coffee urn and a surreptitiously concealed carton of wine, appeared on trestle tables rapidly assembled in the waiting area. My colleagues of the quintet, along with twenty-three committee members and spouses filled the otherwise drab and sombre quarters.

While the arresting officers completed their charge documents, a paper plate loaded high with an assortment of tempting hors d'oeuvres was passed across the wooden gate that separated prisoner from public. Somebody on the committee poured me a glass of wine and was about to hand it to me. A stern voice intervened. "Alcohol cannot be consumed on that side of the fence." I stood there, forlorn and parched.

A lawyer, summoned by the committee, finally arrived, and within minutes I was released on my own recognizance on a $200 bail bond, with the promise that I would appear at court the following morning. "See you in court," said the departing Mounties.

The lawyer bid me good night and promised to call for me at the hotel the next morning. The committee finished off the last of the sandwiches and emptied the wine carton. "See you in court," echoed the committee chairwoman. "My husband and I will be there!"

Fine support indeed. The local police officer turned off the lights and locked the station, apparently confident that no further crimes would occur in Nelson on that Sunday night.

My colleagues and I returned to the hotel, and although dinner was waiting, as promised, it did not take long for the ultimate irony of the evening to sink in. In those days hotels were not permitted to serve alcohol on Sundays. The Lord's Day Alliance prevailed, and I still could not have my glass of wine.

Next morning, soberly, we trooped down to the courthouse. Never before had the visitors' gallery been so fully occupied. I spied the committee chairwoman, but not her husband, along with several members of the board of directors, as well as all of my supporting colleagues. At the front of the courtroom stood the two RCMP officers, resplendent in their dress uniforms, ready to give testimony. My lawyer, obviously in familiar surroundings, chatted amiably with them and with the court stenographer. I was not without apprehension. Clearly, my legal advisor was not a music lover. He had not been one of the 450 Nelson citizens present at the concert.

I stood in the prisoner's dock, separated from the public by an unlocked wooden gate that looked suspiciously similar to the one which had prevented my precipitous escape from the community police station on the previous evening.

"All rise for His Honour Hubert M.," declared the bailiff. We rose and court was in session, my case miraculously advanced to the first hearing of the day. The judge entered. He was none other than the missing husband of the committee chair, occupant of row 3, seat 17 at Sunday afternoon's concert.

He listened impatiently to the charges, then addressed the crowded room. "I am asked to pass judgment on a hit-and-run incident, alleged to have happened yesterday afternoon on Highway 6, just south of our city," he declared. "The matter of the 'hit' is not in dispute and is already in the hands of the respective insurance companies. The matter of the 'run' is utterly facetious. Along with 449 other citizens of our city, I was present yesterday afternoon when the defendant, clearly not on the run, announced to our concert audience that he had struck a vehicle at the ski slope and had duly reported the incident to our local community police service. I have no doubt about his statement, which barely needs repeating here unless the charging officers wish to dispute it." He looked (maybe "glared" is too fierce a description of his annoyance) in the direction of the uniformed pair. They shrugged their shoulders in temporary defeat. His Honour continued, "I therefore dismiss this case as entirely capricious and frivolous." The bailiff handed a document to my lawyer, which gave us a complete and absolute discharge.

The bail bond was returned to me. The lawyer presented his bill instead. We headed south, through the snow, to return the damaged Dodge to its rightful rental ownership in Spokane, lest it be charged, once again, with illegal entry into Canada.

⌣ THE COCKTAIL BASSOONIST

The thriving Canadian "organized audience" provided me with an unexpected opportunity to play and to tour as a soloist as well as in ensemble. Each concert society operated on the inviolable economic principle that they would spend no more on their concerts than they successfully raised in their membership drive. Often a community found that it had spent the majority of its available budget on one or two higher-priced feature attractions. Then they inevitably looked helplessly to me. "We have only a small sum left, and we still need another concert. Can you find us something at the right time and at the right fee?" I only needed to look in the mirror to find the artist who was most readily available and certainly easiest to negotiate with.

One such concert took place in Churchill, a town in the far north of Manitoba on the edge of Hudson Bay. Overture Concerts had organized Churchill's first concert committee in tandem with the more easily accessible mining centres of Thompson and Flin Flon. Normally, all three towns would have been encouraged to present the same artists to economize on travel costs. But this was an opening season, and the other communities had started their series earlier in the year. We needed an attraction that could be sent, inexpensively, to a single isolated location. I was conveniently available.

The townsite was originally a Cree and Chipewyan hunting settlement. In the seventeenth and eighteenth centuries it became a storehouse for the fur trade. By the middle of the twentieth century, modern commerce changed the nature of the town, as well as its population, once again. Located hundreds of kilometres closer to world markets than the major east or west coast ports, Churchill became an important grain shipping port. Although Hudson Bay was only free of ice and open to ships for three months each year, a railway was built to transport the grain from prairie to market.

In the 1950s and 1960s, Churchill was the year-round site of a high-tech joint Canadian–American rocket-testing range. More recently the town has become renowned among ecotourists as "Polar Bear Capital of the World." So there were many reasons to visit Churchill other than to give a bassoon recital.

I left Winnipeg on a bright and sunny wintery day, one of those special times in the north when the sun illuminates miles of frozen lakes and un-blemished snow with its glowing reflection, and the plane's tiny shadow, immaculately shaped like a toy, follows unerringly, gliding smoothly over the landscape spread out below.

Once in the village, I was awed by the polar bears, intimidated by the rocket range, delighted with the audience (as I hope they were with the performance) and finally, to my astonishment, pampered with a caldo verde and bacalhau à minhota, served at an extraordinary Portuguese restaurant miraculously located in this tiny isolated village north of the fifty-fifth parallel. The owners were apparently as entranced by the concert as I was by their cuisine. "Why don't you stay a while, a month or two? Entertain our dinner guests with a few tunes each night. At least while the cod supply lasts?" they asked.

I declined a new career as Cocktail Bassoonist and early next morning headed to the airport beneath troubling skies. How quickly the weather changed! An early morning announcement hinted at travel problems to come: "The aircraft has not yet left Winnipeg. It may not be able to land here, in which case there will be no flight out today!" Nonetheless, baggage was checked in, and then began the day-long waiting game.

A modulated voice solemnly informed us at 2 p.m., after a seven-hour wait in the cavernous hangar that had been converted into an airport ter-minal, that the flight was, indeed, cancelled for the day. The voice prob-ably belonged to Peter Mansbridge, later to become the iconic anchor of *The National*, CBC TV's evening newscast. The voice continued, "Please claim your baggage at the front of the terminal." Since he was the one and only airline employee, it was he who also trundled the baggage cart back to where we all stood. A belated "Thank you, Peter!" Churchill had no road connection, but there was a thrice-weekly passenger train that meandered the 1,700 kilometres to Winnipeg in forty-two hours. With blizzard con-ditions threatening, an outbound flight seemed highly unlikely for the next day or two, so Churchill's one and only taxicab spent the next three hours shuttling between airport and town—eleven times in total—to carry the stranded passengers and assorted baggage to the railhead.

Railhead? There was no railway station, as such. The train simply arrived and parked on a stretch of track between the hotel and the few stores that constituted the downtown shopping centre. Train #693, northbound, arrived just as the first of the refugees from the airport were coming into town. It snorted and grunted and ground to a grudging halt, disgorged its passengers, and then shuffled up and down the tracks until it found what its engineer must have thought was the perfect parking place. Only then did the taxi risk crossing in front of the locomotive. One carload got out, and the taxi driver headed back to the airport for the next set of passengers.

∼ A MIDNIGHT AGM

I realized that the route of the railway passed through the city of The Pas, one of the few Manitoba mining centres that had not yet been approached about forming a concert society during the organizational frenzy of the past few seasons. At last here was a chance. Quickly, I changed hats from yesterday's concert artist to tomorrow's community organizer.

I ran my finger down the timetable. The train reached The Pas on the second night of our railroad odyssey at 11:35 p.m. It stayed there exactly twenty-five minutes. Would anyone want to come out to meet the train at such an hour on what promised to be a very stormy night?

Attached to the solitary pay phone in the hotel was a bedraggled copy of the telephone directory for the entire northern region of Manitoba. I found the phone number for the public library of The Pas and called my one and only contact in that city. The librarian's name was Susan, not Marian, but I was still the Music Man, happily whistling the tune of "Seventy-six bassoons..."

"Yes," she said, "I am very interested personally, but you must admit, it's not a very convenient hour." I did admit. "And it isn't an easy night to get around." I agreed. She continued, "I'm not sure anyone will get out at that time, but I will ask around. Thank you so much for calling. Have a good trip. It certainly is a nice idea."

"Seventy-six bassoons" switched to a minor key. I boarded the train and settled down for that slow, majestic journey across miles and miles of Canadian Shield. I watched as we crossed vast open spaces of barren tundra, frozen lakes and gigantic bare rock forms. Sometime in the night we crossed the treeline, and by morning the tundra was replaced by stunted boreal forest. We stopped at Herchmer, Weir River and Gillam, at Ilford and Pik-witonei, at Thicket Portage and Wabowden, at Cormorant and Atikameg Lake. Darkness descended for a second night, and The Pas was still seven hours away. Who would be crazy enough to be waiting for me in the middle of the night?

The arrival at The Pas was accompanied by the usual squealing of brakes, hissing of steam lines, and shouting of passengers and train officials. I went to the door of the train, pulled it open against a howling wind, and was almost blown back into the carriage by a blast of snow. Suitably bundled, I pushed my way through to the platform and looked around to see if my hardy librarian had braved the minus 35 cold and wind.

I had underestimated the power of music. A small group of men and women huddled under the solitary platform light. One of them motioned to me furiously. "Mr. Zukerman? Quick, over here, it's a little warmer." We stepped inside a baggage loading area. There were seven of them, and the spokesperson was none other than Susan, the librarian. "Seventy-six bassoons" changed back to a major key.

"We don't have much time," she continued, "so we've already formed our committee. I'm chairman, Gerlinda is secretary. William, the local newspaper editor, will handle publicity—he is babysitting tonight and couldn't come. Harold here will take on membership. We think with the town population at three thousand we'll have a membership of between 150 and 200. What's our next step?"

I was amazed (and delighted) at their efficiency, and assured them that there would be a choice of splendid touring possibilities once their budget was in place. I quickly outlined a campaign strategy. We would provide materials, subscription forms, membership record books and suggestions for publicizing a membership drive. The train whistle screeched our impending departure. The committee thanked me for the visit. They quickly signed papers of affiliation, and I returned to the warmth of the train, while they went home to relish what they had started for their community. Never in the history of "organized audience" had a local concert association been founded in so short a time!

On board the train I tried to sleep as we plunged on through the night. Sturgis, Mikado, Kamsack, Gilbert Plains and Glenella still lay ahead of us.

With luck I would arrive at Winnipeg in time for my next engagement in the nearby university town of Brandon. I needed to change hats. I was returning to the world of the soloist.

~ THE MANITOBA MAGNET

Brandon was the seat of a remarkably active school of music. The school was founded in 1906 and since then had assembled a fine faculty, built a splendid recital hall and attracted students from across Canada and from overseas. As a result, it maintained a prestigious concert series for visiting artists. I had the good fortune to be invited to play for an audience of students, faculty and community members.

As I played, I glanced into the audience and caught the eye of a strikingly attractive young lady in the third row. A fleeting smile suggested that she was actually en-

Erika Bennedik, the Manitoba Magnet. Photo: Reinhard Bennedik

joying the bassoon repertoire. Such a tantalizing sense of involvement! Yes, and perhaps such self-deception. My eyes strayed a second too long, and suddenly the page of music was a blur. I was on the edge of losing my place.

I had a momentary vision of stopping the concert. I would first apologize to my pianist, then to the lady in question lest, by some quirk of etiology, the moment might be attributed to her blameless soul. In contrition, I would invite her to join me backstage after the concert. Finally, I would apologize to the audience at large and start the piece again. The concert would resume and conclude in splendid good humour.

Well, it didn't happen quite that way, but there was no question. I was smitten.

The direct outcome of that chance encounter was an astonishing increase in the number of my business trips to Manitoba. The mysterious lady from row three—no longer so mysterious—and I became the closest of friends. With this marvellous Manitoba magnet, new concert societies flourished throughout the region, even reaching deep into adjacent northern Ontario.

Looking back, I realize that at that memorable concert I may have nearly lost my place, but I gained a partner in life. Erika and I have now known each other for nearly sixty years, and we still celebrate that concert as one anniversary among many.

The New Era

A moment of musical magic descended on Vancouver when the Queen Elizabeth Theatre was officially inaugurated by Her Majesty the Queen in the 1959–1960 season.

The Vancouver Symphony, in particular, had cause to celebrate. Six months earlier, big industry had prevailed and the orchestra had been tossed out of the Orpheum Theatre. The Sunday afternoon concerts moved to the ancient and decrepit Georgia Auditorium. There the orchestra ignominiously shared rental time with weekly mud wrestling.

Much hope was in the air when the first manager of the gleaming new hall greeted Her Majesty at the opening ceremony on July 5. By September 15 he was in jail for embezzlement that had occurred during construction. The ceiling, four feet lower than prescribed by the architect, resulted in an irreparable acoustic affliction. The orchestra may have been rescued from a dingy auditorium, but in the new theatre it suffered from acoustics as muddy as the wrestling that remained behind at the old Georgia Street venue.

We were as yet oblivious of its acoustic failings when Queen Elizabeth II came to visit. Protocol for the occasion was explicit. "The Royal party enters the auditorium and is guided to their seats. The entire audience rises when their Majesties are standing at their designated seats, a cue is given to the orchestra. Six measures of the national anthem are to be played."

I had put together the orchestra for the occasion, but they were in the pit and they could not see directly into the auditorium. I had been instructed to stand on the edge of the platform and signal to my colleagues in the pit when they should begin the truncated anthem. The Royal party arrived at their seats. The equerry signalled to me. I cued the concertmaster, who gave the necessary downbeat. As the first note was sounded, I hastened offstage to resume my place in the pit.

Meantime, the strings dutifully played "God Save the Queen" in the traditional key of G major. The brass and woodwinds, inevitably much louder, commenced their six measures of "O Canada" in the key of E-flat major. The resulting cacophony either confirmed the new theatre's problematic acoustics or announced Canada's emerging political dichotomy.

Her Majesty smiled throughout and sat awaiting the start of the concert. Perhaps she was prepared for a wildly contemporary program, full of polytonality? Down in the pit, I expected to encounter musical chaos and confusion. "Did you hear what happened?" I whispered.

My colleagues looked mystified. "Is anything wrong? Were we out of tune?" Presumably God had saved the Queen—and the future King—from both musical and political dissonance.

⮞ TOUCHES OF ROYALTY

Many musical instruments lay claim to royalty. The organ, the violin and the piano are each lovingly referred to by their practitioners as "the king of all musical instruments."

Nobody, as far as I know, has claimed that title for the bassoon, and I am not willing to suggest that my later critical coronation as "High priest of the bassoon" elevated either me or my instrument to the ranks of priesthood or royalty.

Nonetheless there were other encounters with kings and queens, princes and princesses, and perhaps, with my bassoon in hand, I succeeded in charming some of them into beautiful frogs or tadpoles.

Some years previously, at the Empire Games, Prince Philip had represented the Royal Family. He was witnessing the sculling events on the Vedder Canal, near Chilliwack. I had driven several of the athletes to the canal for the races and was standing close to the Prince as he reached down to shake the hand of a winning rower.

As he put his foot forward for support, he began to slide dangerously on a muddy stretch of the platform. As the nearest human being, perhaps the only one who witnessed the potential disaster, I reached out and extended my arm. The Prince held on and recovered his balance. That was the first time that I truly touched royalty.

To recount another royal event, I must now invite you to the village of Bella Coola. Let me set the scene.

With its population at the time of approximately 2,750, including the surrounding area, Bella Coola had successfully organized a concert society. As with every new town, I needed to find performers willing and able to appear for the new series.

I rapidly discovered that it was not easy to get in and out of Bella Coola. The village lay deep in a coastal fjord, on the edge of what is now known as the Great Bear Rainforest, and although it was one of the few coastal settlements that could actually be reached by road, it was a precarious six-hour drive from the nearest town of Williams Lake, and sixteen hours by road from Vancouver.

The highway into the Bella Coola Valley is fondly known as "The Hill." At the time, it was a terrifyingly steep and narrow unpaved route of hairpin turns and switchbacks. It descended 1,487 metres to the valley floor at grades up to 18 percent. The road was devoid of guardrails, and in places it was only wide enough for one vehicle, bordered on one side by cliffs and on the other by a drop of hundreds of metres.

Seaplanes could land at the village dock, and there was a small airport fifteen kilometres inland at Hagensborg. Winter weather was notoriously severe, and flights were both expensive and unreliable—frequently diverted to Williams Lake or returned to Vancouver.

There was a third way to reach Bella Coola. The venerable steamer *Northland Prince* plied British Columbia's coastal waters, serving as freighter and public transit for dozens of isolated communities. It was the weekly bus to the north. It sailed through the turbulent waters of Hecate Strait to Bella Coola, Ocean Falls, Kitimat, Prince Rupert and Stewart.

The forward part of the ship was devoted to freight, and the *Northland Prince* transported a panoply of items ranging from house furnishings to horses, generators to garbage cans, refrigerators to rocking chairs, and microwaves to motorcycles. The superstructure rose elaborately aft, like an ornate wedding cake, with layer upon layer of bridges, cabins and common spaces. The ship served as a post office, bringing the mail and the occasional mail-order bride. It was the library and a floating bank. When the circuit magistrate travelled on the *Northland Prince*, the lounge was converted into a courtroom.

In a moment of fevered imagination, I had a dream of taking John Avison's CBC Radio Orchestra to Bella Coola aboard the *Northland Prince*. Why shouldn't the lounge of the old freighter be turned into a rehearsal hall for an orchestra? I was the newest member of the band, and John may have still thought that I was a "brash young upstart," but when I suggested the idea to him, he was intrigued by the possibility.

Bella Coola was delighted at the prospect of an orchestral visit. So too were the other towns and villages along the marine highway.

But we were at the mercy of the tides. With the navigating officer I worked out a schedule that would allow us to sail into the various communities along the route and stay just long enough to play our concerts. The ship would maintain steam while we went ashore. As soon as we returned, it would hoist anchor and sail through the night, arriving at the next community in time for another concert. The *Northland Prince* would be our rehearsal hall, cafeteria and hotel, as well as transportation between the coastal communities.

It was a brilliant, expensive and insane proposal. But somehow it worked out.

A few months before the actual tour was to take place, I thought it wise to conduct a trial run of the itinerary. I set off aboard the *Northland Prince* in company with a violinist friend, John Chlumecky. Together, we visited each of the towns on the proposed route. To our relief, the logistics seemed to work perfectly well.

Now a brief note about Mr. Chlumecky, for here my tale of royalty in the Canadian wilderness starts to unfold. John, whose given name was actually Johannes, was a scion of some long-lost Moravian nobility. One of his many uncles twice or three times removed, the Baron Leopold von Chlumecky, had served as transport minister in an early-twentieth-century Austro-Hungarian government. In 1941, Johannes escaped with his father from their native Czechoslovakia to England, only to be deported to Australia as an "enemy agent."

After the war, the Chlumeckys ended up in Vancouver. Johannes had lost the fluent use of his native Czech. His German was spotty at best, and in the dusty Australian internment camp of Hay, NSW, where he spent four mind-numbing years of utter boredom, he acquired only rudimentary English. But he was a passably good violinist, and he didn't need much in the way of language skills to play in the embryonic 1959 Vancouver Symphony and the CBC Radio Orchestra. There we became good, if taciturn, friends.

John fell ill just before the actual tour took place, and the orchestra embarked aboard the *Northland Prince* one violin short. CBC TV had decided to send a film crew along with the orchestra. Their documentary, *Orchestral Passage*, was one of the earliest CBC colour productions. When it went on the air in Vancouver, the CBC switchboard was inundated with calls. "The colours are all wrong," complained one irate caller. "The faces are all green or yellow," railed another.

In fact, the colour on that early TV production was exceptionally clear and accurate. Imagine the tossing and rolling, the pitch and yaw as the ship entered the notoriously stormy waters of Hecate Strait. As the orchestra tried to rehearse, one by one the musicians left their seats, heading for the railing at the side of the ship. In the end, while empty chairs and music stands slid across the floor of the lounge, only a single violinist and the conductor remained standing.

The cameras did not lie. Never before in the history of music had the "Blue Danube Waltz" been given so many unexpected pigments, nor had it ever been so theatrically transformed into a Technicolor version of the Haydn *Farewell* Symphony.

After a harrowing, sleepless night the orchestra arrived in Bella Coola for the first concert. It was, I suppose, poetic justice that long before the orchestra's battle with the seas of Hecate Strait, John Avison had scheduled the opening work on the program: Mendelssohn's concert overture *Calm Sea and Prosperous Voyage*.

The concert was a resounding success, and well before ebb tide the orchestra returned to dockside, where the *Northland Prince* was straining at its hawsers, ready to depart for an overnight journey to the next concert at Ocean Falls.

In those few minutes, while stage manager Judith Fraser reloaded instruments and music stands aboard the ship, I chatted with members of the local committee. One lady recalled our earlier visit. "Where is your friend," she asked, "the violinist of royal descent?"

Of course I knew of Johannes's background in faded European nobility, but I did not recall that I had told anyone in Bella Coola (or anywhere else) that he was descended from aristocracy, let alone royalty.

Out of curiosity I asked, "What on earth made you think there was a royal connection?"

She looked puzzled. "What else could we believe?" she asked. "You always addressed him as 'Your Highness.'"

Only then did I realize that I had never used his anglicized name. It hadn't taken long for "Yes, Johannes. No, Johannes. Yes, Johannes. No, Johannes" to morph into "Yes, Your Highness. No, Your Highness." Royalty had indeed touched that quiet corner of the West Coast.

∽ A GIFT TO BE SIMPLE

At one of the first events in the new Queen Elizabeth Theatre, I was invited to give the world premiere of a new bassoon concerto by Murray Adaskin.

This was a daring move for an orchestra that played notably little contemporary music. The Vancouver Symphony seldom invited players from its own ranks to appear as soloist, and in any case, the bassoon was rarely featured as a solo instrument. But Murray Adaskin was already well known as an important Canadian composer. Change was happening.

Adaskin was head of a one-man music department at the University of Saskatchewan, and in the late 1950s he was also conductor of the Saskatoon Symphony. I had met him briefly when the Vancouver orchestra had played one of his early works, so I knew of him as a composer and he had heard me play in the orchestra.

Some months earlier, I was in the midst of a rugged organizational trip in the far north of Saskatchewan when I read in a local newspaper that the Saskatoon Symphony would be giving the world premiere of a new work by Adaskin, his recently completed *Prairie Suite*. Although I was many miles away from Saskatoon, I decided to try to attend the concert. What looked like a perfectly ordinary secondary road on the map turned out to be the

George with Murray Adaskin.

Carrot River Cutoff, a Department of Natural Resources forestry trail better designed for jeeps and four-wheel drive vehicles than a compact rental car. When I arrived in Saskatoon four hours later I was weary, dusty and in need of a stiff drink.

Murray's music department at the university was housed in two rooms in the Agriculture Building. Earthy farm aromas filled the air in his teaching studio. I found the Maestro in great despair. "Thank goodness you are here . . . do you have your bassoon with you?" He waved a sheet of music in front of me, and I recognized his immaculate music penmanship. In those days before computer notation programs, the best music copyists achieved a form of elegant calligraphy, and Murray was a master of the art. "Our bassoon player has just called. She is ill and cannot make it tonight."

"But I don't have a bassoon with me. I'm on a business trip!"

"We'll get you one," he insisted. "You have to play tonight."

"But I haven't rehearsed."

"That doesn't matter. You are a good sight-reader. You know my style. I'll cue you."

"The union will not let me perform with non-union members."

"Our second clarinetist is the union secretary. We'll obtain a special waiver for you."

"I don't have any decent stage clothes."

"That doesn't matter . . . just dust off a little, you'll be fine! Here's your music." And with that he thrust the music and a clothes brush into my hands.

A borrowed high school bassoon appeared, complete with three ancient reeds—one caked solidly with lipstick, one cracked down the middle, and a third that was made barely playable after ten minutes of ardent scraping with a borrowed kitchen knife. An hour later I was on stage sight-reading the bassoon part of a world premiere under the composer's baton.

Murray's *Prairie Suite* was a triumph that evening. Saskatoon symphony-goers in the late 1950s were no more disposed to contemporary works than those in Vancouver. Yet many in the audience that night sensed the significance of the performance of a work that was so obviously inspired by their province. It was a joy for me to participate in such an evening of community music-making.

A year later a package arrived in Vancouver. It contained the score of Murray's bassoon concerto, which he had written during the intervening summer and dedicated to me. I look upon that gift from his heart as the finest concert fee I ever received! I premiered the concerto in 1960 with the Vancouver Symphony.

Murray had a lifelong appreciation of the bassoon, and he wrote several other works for me, including a quintet for bassoon and string quartet, his Vocalise no. 2 for solo bassoon, and a remarkable trio for violin, bassoon and French horn (his Divertimento no. 3). I once asked Murray if he would consider writing a second bassoon concerto. "Just think of it," I said, "if there were two bassoon concertos . . . whenever I would suggest the Adaskin to a conductor, he or she would be compelled to ask, 'Yes, but which one?'"

∼ THE FIXER

As the 1960s dawned, a cornucopia of musical opulence began to offer its bounty on the stage of the "Queen E," as the new theatre soon became known. Both local artists and visiting groups found a place on the new stage that hosted symphony, opera and ballet.

And then came Nicholas Goldschmidt, like a comet flaring across the night sky, with a dazzling lineup of internationally renowned artists who visited the city under the banner of the Vancouver International Festival. In a series of summer festivals, Goldschmidt brought to Vancouver Glen Gould, Joan Sutherland, Oscar Peterson, Harry Belafonte, Herbert von Karajan, Anna Russell, the New York Philharmonic with Leonard Bernstein, the Hungarian String Quartet, the Peking Opera, Bruno Walter, the Red Army Chorus, the Kingston Trio, the New York City Ballet, the Juilliard Quartet, the Moscow Circus, Charles Munch, Margot Fonteyn and Rudolf Nureyev, Igor Stravinsky, and the Mormon Tabernacle Choir.

Belgium-born Nicholas Goldschmidt came to North America in 1937 and immediately began directing opera schools, first at the San Francisco Conservatory and Stanford University, then at Columbia University before serving as the first music director of the Royal Conservatory Opera School in Toronto. In 1950, he helped launch the Royal Conservatory Opera Company, which became the Canadian Opera Company in 1977.

"Niki," as he was fondly called, was a daring and innovative arts administrator. Once settled in Canada, he proceeded to convert his dreams into a seemingly endless pageant of glorious national musical events. During his fifty-four years in Canada, Niki's imprint was everywhere. He founded the Guelph Spring Festival, the Vancouver International Festival, the Algoma Festival, the Ottawa Summer Festival and countless choral festivals across the country. In Canada's centennial year he led a national arts festival that visited large and small centres alike in all ten provinces and the two territories that existed at the time.

Niki coupled his extraordinary organizational skill with an equal versatility as a performer. He was both a conductor and a singer, and he imbued everything he undertook with unabashed enthusiasm and love for the music.

I first met Niki when he arrived in Vancouver in 1957 for the University of British Columbia's summer music school. He conducted what may well have been the city's first opera, a production of Mozart's *Così fan tutte*. I should not have been surprised when I next saw him at work self-accompanying Schubert songs at a fundraising gathering for wealthy patrons. (I should add that I was there as a backstage assistant, not as one of the evening's guests!)

Perhaps Niki sensed a parallel to his own career when he viewed my early steps in management and on the concert stage. In 1959 he engaged me as his assistant at the Vancouver International Festival. I soon found out that this was an assignment without a job description. Here are a few of the tasks I was asked to handle in my first week as Niki's assistant: I located two tympani and a triangle for an ensemble whose truck had broken down outside Chilliwack. I purchased a bouquet of flowers to present to a visiting soloist upon the completion of her recital. I arranged for a piano tuner to stand by to re-tune the piano during the intermission of a concert by a notably heavy-handed pianist. I organized an extra telephone line for the festival office and for a teletype machine. I met Leonard Bernstein and the New York Philharmonic, with four rented highway coaches, on their arrival at Vancouver airport. I located a doctor to write a prescription for a soprano who had experienced a troubling "throat tickle" on the morning of her concert. I changed one of the buses for the New York Phil back to non-smoking. I switched the hotel room, not once but three times, for a very temperamental tenor. I located four rusty and ancient folding music stands for a string quartet that preferred see-through wire devices to the heavy metal music racks in general theatre use. I trolled downtown newsstands for a Pittsburgh newspaper so that a visiting violinist could see his (favourable) review from the previous week. And I made sure there were no cucumbers on Niki's lunchtime sandwich.

Part of the job also involved contracting the orchestral players for the festival. Contracting is a peculiar business, an aspect of the music profession that serves as the link between performers and employers. It was not lost on me that in Britain the contractor—rather sinisterly, I always thought—was known as the "fixer."

So fix I did.

I needed to assemble an eighty-five-member festival orchestra to play for some of the world's greatest conductors. The Vancouver Symphony had dispersed for the summer, and many of the key players were away from the city.

The union grudgingly granted permission to bring in some players from Seattle and Portland, but the majority were from our own freelance corps of orchestral players. The orchestra made up for its lack of experience with an amazing surfeit of enthusiasm.

Bruno Walter was ineffably polite, courteous and benignly tolerant of such an undisciplined pickup orchestra. With Charles Munch, the orchestra's weaknesses fell away before his Gallic effusion. Stravinsky didn't mind wrong notes. He was more concerned with the overall shape of his works, and we didn't disappoint him with our Vancouver performance of *Le Sacre du printemps* about fifty years after it was first premiered in Paris.

However. It was clear from the start that our summer-assembled festival orchestra was far below acceptable standards for Herbert von Karajan. Less than an hour into the first rehearsal he stopped abruptly and, pointing to the rear of the second violin section, singled out one individual player after another, ruthlessly demanding that they each play a particularly difficult passage. When they froze into terrified paralysis or broke down in quivering tears, he simply ordered them off the stage. It was a display of imperious orchestral tyranny.

As contractor, I had to intervene. I stopped the rehearsal and declared an intermission. My orchestral colleagues breathed a sigh of relief.

Karajan was enraged. He would not be told when to stop. He demanded transportation back to his hotel. For all I knew he was about to summon a private jet to whisk him away. Niki, with multilingual power, cajoled, begged, importuned, entreated, wheedled, beseeched the Maestro to reconsider. Karajan finally agreed to carry on.

We left the decision to continue the rehearsal up to the players. Seventeen more of them opted not to play. Since humiliation wasn't yet among union-forbidden actions, we settled for full pay for everyone on the original contract.

With his frigid mirror-practised smile, Karajan relentlessly beat Beethoven's sixth symphony into submission with only forty-two of the seventy-eight players originally hired for the engagement. It was a joyless pastoral, but at least Karajan had fulfilled his contract. I'm not sure what, if anything, I "fixed," but I had avoided a musical massacre, and Niki Goldschmidt continued to employ me for the festival contracting.

⌇ STRIKE ONE!

Vancouver's main season symphony orchestra blossomed with pride in its new home. For the first time in its history, rehearsals were conducted in the same place as the performances. New players joined the orchestra. Audiences were enthusiastic, the traditional Sunday afternoon events were well attended and the silver screen at the Orpheum remained unscratched. The quality of the symphony was growing, but the season remained at twenty-three biweekly concerts. This was no longer acceptable to the musicians. More to the point, this was no longer acceptable to the city. Vancouver needed more from its symphony orchestra.

By the early sixties, it had become clear that the orchestra's board and management were unlikely to voluntarily increase the yearly playing activity. Negotiations between the union and the symphony society collapsed, and we suddenly found ourselves unemployed. The musicians were not on strike . . . we were simply not re-engaged.

We formed a picket line outside the theatre and handed out leaflets describing our predicament. The musicians were not pressing for higher fees. We were asking for an expanded season of twenty-six weeks of work.

In their distress, my colleagues turned to me, thinking that my involvement in the world of concert presentation would somehow qualify me to manage an orchestra. They asked me to organize a protest concert in place of the event that should have launched the season.

The symphony society fought us at every turn. Under no circumstances could we have access to their mailing list. The city would not rent us the hall. Artists' managements declined to let their soloists appear for us. The metropolitan newspapers would not run our advertisements. The music library was not available to us. Even our union denied us the benefit of the symphony-negotiated playing rate.

At each step we fought back. We created our own mailing list. A benefactor rented the theatre for us. We found a conductor and a guest artist willing to defy their managers. We advertised in the suburban press and on radio. We sat up at night copying music instead of depending on libraries or rentals, and we happily agreed to pay each player the minimum scale for performance—without the faintest idea whether the money would come back to us from ticket sales.

On November 17, under the neutral name of the Vancouver Orchestra, we presented our gala concert, which was attended by 650 supporters. The program was unabashedly symbolic: Brahms's *Tragic* Overture, Hindemith's *Symphonic Metamorphoses* and Haydn's *Farewell* Symphony.

We only survived financially when the musicians unanimously agreed, defying a ruling by the union, to donate 75 percent of their fees to help cover costs. We interpreted all of this as a success, and we were just about to plan a second concert when the symphony society—having already saved itself the operating costs for half the season—suddenly agreed to resume negotiations.

The discussions were painfully slow. They agreed to add a single week to the season and hesitantly acceded to a request for overtime pay whenever rehearsals ran beyond the designated time. In return for these concessions, they demanded that we provide them with the mailing list we had compiled for our concert! Thus the non-strike was settled, and the orchestra returned to work in January. My brief career as orchestra manager came to a grateful conclusion.

It was not, however, the true end of this story. In March, when I should have been discussing my contract for the following season, a bleak silence prevailed. Should I have been surprised when I learned that the newly appointed conductor had already engaged a friend of his from the United Kingdom to come to Vancouver as the principal bassoon? I no longer remember how he justified this decision to the union, but I do recall thinking that some members of the symphony's board of directors would be pleased to know that their work-stoppage "troublemaker" was not on contract for yet another season.

So there, in 1964, my ten-year association with the Vancouver Symphony came to an end. Once again I would have time to organize the hinterland. What I did not know was that my career as a soloist was about to take an astonishing leap forward.

Redeeming Mileage

PRELUDE:

Abandon Ship

Before I enlisted in the military in 1944, my friends bought me a going-away gift—a booklet entitled *How to Abandon Ship*, published for the elucidation of young men about to embark on a naval career.

Twenty years later, when my Vancouver Symphony contract was not renewed, I was reminded of the volume, long since lost and, during military service, fortunately never used. In fact, I had not exactly abandoned the symphony ship. If anything, the symphony had abandoned me, but the result was the same. I found myself in deep musical waters without the equivalent of a life jacket.

Fortunately, I didn't need to tread water for long. Neither the Vancouver Symphony nor I realized it, but by declining to give me a contract they were turning me loose to indulge in all those musical adventures that I could not possibly have undertaken while in their employ.

Although I would continue to play for John Avison's CBC Radio Orchestra, I found myself with lengthy periods of free time on my hands. I could now take more time to organize new concert societies. I could also plan and accept more solo engagements and ensemble tours. The two sides of my existence, virtuoso and impresario, had never before been so clearly delineated, the opportunities for each so ready to be fulfilled. From these two themes flowed a myriad of variations.

∼ TEACHING THE DOUBLE BASS TO FLY

In the opening scene of Shakespeare's *Julius Caesar*, Flavius reprimands a passing carpenter for not displaying publicly the symbol of his profession.

The virtuoso.

Today's travelling musicians would not give Flavius cause for complaint. You need only spend an hour in the departure or arrival hall at any international airport to witness a parade of violins, violas, cellos, double basses, guitars and French horns. Faces may be lost in the crowd, but instrument cases and shapes are instantly recognizable. There you will find us all, either preparing for the tour ahead or returning to earth. Airports are the compression chambers of our worldwide concertizing.

Here, a well-known string quartet. There, a celebrated violinist. Over there, members of a youth orchestra, like a flock of bushtits, swarm through the main entrance. A bemused bassoonist awaits his flight announcement. Trombones and a tuba suggest a travelling brass band. A solitary double bass player trundles his oversize instrument toward one of the many check-in counters. A guitarist takes his instrument along for a summer holiday. They all expect to carry their instruments on board their flights. Not all will succeed.

Conductors, pianists, vocalists and even piccolo players are less conspicuous and usually board their aircraft without a thought for the ordeal of those who travel with large and bulky instruments.

Until well into the twenty-first century, a farrago of confusing and conflicting rules dictated the conditions of air transport for musical instruments. They often differed from airline to airline, so it was seldom possible to be entirely sure that a particular musical instrument would be allowed on board. Size was one of the determining factors. Would the instrument fit in the overhead bin or under the seat in front of the passenger? Or was it a matter of weight? Some airlines allowed nothing over seven kilograms in carry-on baggage. Nobody was ever quite certain who made the decisions. There may have been policies in place, but airline agents did not always know where to find them. Sometimes eligibility was determined arbitrarily at the check-in counter, sometimes by a gate agent at the moment of boarding an aircraft.

Then there was security. Musical instruments had to go through the normal inspection procedures. Bassoons and other woodwinds, with so many metal keys, tended to ring mysterious alarm bells. Under X-rays, the jumble of keys might look sinister. Inspectors brushed them with a talcum-like powder to test for carbon residue and questioned when they had last been fired.

String instruments, which are mainly wood, faced a different kind of problem. Once, at a major Canadian airport, a viola player was on tour with three colleagues, part of a well-known quartet. Her instrument was sent through the x-ray twice, while her colleagues' violins and cello passed through without question. Finally, she was asked to remove all four strings of her instrument, place them in a sealed envelope and check them in as accompanying baggage. The obvious fear was that viola strings, more menacing than those on a violin or a cello, could be used to garrote a passenger in the seat ahead.

Cellos, double basses and other particularly bulky instruments caused special vexation for their owners. The instruments themselves do not weigh very much, but they occupy large spaces. On most airlines, even today, a seat (economy class only) can be purchased for them. Who hasn't overheard a preboarding announcement, "Will Mr. Cello please return to the check-in counter"? Once on board, with a seat purchased, bad jokes abound about whether the instrument is entitled to complimentary meals or wine.

The alternative to buying a ticket for the instrument is to transport it as checked baggage. Apart from the possibility of being lost (imagine a tuba arriving in Sydney, Australia, instead of Sydney, Nova Scotia), there is the constant risk of damage from rough handling and, worse yet, cracked wood from unheated cargo holds.

Faced with such dangers and the frustration of not knowing which rule might be applied on a given flight or a chosen airline, many cellists and double bass players have acquired sturdy wooden or fibreglass carrying cases for their instruments. The cases often weigh more than the instruments they shield. Even that is not always enough to assure easy travel. Some bass players have discovered that these cases—fondly referred to as "coffins"—will not fit through the freight doors of smaller aircraft in commercial operation. Short of chartering and flying their own planes, what else can a player do? It clearly calls for imaginative problem-solving.

Perhaps the story of the "cellinet" tells it best of all.

Years ago, in Tasmania, the cellist of a distinguished Russian string quartet on tour needed to fly from Launceston to Melbourne. He was told, in no uncertain terms, that his cello could not go in the cabin with him, even if he purchased a ticket for it. And no, it could not go as freight because the dimensions exceeded allowable limits on that particular aircraft. The airline's union was in negotiation for a new contract, and "work to rule" intransigence prevailed. Members were unprepared to allow any flexibility in their strict interpretation of the rules. It would seem that there was no way the musician could possibly be in Melbourne with his cello in time for a concert that same evening.

Ever resourceful, he knew that the ground crew that supervised boarding of aircraft had been provided with a list of those musical instruments that were permitted on board as hand baggage. Although "cello" was clearly not included on their list, he cheerfully marched up to the gate, carrying his instrument. "Is it okay," he asked demurely, "if I take my clarinet on board?" The young gentleman at the airbridge reached into his pocket and brought out the list. Licking his fingertip, he slowly scrolled down from the top. "Piccolo, flute, trumpet, violin, oboe, clarinet . . . why yes, sir. There it is. That will be just fine. Welcome aboard," he said, motioning cellist and cello inside.

Bassoon as You're Ready

≈ HAVE BASSOON, WILL TRAVEL

And now I must tell you how my bassoon has fared in its extensive world-wide travels. During my years of touring it passed through countless airports around the world. It folded up neatly into an oblong carrying case that fit in the overhead bins of most commercial aircraft. The case was designed with multiple zippered pockets that allowed me to carry copious pages of music, as well as a spare toothbrush, an occasional sandwich and a change of underwear. Older aircraft did not have closed bins above the seats, so very often I had to slide the instrument under the seat in front of me. It dutifully conformed with all the regulations.

Although my instrument journeyed over a million miles with me, it has never been rewarded with loyalty mileage points. Much of its travel (and mine) occurred before loyalty programs had been widely established in the airline business. Considering the multiplicity of destinations to which I travelled, it is not at all certain that any one airline would have earned my loyalty, nor I their mileage points.

Instead of dreaming about all the trips I might have been enjoying in my retirement, I invite you to join me while I reminisce about some of those that really happened.

≈ RED CARPET: GIB—GIBRALTAR

Apart from Belfast International Airport, where, during the times of "the Troubles," *nobody* carried *anything* loose on board any aircraft, the only time my bassoon and I were compelled to travel separately was en route to Gibraltar.

The scene is Gatwick Airport, shortly before the departure of Gibraltar Airways' daily 4 p.m. flight. I have checked in comfortably early and am sitting in the departure lounge when the flight is called. I stride to the gate with my bassoon.

"Excuse me, what are you carrying there?"

I have my standard answer for these queries: "It's my bassoon. I always carry it on board. It will fit easily under the seat."

The agent looks down at my case and shakes his head, sadly. "I'm sorry, sir, but you will have to check it. We have a weight limit for carry-on items," he says.

The argument continues, becomes more heated, and the line of passengers behind me is growing impatient. One of the pilots passes on his way to the cabin. "You'll have to check that," he says, pointing to my instrument.

"I have never checked it in my life"—I don't mention Belfast—"and it is too risky placing it in an unheated baggage hold. The wood might crack."

The purser joins the dispute. "We can refund your ticket if you choose not to fly," he says. They know that I will not take that option. There are no other flights that evening, and I have a rehearsal scheduled for the next morning. Reality sinks in.

In desperation, "Will you let me carry the instrument to the hold and see where it is loaded, and maybe place it there myself?" I ask. The purser points out to the tarmac alongside the aircraft. Armed military police stand with their automatic weapons loaded and ready. The airport is on high alert. There is no way I could be permitted to join the baggage handlers on the tarmac. For only the second time in my life on a commercial flight, my bassoon and I are separated.

We land at Gibraltar one hour and forty minutes later. As the aircraft pulls up to the gate, there is an announcement from the pilot's deck: "Would passenger Zukerman please proceed to the front of the aircraft." I dutifully edge my way past dozens of other travellers, equally impatient to disembark. I am filled with trepidation. Why this strange, imperious summons?

The door swings open, and I am personally greeted at the top of the stairs by the Gibraltar airport manager. "We received a message from Gatwick that your instrument should be handled with the utmost care," he announces. A red carpet is laid out below the steps, and I am invited to walk down, ahead of all the other passengers. At the foot of the stairs a baggage handler gently carries my instrument, first item removed from the gaping hold, and places it securely in my arms. Only missing is the royal purple serving cushion. What a joyous reunion!

Oh, that our musical instruments should always enjoy such gentle airline treatment! Fortunately, for most of my travels, I was able to hold tight to Heckel #9174.

⌣ TERCEIRA CHEESE: TER—LAJES, TERCEIRA, AZORES

I remember a poem from school days: "At Flores in the Azores, Sir Richard Grenville lay, and a pinnace, like a flutter'd bird, came flying from far away." Those are the opening lines of Alfred Lord Tennyson's naval saga of *The Revenge*. Alas, I never savoured the gentle breezes of Flores, but other islands of the Azores archipelago are equally alluring and full of memories from my early touring days.

In 1978 I completed a remarkable tour of those islands, including concerts in Santa Maria, Terceira and San Miguel. The tour concluded in the town of Angra do Heroísmo on Terceira. It was a logical touring plan, since in those days Pan American Airways served the Azores with daily flights from that island to Boston. There I could connect to Air Canada for the flight home to Vancouver.

The Angra concert was held in a wonderful baroque church overlooking the municipal gardens of the city of thirty thousand. The chairman of the concert organizing committee was a teacher at the local all-boys high school, and after the concert I joined him and his committee colleagues for a late-night supper. There, in a tapas-like setting that allowed ample choices of a widely varied cuisine, we indulged in many samples, including splendid wines and cheeses of the region. I particularly enjoyed a cheese from one of the outer islands, a delicious dry Queijo do Pico fromage de vache with a piquant herbal flavour.

Leaving the restaurant, my host turned to me. "Would you be able to play for our school tomorrow? Your plane is not until two in the afternoon." I was delighted and immediately accepted.

Early the next morning, the teacher came for me with a VW Beetle, already packed with two students. Somehow my luggage, bassoon and I managed to fit in, and we headed down narrow village streets to the school, which lay along the route to the Terceira airport. It was still early, and businessmen in traditional British office uniform of bowler hat and umbrella rode sidesaddle on a seemingly endless parade of donkeys, all heading toward the city centre.

As we arrived at the school, my driver-host coughed and apologized lightly. "I am afraid we have no money for a fee." I had hardly expected anything, and had accepted for the sheer pleasure and unique opportunity of playing for youngsters on a relatively isolated island. And so I played to five hundred high school boys who stood in rows of thirty, listening attentively to Gabriel Pierné, Wolfgang Amadeus Mozart, Johann Wenzel Kalliwoda and Elliot Weisgarber as if they had been waiting for this event for all of their growing lives!

After the concert, a senior student came forward and greeted me in fine fluent English. "We are sorry, indeed, that we have no fee for you. We understand you were well taken with the Queijo do Pico cheese. We would like you to take a sample home." With that, the sample appeared at the back of the hall. Some sample! A huge wheel of cheese was rolled down the centre aisle toward me. Nothing in the negotiated annals of bassoon recitals has ever equalled such a payment.

And so back to the VW—driver, bassoon, two students, suitcase, me and now the cheese somehow all squashed in, and before long we were at the airport, cramped, happy and inhaling the magnificent aroma of the Pico fromage. This was many years before tight safety regulations sealed airports in cocoons of security, and we whisked through the terminal to the Pan Am Quonset hut check-in area. The aircraft had just arrived from Lisbon and was sitting invitingly on the tarmac. It was an early DC-8 jet. (Pan Am was the first to operate jets on its major international "Clipper" service across the Atlantic.)

My suitcase and also the bassoon were weighed. "You are just barely overweight, sir," the extra polite and, as I soon discovered, extra zealous passenger agent told me. "We will not charge you." Before I could thank him, he added, "However, are you planning to take that—object?" He pointed at the cheese.

"Why, yes," I explained, "it is my fee from the school."

"Hmm. Yes . . . well, would you mind placing it on the scale?" It registered 17.5 kilos. "I am terribly sorry, sir, but the excess rate is $34 per kilo." He made a rapid calculation. "Unfortunately, for that cheese you will have to pay $595."

There was a voluble exchange between the head teacher and the agent in very loud Portuguese. It was promptly echoed in English as I did battle with the passenger supervisor, who had emerged at the sound of the altercation. The polyglot voices of other passengers who saw their flight delayed over a pointless argument were raised in supporting cacophony. We shouted and railed and protested until it was virtually time to board, and at that sad moment it looked as if the cheese might stay behind on the island of Terceira.

At that moment King Solomon arrived on the scene.

Well, not the king himself, but his earthly representative in the resplendent uniform of the Pan Am pilot. "What's all the ruckus?" he enquired, as he strode toward his waiting aircraft. A dozen voices, in English and Portuguese simultaneously, outlined the case for and against the cheese. The cheese itself sat silent and pungent.

The captain studied the cheese, the protagonists, the staff, the many irate passengers, and reached his decision. "What the hell!" he said. "Sure, we'll carry the cheese to Boston on the following terms. Cut it in half. You keep half. The other 50 percent is divided among the passengers and crew for tonight's transatlantic dinner. Do we have a deal?"

"Yes," I replied. "Yes," agreed the ticket agent. "Yes," confirmed the supervisor. "Yes," echoed a chorus of waiting passengers. "Yes," breathed the victorious cheese as we rolled it to the gate and the waiting aircraft.

On board, in the confined tubular space of a DC-8, the surgery was performed by a senior cabin attendant. (Is cheese-slicing among the skills taught in their training programs?) The aroma of Queijo do Pico cheese filled the cabin. My remaining half had to be cut in two to fit in two overhead racks. The bassoon had to sit beneath the seat ahead of me for the entire trip. It was well worth the discomfort.

The journey to Boston, a six-hour flight with a ninety-minute dinner service, turned into a glorious party, culminating in a handsome portion of cheese for each passenger and crew. My best concert fee, ever, wafted me home in aromatic style.

⌁ THE ATM BASSOON: TRN—TURIN

European trains are not always as glamorous as their names suggest, and it was not unusual that the Simplon Express was delayed for hours in traversing its namesake tunnel. Instead of arriving in Turin on the River Po at a sensible dinner hour, we steamed into the Stazione Centrale at a depressingly late hour just before midnight.

For some obscure reason I had not made a hotel booking, so I took a room at the nearest available Hotel Centrale d'Stazione, once the city's most glamorous hostelry, now reduced to the status of a seedy railway hotel. The room was curiously spartan and possessed of a strangely warped door that would not close securely. Well, touring is full of such nights, so despite a restless sleep interrupted by constant unidentified traffic up and down the corridors, I was up the following morning and off to a rehearsal at the concert hall with the splendid Turin radio orchestra, conducted by an unknown of the day, Claudio Abbado.

It seemed pointless to change hotels; my clothes were hung up, my toilet kit laid out and the room was comfortable enough. It was hardly secure, but then my bassoon was with me and there was little of value in the room during the day. I would only need to stay for one more night, since early the next day, immediately after the Turin concert, I was on my way to Berlin.

Rehearsals went well, with a chance to play Murray Adaskin's scintillating one and only bassoon concerto, written for me ten years previously, and as an antipasto, the wondrously tuneful Andante and Hungarian Rondo by Carl Maria von Weber.

Despite much happy music-making, there were rumblings among the musicians of this fine orchestra clearly not concerned with musical matters. This was the first rehearsal following an abrasive strike of three weeks' duration, a strike initiated when paycheques failed to clear at the bank and the musicians discovered that, as civil servants of the city of Turin, they were subject to the frequent and progressive bankruptcy of their city's treasury. The strike had been settled by a unique agreement. The musicians would play, provided that the national broadcast agency (with funding coming from Rome) would pay every performer in cash at the intermission of each concert.

The new understanding applied equally to conductor and soloist. And so, at intermission of the concert that evening, a small army of accountants and bookkeepers arrived at the hall with a steamer trunk loaded with crisp new 10,000 lira notes. This was before the euro became the common currency of Europe.

I waited patiently in my dressing room while they counted out the conductor's five million—a tidy package of five hundred of the crisp new bills. His door clicked shut, and there was a discreet knock on mine. My fee on this occasion included a reimbursement of a hefty overseas airfare; 280 of those singular denomination banknotes were counted, then carefully recounted and finally handed to me in a plain brown paper bag.

And so, clutching the equivalent of $2,500, I returned to my railway hotel after the concert. There I suddenly recognized the enormity of the risk posed by the door that could not be locked, and by those constant nighttime passages of so many of the hotel's temporary occupants. I sat on the edge of my bed contemplating the dilemma, very reluctant to fall asleep with so much cash on my person.

The solution came to me as a revelation. Slowly I stuffed the notes into the bell and long tenor joint of the bassoon until not a glimmer of light could be seen through any of the holes of the instrument. Satisfied, I closed and zipped the case shut, placed it beneath my bed, and managed a fitful sleep. I was reminded of the words of Bill Waterhouse, British virtuoso bassoonist, erudite scholar and teacher, who wrote so glowingly of the "noble bassoon." How many times I had argued with him that, in fact, our instrument's epithet should have been, first and foremost, the "lyrical bassoon." Indeed, in the Weber that I had just played, the instrument clearly lived up to that name. But maybe both Bill and I were wrong. At this point, it had been turned into a "lira-full" bassoon.

The alarm rang at 5:30 a.m., and with my cash-laden instrument in hand I grabbed a roll and a coffee at the hotel buffet and dashed for the airport bus. Once on board the flight I promptly collapsed in my seat and slept for the full hour and ten minutes of the flight to Berlin.

Only when I descended from the plane into the old Tempelhof Airport terminal did I suddenly foresee a possible difficulty. In the days before the wall came down, passengers had to go through a form of customs clearance on entering Berlin. We stood in line awaiting inspection. Imagine the strange look of the customs officer if, upon probing the bassoon, a shower of 10,000 lira notes, all brand new, fluttered out before his eyes. There was probably no regulation forbidding the import of Italian currency—but perception is everything, and the mere contemplation of how it might appear was enough to send tremors of nervousness through every fibre of my body.

In fact, nothing happened. No close inspection. No probe. No shower of 10,000 lira notes. That afternoon, in my sanitized Berlin hotel room, near the Sender Freies Berlin radio station, I carefully extricated the bills from the bassoon and recounted them before seeking a bank in Berlin that would exchange that many Italian notes for Canadian currency.

⌣ TURN WHEN I NOD: MRU—MAURITIUS

In Mauritius, concerts were held at the site of an old sugar mill overlooking a magnificent beach, which stretched with golden sand and azure waters as far as the eye could see. Evenings were warm. There was always the gentlest of breezes. The stage, in the outdoors, was set at one end of a pool that was surrounded on all sides by seats for the audience. My pianist, an executive of a large sugar company, had recruited his son, a senior pilot for Air Mauritius, to act as page-turner. The young man could not read music but had been carefully instructed by his father: "Whenever I want you to turn, I'll just nod."

Unfortunately, under pressure of performance, the pianist began to nod involuntarily. The obedient son performed dutifully as instructed, only to find the page determinedly turned back by his father. As the piece progressed the music was more complex, and the pianist became increasingly agitated. Singular nods became a convulsive series and the pages were turned frantically—in each direction. Finally, knocking aside his son's uplifted hand, our valiant pianist plunged on with the performance. I skipped measure after measure to catch up to whichever page had just been turned!

We had arrived at a less turbulent moment in the piece when a sudden breeze caught the music and gently wafted it off the piano and into the reflecting pond. Without hesitation, the pilot-cum-page-turner waded into the middle of the pool to retrieve the soggy pages. At the keyboard, his father simply threw up his hands in despair, while I did my best to improvise a lengthy cadenza. The score returned, soaking wet, and we continued as if nothing had happened. In any case, nothing dampened the spirit of the rest of the concert.

Three days later I flew back to London on Air Mauritius's new Airbus A300 with the son at the controls. I nodded my head when I thought that it was time for him to turn to land on Heathrow runway 27R, but I don't think he noticed. It was clear that he was a far better pilot than page-turner.

~ PIANO IN THE PASSING LANE: PER—PERTH

Everyone in that far corner of Western Australia knew that the old disused church had been converted into the Centre for the Arts. There was no sign at the door to announce its existence. But neither was there a cross in the forecourt to challenge its new identity. It sat in a seldom mowed and never weeded half acre at a dead end of a bleakly dark and inconspicuous street. Perhaps the location foretold just where the Centre lay in the hearts of the municipal authorities.

Nonetheless, this street to nowhere had an important role to play in the very essence of the town. The entire south side was lined with public houses. Eleven pubs, one after the other, competed for nightly patronage. Their facades stretched along the sidewalk to the end of the pavement and were illuminated by a solitary, unshaded 60-watt bulb that swayed aimlessly across the street between two deserted storefronts. The last of the pubs adjoined the site of the arts centre. At some point it must have become clear to the city fathers (and mothers) that in an unequal battle between piety and inebriety, the old church was unable to withstand the competition. Now, by the act of conversion, the arts centre was being given its chance to survive in this alcohol-infused setting. This time the battle would be between art and booze.

It was to this dreary setting that I arrived for a concert with Michael C., my pianist colleague from the university where I had the good fortune to be spending a season as "artist in residence." Part of the assignment involved outreach to smaller centres throughout the state. This was an activity that gave me particular pleasure because of my parallel involvement at home.

As we drove up, we could see that there were trucks and motorcycles parked haphazardly along the road outside respective drinking establishments, although not a single vehicle stood before our concert venue. "Not to worry," opined Michael, "this is one of those towns where everyone turns up at the last minute." We strode down the driveway, past an upturned trash can, beside the unweeded flower beds, and pushed open the door. Through dim evening light we saw rows of pews separated by an aisle designed for no more than a very thin bride and groom. Where the altar had once dominated, now there was a bare platform.

Michael clambered up a rickety set of stairs and marched across the stage, anxious to try the piano that he would have to play that evening. By the time I joined him on stage a billowing cloud of dust had covered the entire unswept area. "The piano must be back here," said Michael through the miasma. The cloud settled into a musty haze. Guided by dim work lights on either side of the platform, we groped our way toward the rear wall. Apart from the layer of dust, which had resumed its role as floor cover, the stage was completely bare. There was no piano.

"Perhaps it's downstairs in the rehearsal room," I suggested. The stairs down were even more precarious than the few that had led us onto the stage. There we discovered dressing rooms that might well have been mistaken for a row of subterranean prison cells had they not turned out to be as unlocked as they were unlit. They had not been occupied for weeks and were shrouded in gloom, with half of the lights burnt out. We pushed open one creaky door after another but found no piano anywhere.

We chose the cleanest of the eight sepulchral chambers as our dressing room for the night, and there I set my bassoon, hung my concert clothes and soaked a hopeful reed, while Michael continued his search of the dismal building. "There must be an instrument here somewhere," he muttered. "Maybe they have it locked up . . . somebody will be here shortly." And sure enough, as concert time approached, somebody did turn up. The chairwoman of the local arts council sailed majestically through the front door and arrived imperially at the foot of the stage.

"Good evening," she boomed, grasping me by the hand and shaking it ferociously up and down several times. "Welcome! I recognize your photograph." She stopped suddenly and looked at Michael. "Who is he?" she demanded. I introduced my pianist for the evening.

"But we don't have a piano!" she proclaimed. "Besides, they didn't tell us anyone else was coming."

Michael looked at her incredulously. "An arts council without a piano?" he queried.

"Nobody said that we needed a piano for this concert so we sent ours away for repairs," came the rumbled reply.

"Well," replied Michael with generous equanimity, "we'll just have to find one somewhere, won't we, ma'am?"

"That will be impossible," Madame Chair reverberated. "There are no other pianos anywhere in town." And with that she stared belligerently at Michael and smiled conspiratorially at me. "You'll just have to give us a solo concert tonight, won't you, Mr. Zukerman?"

"Madam," interrupted Michael, "there are at least eleven pianos in this town that I know of." He pointed to a vague spot somewhere along the south side of the street.

She sputtered, "You can't mean those . . ." She hesitated to use the word "pubs?"

"Indeed I do," rejoined Michael. "Even if their patrons are already two sheets to the wind, the pianos will have remained sober. Out of tune, yes, sloshed, no."

By this time the first members of the audience had arrived and were caught up in the drama being enacted before their eyes. This was clearly far better theatre than the advertised recital.

Michael persisted. "In each of those pubs, there is a piano. We shall go and find one. Gentlemen," he singled out the front row of well-dressed men, "who would like to visit the pub next door?"

Of course, this invitation was hard to refuse. These gentlemen, who had dressed so splendidly for the evening, might well have come to the concert with a modest degree of trepidation, perhaps gently encouraged, even persuaded, by their respective spouses. Was it really possible that they were now being invited to a pub crawl?

No sooner was the proposal made than eight handsomely attired gentlemen rose as one and followed us in single file down the narrow aisle, out of the church and straight to the entrance of the old and faded Swan and Lion. The bartender looked up with delight at the prospect of ten prosperous-looking customers so early in the evening.

"Mind if we look at your piano, mate?" Michael asked.

"Be my guest," replied the publican.

We all trooped to the rear, where indeed there was a very ancient and decrepit piano in appalling shape. Michael tried a few notes and sadly shook his head. We turned to leave, but the niceties of pub life could not be ignored. It just wasn't done to ask a pub owner if we could borrow his piano, and then leave without sampling his wares. Michael called for a round of Guinness for everyone. The volunteers quaffed copiously and only then did they follow us out the door and down the street to the Pelican Arms.

There the piano was equally execrable, and once again protocol had to be observed. A round of Whitbread ale prepared the volunteers for the next stop. They were finding the concert evening far more enjoyable than they had ever anticipated. Two more establishments were called upon, and two more abominable pianos were rejected before we arrived at the Cock and Bull, where Michael patiently repeated his request.

"Sure, mate," replied the lass behind the bar, "play us a tune while you're at it, will you, luv?"

The volunteers, by now well-trained, were already assembled at the bar even before Michael had located the piano. While they sipped a round of Black Isle, their fifth pint for the night, Michael tried the piano. This one seemed quite playable, although badly out of tune. He obliged the pub patrons with a short tune—a prelude from the "Coffee Cantata." Nobody appreciated the subtle irony of his choice.

Michael joined us at the bar. "Would you mind very much if we took the piano over to the arts centre for the evening?" he enquired.

"Sure mate, if you can figure out how to move it. It weighs a pretty ton or two."

The assembled volunteers fortified themselves with a supplementary round of Pitfield and prepared for the task at hand.

Indeed, this particular piano was a gigantic piece of furniture. It was, perhaps, one of the last pianos ever to have been transported to Australia aboard a nineteenth-century convict transport vessel. It was a massive, Brobdingnagian monster, embossed with much decorative carving, possessed of colossal bulbous legs, a mammoth sound board towering above the keyboard, and an immense music rack designed for a complete Bruckner symphony without page turns. It was the *Titanic* of pianos.

Michael cracked the verbal whip, giving encouragement as his volunteers put their shoulders against the instrument and valiantly attempted to overcome the inertia of centuries. Slowly, slowly, slowly the instrument inched forward on wheels that had probably not turned during the entire twentieth century. Once it emerged from the Cock and Bull, the piano was pointed toward its destination, and the beast was pushed and shoved down the middle of the street to the arts centre. Astonished drivers cautiously steered to one side or the other to let the piano pass.

Imagine the extraordinary parade. I was in the lead in white tie and tails. Michael, in splendid tuxedo, followed up in the rear, while our band of eight happy and well-lubricated concertgoers nudged the instrument on its way past the cheering patrons at the pubs whose pianos had been rejected for duty—past the Swan and Lion, past the Pelican Arms, past all the others, down the street toward the old converted church.

When we reached the Centre the doors were flung open, and with a triumphant flourish the instrument was wheeled down the aisle to the front of the hall. There, with one last gargantuan heave, it was hoisted onto the stage. The cloud of dust that engulfed the piano was even thicker than the one that Michael and I had encountered earlier in the afternoon. A great roar rose from the assembled audience. The heroes of the evening, that gallant team of piano movers, took their well-deserved bows, then dusted their hands, smoothed their suit jackets and resumed their seats as members of the audience. The stage was left to us.

Of the concert, all I remember is Michael's unflinching efforts at that piano. He coaxed sounds from it that clearly belied its beer-soaked appearance. Between us, Corelli, Mozart, Spohr and a splendidly acrobatic Rossini somehow prevailed.

When the concert was over, we left as quickly as we decently could to head back to the city. As we drove, we tried to imagine the piano on its return journey. Would the arts council find volunteers to revisit the Cock and Bull after hours? And once underway, would the piano veer to the left of the road, or would it take the passing lane?

The more I thought of it, the more I suspected that it would probably remain on that bleak stage at the arts centre, patiently awaiting the cloud of dust from the next visiting ensemble. At least until the arts council piano returned from the repair shop, the Cock and Bull's behemoth would be a fitting gift from the town's drinking population to those who would rather drink from the Pierian Spring.

⌇ CHAIRMAN MAO'S TRIUMPHANT MARCH: HRB—HARBIN

There were probably more accurate divining rods than a vintage Heckel bassoon with which to test the spirit and mood of China in the late 1980s. Yet my instrument was as fine a dowser as any forked twig when I became the first bassoon soloist invited to the People's Republic.

I visited China only once, and it was at an extraordinary time: just a few months before the June 1989 brutality of Tiananmen Square. Many peaceful student demonstrations were already taking place. Wall posters and protest gatherings brought with them the faint expectations of change. The era of the Cultural Revolution (1966–1976) seemed to be over, and China was opening up once again to the outside world. The atmosphere was full of anticipation, and the political excitement could be felt everywhere. An opportunity for me to perform and to teach at conservatories in Beijing, Shanghai and Xi'an was just one surface reflection of these pending changes.

Arriving at the Beijing airport was a startling contrast after my many trips to the Soviet Union. Here was a country with a smile, a cheerful greeting at immigration, a green "nothing to declare" line at customs. This is not to suggest eternal happiness, or a chorus line from a musical comedy, but certainly on a person-to-person basis, the Chinese appeared to be comfortably relaxed in their dealings with foreign visitors.

Although it was clear that there were orchestras re-emerging in major cities I had very little idea of the level of Chinese bassoon playing. Violinist Isaac Stern's remarkable tours had shown that musical conservatories were flourishing in the larger centres. Whether interest in Western music had spread from the more popular piano and string departments to the orchestral woodwinds was yet to be discovered.

I knew that my Chinese colleagues had little access to printed scores of bassoon music. With this in mind, I took with me a wide selection of published works for the instrument. I willingly wrote off the excess baggage expenses to goodwill, and travelled content in the knowledge that generations of Chinese students would have the chance to learn some of the important works of the bassoon repertoire. It was heavy stuff at seventeen dollars a kilo.

The professor of bassoon at the Beijing Conservatory was Dia Yun Hua, one of China's few female bassoonists. When I met her, she had not played her bassoon professionally since before the Cultural Revolution. In common with so many middle-aged professionals, she had her tales of brutality and indignity from that sad period in China's history—which went a long way to explaining why she preferred to derive her musical satisfaction through the reflected glories of her students. And there were many of them, thirty-one in Beijing alone, including a father-and-son team from Inner Mongolia. There, in the shadow of the fabled monument to Genghis Khan, they had built their own bassoons, following instructions from an 1889 Heckel catalogue that had somehow reached them in the capital city of Hohhot. Now they were here in Beijing to learn how to play the instruments they had carved by hand.

While my concert performances were cheerfully tolerated, the classroom rather than the concert stage was the focal point of my visit. Like blotting paper, the students absorbed everything, from beginners' studies to the most challenging concerti. That was hardly surprising in a nation where on early morning TV you were just as likely to catch an English grammar lesson as detailed instructions on how to construct a steam turbine in your backyard.

I wanted to find out what was being created in Chinese musical circles. Mostly I discovered traditional folk music adapted for Western instruments. At that time there was little serious art music being written, although I did attend one orchestral concert in Beijing consisting entirely of twelve-tone music. The vast majority of what I was shown was characteristic, charming, nostalgic, monochromatic, but always suggesting some faint, hidden enchantment. The piano accompaniments were deliciously florid and decorative, and the solo parts were colouristic and descriptive. Where they had not captured the particular attention of the Red Guard, the folk tunes had been allowed to retain their titles: "A Shepherd's Song," "Birds in the Trees," "The Herdsman's Lament"—all simple pastoral poetry in music. Or so I thought.

Ms. Dia introduced me to many such pieces, including one of her own arrangements, which she had created during her exile in the countryside. Though she had been deprived of her instrument, the Red Guard could not erase her innate musicality, and she had been able to transcribe for the bassoon melodies that she recalled from her childhood. One particularly poignant piece was based on a delicate pastoral melody. Ever the teacher, Ms. Dia coached me carefully on the work—gentle, lyrical, even sentimental—and I played it as a warmly received encore at my programs in Beijing, Shanghai and Xi'an.

At the end of the tour I also played the piece in Hong Kong, and my pianist there burst out laughing when he read the characters at the top of the page. The piece, he explained, had been renamed "Chairman Mao's Triumphant March to Victory through the 7th Valley of the Yangtze River." Ms. Dia had retained the pastoral melody, but lest it fall afoul of the Red Guard, she had adopted a title that presumed to convert a serene folk song into a more acceptable military march. I was reminded of the other great socialist nation of the early twentieth century, where I had encountered a magnificent oratorio written for massed choirs and symphony orchestra entitled "Cantata in Praise of the Steel Workers of Smolensk on Completion of Their Second Five-Year Plan." In both cases, the music rose far above the chosen title.

On my last night in Beijing, there was a phone call from the Canadian embassy. Could I delay my return home? "The Chinese state agency would like you to play a concert in a small provincial city up north."

I suspect that neither the agency nor the embassy realized how precisely they had pressed the right button! Here was a chance for me to parallel my small-town experience in Canada. I had visions of Kenora, Red Deer, Brandon, Swift Current, Yellowknife, Cranbrook, Port Hardy. "Of course, I would love to visit a small provincial city," I replied. "When do I go? Where are they sending me?"

I did not have an answer to either question until I was picked up and taken to the airport the following day. There I was handed a boarding pass. I looked at it with amazement. I was headed to Harbin, population 6.5 million. This was their small provincial city.

There had not been time to send the music for the piano accompanist ahead of me, but I was assured that there were many competent and experienced pianists available. Unfortunately, the young lady who arrived at the rehearsal wasn't one of them. Understandably, she was not familiar with the bassoon repertoire. She was also a painfully slow sight-reader and had little experience working with other musicians. Ten minutes into the rehearsal I knew that it would not be possible to put together a suitable program.

We called an intermission and I spoke to the concert organizer, who was full of sympathy and understanding. "Please, don't worry," he said. "Everything will be taken care of. We will make another rehearsal this afternoon."

I returned after lunch to find another young lady poised at the keyboard. We began to work and I found myself facing the same problem. Like her colleague from the morning rehearsal, the new pianist was not an ensemble player and could not handle a widely varied Western repertoire. By intermission I was ready to suggest a full program of works for solo bassoon. "That really will not be necessary," I was sternly informed. "We will fix the problem. There is time for rehearsal tomorrow morning before the concert." Before I could argue, they escorted me to a splendid banquet for the entire faculty of the conservatory. As the twenty-third course arrived on the gigantic revolving lazy Susan, I was still wondering who would turn up at the piano for the final rehearsal.

I found out soon enough. Next morning, when I walked into the rehearsal room, I was astonished to see both young ladies from the two previous rehearsals. "We have worked it out," one of them quickly explained. "I will play the left hand and my friend will play the right hand. Everything will be just as you want."

There was no time for further changes. We rehearsed as best we could, and somehow we ploughed through the concert. An enthusiastic Harbin audience of 1,300 students heard one of the most astonishing four-hand piano accompaniments ever devised!

Festooned with floral bouquets, I returned to Beijing and packed for the journey onward to Hong Kong and home. I now had an extra suitcase of Chinese bassoon music to carry. The return excess charge was nearly double what I had paid outbound. The entire hard currency fee for the tour was less than the combined excess baggage charges, but I never claimed that I had gone to China to play the bassoon in order to make money. One of the Chinese administrators summed it up aptly. "Don't they pay you a salary at home?" she enquired. "We cannot understand why you need to ask for a fee when you visit another land!"

⌁ THE UNCHANGING KEYBOARD: JNB—JOHANNESBURG

Visiting South Africa in the late 1980s and 1990s was both a revealing and a harrowing experience—revealing, because by then it was possible to see the nation's potential (Nelson Mandela was released from prison in 1990, and became president in 1994), but also harrowing because so much of apartheid still remained. The very act of visiting the country could be seen either as some kind of support for the withering regime, or as an outstretched hand to a beleaguered people.

Touring artists have often faced dichotomies like this. Wherever in the world such monumental social and political upheavals occurred, we were compelled to decide whether to boycott or to encourage music, even if it was in a despised regime. Boycotting inflicted a strong political (and artistic) penalty, and often harmed the victims as much as the oppressors. Encouragement might appear to offer some kind of acceptance of the regime, but was also a lifeline for colleagues desperate for musical contact with the outside world.

Even as South Africa was slowly creeping away from apartheid, musicians' unions outside Africa called on us to apply one more turn of the screw—namely, to boycott. Our fellow musicians in Africa begged us to come, to include them in the greater musical changes happening around the world.

I made a personal decision. Our music was also their music, and many of them shared our dedication to excellence, beauty and enlightenment. The keyboard never changed. Black and white keys were always equally significant.

Eric Atwell, who managed my South African tours, was an outspoken rebel in his youth and an eccentric iconoclast in his later years. He was imprisoned briefly by the regime, and even after his release he risked further jail time by writing a stream of provocative letters to the editor of any newspaper that dared to publish his fervent anti-apartheid cries for justice. By the time I met Eric, he was living in Port Elizabeth, where he divided his time between classical music and wildlife conservation. He had launched a network of active concert societies, for which I was invited to perform. I felt a kinship with him for this activity, which paralleled in so many ways exactly what I was doing with smaller western Canadian centres.

Eric sent me to play a concert at the town of Alice in the Eastern Cape, home of the University of Fort Hare. The all-black campus boasted Nelson Mandela, Oliver Tambo and Robert Mugabe among its most renowned students. Many members of the future governing party, the African National Congress, took their university training at Fort Hare, and it had a well-deserved reputation for academic excellence on one hand and affirmative action on the other. In African universities, affirmative action was probably more important, but no less contentious, than it was anywhere else in the world. The mantra of the university had become "pass one, pass all." Affirmative action often produced skewed results that challenged its success though not its intent.

When I was there in the late 1980s, the separation between community and campus was deep, and neither seemed to be trying very hard to heal the rift. On one side there was a modern, heavily politicized, public institution with gleaming student and classroom buildings. On the other side was the village, with a much older countenance. The village had its own racial divide and an even more clear-cut separation between classes of wealth. If apartheid was being overcome, at least in some of its more blatant manifestations, little had occurred to erase differences between the very wealthy (whether black or white) and the very poor.

Alice remained a small, conservative, church-oriented African village. No surprise, then, when driving down the highway from Cape Town, to approach the town with its strung-out industrial and commercial zone and encounter many signs announcing a variety of church services for the believers. A picture of Jesus stood prominently at the corner of the highway and College Drive. The Saviour's message was strong and clear: "Jesus never fails." Was it a further reflection of the gap between town and gown that somebody had scrawled below it the perfect Fort Hare response: "Pass one, pass all!"

On another of Eric's memorable tours, he arranged a prestigious appearance for me with the State Symphony Orchestra in the capital, Pretoria. Now, a wandering bassoonist may feel vulnerable when he turns up as soloist with an important symphony orchestra. After all, the bassoon players in any major orchestra are unquestionably leading exponents of their instruments, and although they have opted for the security of an orchestral position, each of them is familiar with much of the repertoire that the soloist plays. My first action at any rehearsal with an orchestra was to introduce myself to my colleagues. In many cases they knew of me. Very often I was also personally acquainted with them. We are a small world.

I didn't realize exactly how small until I came face to face with the four Pretoria bassoonists. As I shook hands with them, I realized how much my peripatetic touring had influenced the world of the bassoon. One by one, they recounted how they had each begun to play the instrument after hearing me in recital, at a school concert or on recordings. One of them was from Brisbane, Australia. He had attended a recital that I had given in Toowoomba fifteen years before and decided then and there that he wanted to play this instrument. The second player was from Calgary. He started playing the bassoon after hearing my early recording of the Mozart concerto. "I wore the disc out listening to it so often," he told me. The third young player was from Johannesburg. He had been studying violin but felt that he could never reach a good professional level. His teacher had suggested that I should have a chat with him and show what the bassoon could do. Obviously what I showed him worked. He immediately decided on his future career.

The last player in the Pretoria State Symphony was a young man from Northern Ireland. He had heard me perform, and fell in love with the bassoon, at a youth concert in Belfast during "the Troubles." I

George inspiring the next generation of bassoonists.

had entered his school through a series of double-padlocked iron gates. Security was intense. Children, like their parents, lived in daily apprehension of bomb blasts and senseless attacks on innocent targets. An eight-year-old listened intently for thirty minutes, then was the first to raise his hand with a question. "Mister," he said, pointing at the bassoon, which had veered ominously toward the assembled children, "do you have a licence for that thing?" There in Pretoria, the second bassoon player of the State Symphony Orchestra reminded me that he was the youngster who had asked that question in Belfast fifteen years earlier. Licensed or not, I believe I earned the right that evening in Pretoria to play my heart out for my four orchestral colleagues.

∼ THE ATTACK OF THE WINGED TERMITES; PPT—PAPEETE

I would never have undertaken an extraordinary tour of the Society and Loyalty Islands of French Polynesia had I been forewarned that my bassoon might be devoured by termites.

In Tahiti, the concert was at the Maison des Jeunes. The theatre consisted of a ringed platform, open at the sides (thus well and truly air-conditioned), with a roof that shielded performers from the blazing overhead sun. It was set on Papeete's waterfront, near the exotic Paofai Gardens. Directly in front of the hall rose the Disney-like mountains of the island of Moorea. It had rained in the morning, and a faint mist rose from the surrounding beaches, adding dappled mystery to the magical view of that fabled island.

Just before we were to begin the concert, the stage manager took me by the arm and muttered four words: "Attention à la migration!" ("Watch out for the migration.") It was a strange warning just before the start of a bassoon recital. Was it theatrical slang for "good luck"? The Polynesian version of "break a leg"? In any case, I certainly had no idea what a migration looked like, or why I should expect one to interrupt the concert.

It did not take long to find out. Halfway through the first work on the program, the hall turned strangely dark. At first the faces of the audience seemed blurred. Then the edge of the concert platform disappeared. When I turned toward my pianist, I could see neither her nor the piano. The sounds that reached me from less than three feet away were muffled by a vast host of invading insects. I tried to play on, but then I actually felt "la migration."

Insects covered my face, arms, legs, their wings flapping furiously, desperately, blindly. The entire theatre, audience, stage, piano, soloist and my poor wooden bassoon were enveloped in a swirling yellow cloud. The swarm did not linger. In moments they had passed onward on their relentless flight to their new breeding grounds.

Only later did I learn that these were termites from Moorea. Once every seven years, generally after a rainfall, they migrate in gigantic slow-moving swarms to breed in the mountains above Papeete. The theatre lay directly on their route. In setting the time and date for the concert, the local organizers had paid no more attention to their stage manager's warnings than had I.

Later that month I met an entomologist in New Zealand, and from him I learned two important and gratifying nuggets of information. First, he informed me that dry-wood termites (*Coptotermes formosanus*) are a particular delicacy when salted, roasted or fried in their own fat, or even when consumed raw. I was happy to know that I would not have suffered incurable intestinal affliction from the dozens that I swallowed in the course of their flyby. The second fact was also cause for great hosannas of relief. These winged termites were definitely not of the bassoon-eating variety. Even if they had stayed for dinner, my bassoon would have remained intact.

∿ A HORSE CALLED STRAVINSKY; AKL—AUCKLAND

In Auckland, New Zealand, the conductor arrived at rehearsal in a state of great excitement. On the podium, instead of the usual conductor's score, he placed the morning newspaper, open to the sports section. In the middle of the page he had circled an item in bright red, then added several exclamation points lest anyone missed its significance. "Rehearsal can wait," he announced. "A horse called Stravinsky is running in the third race at Pukekohe." Was it only a coincidence that the orchestra was rehearsing Stravinsky's *Firebird Suite* for the concert that week?

Pukekohe is one of Auckland's many racetracks. There are fifty-two tracks throughout New Zealand, and over 350 in neighbouring Australia. Not surprisingly, betting on the horses is a popular southern hemisphere diversion, and musicians are not immune to this national obsession.

Instruments temporarily neglected, the members of the orchestra gathered around their Maestro and studied Stravinsky's track record. The odds were heavily against our horse. Maybe a last-minute bet of confidence would provide unexpected encouragement for both horse and jockey. The players dug into their pockets for whatever loose change they found handy. The conductor and I added our contributions, and together we pooled $118, which was carefully counted, recorded and handed to one of the apprentice second violinists, who was dispatched to the nearest betting shop to make sure that our wager was duly placed.

Only then could the rehearsal commence. At precisely 11:23, a special intermission was declared, and we all gathered around a portable radio to hear the live broadcast of the race. On long races of over eight furlongs, jockeys often hold their mounts at the rear of the pack, waiting for opportunity, as the other horses tire, to drive through to a win. Stravinsky stayed back, comfortably and safely as the race began. We were sure he would find his pace and sprint ahead to a glorious win. Unfortunately, his jockey seemed to forget the second half of the formula. Stravinsky never changed his position and came in ninth in a field of eleven thoroughbreds.

In contrast, on the concert stage later that week the original Stravinsky was an unqualified success. True, the *Firebird Suite* had the benefit of a dry, well-heated theatre. Poor Stravinsky, the horse, had to run on a muddy track.

As I continued my tour, first in New Zealand, and then crossing the Tasman Sea to Australia, I discovered that breeders in both countries had chosen an astonishing array of musical names for their favoured racehorses. As a result, over the years I have won splendid returns on horses named Borodin, Allegro, Prince Igor, Petrouchka, Italian Symphony, Haydn's Choice and Seductive Tune.

In the town of Tennant Creek, in Australia's Northern Territory, there were no electronic booking connections in the 1970s. To place a bet, one visited the bookie. I wandered down the main street, built immensely wide in the gold rush days of the late nineteenth century to accommodate the turning radius required by camel trains, and introduced myself to a friendly bookmaker who gladly took my bet—both ways—on a horse called Hornpipe. I told him that I was playing a concert starting at 7 p.m. He said that he knew all about the concert and was actually planning to attend with his family. "I'll let you know if your horse places."

As I strode on stage to begin the evening's recital, to my delight, I saw the bookie, his wife and four children seated in the front row. I could not miss his friendly oversize wink. The musical horses were paying off again!

At intermission, my private bookmaker came backstage, extracted a large envelope from his pocket and proceeded to count out my winnings. With due respect to the Arts Council of the Northern Territory, I never did tell them that the bookie's payoff that night exceeded by 150 percent the fee that I received for the evening's concert.

⌁ KEY CLICKS ARE FOREVER: PHL—PHILADELPHIA

My well-travelled bassoon, like any mechanical device, needed maintenance from time to time. Whenever repairs became necessary, I would embark on a pilgrimage to Philadelphia, where I would place my precious instrument in the hands of W. Hans Moennig.

Hans firmly believed that all the best woodwind instruments in the world belonged to him. The hundreds of instrumentalists who flocked from all over the world to his Philadelphia instrument repair workshop were his family of players, and he made a compact with each of us. He entrusted "his" instruments into our temporary custodianship, and as long as we treated them reverently, and played them reasonably well, he would keep his side of the bargain, and make sure that his instruments—to the extent that we allowed him—would be kept in shape and would always play well.

W. Hans Moennig was a master instrument repairman and a remarkable craftsman. He drew players from as far afield as Tokyo, Vancouver, Sydney, New York, Moscow, Mexico, Berlin and Prague to his cramped Philadelphia atelier. It was conveniently located, equidistant between one of Philadelphia's railway stations and the Curtis Institute of Music on Rittenhouse Square. There, in the second half of the twentieth century, he held court as the indisputable repair guru of our woodwind world. He played his lathe as elegantly as any of us would play our instruments. The flame on his Bunsen burner was as steady as a violinist's bow. His screwdriver moved as surely as a conductor's baton.

To take your instrument to W. Hans Moennig's—if you could secure an appointment—was an act of homage, a pilgrimage, a wind player's crusade. His world of instrument repair was divided in two, himself and his "enemies"—a generic term under which he classed everyone who did not share his understanding, skill and sensitivity when it came to judging the tension in a spring, the suppleness of a pad or the perfect alignment of a new key. Hans's special enemies were the instrument makers of East and West Germany and Czechoslovakia. That encompassed the vast majority of the world's finest instrument makers in the post-war years. In particular he reserved a love-hate relationship for the famous Heckel factory. They were renowned around the world as the makers of the finest bassoons.

It was not that he failed to appreciate their work. He grudgingly admitted that they made splendid instruments, but he firmly believed that none of them could play decently until he had worked on them, and he could not permit "his" players to perform on these new instruments until all the sins of the original makers had been rooted out. It was not surprising that at one time or another virtually every Heckel bassoon in North America, and many from other corners of the world, were brought to Philadelphia so they could pass through W. Hans Moennig's Daedalian hands.

When I first turned up at that famous attic, I had just returned from my year in the Israel Philharmonic, and I arrived, innocently, with a virtually new Heckel bassoon.

By its very provenance, it became one of Hans Moennig's precious possessions. That I had played it for a full season before he had a chance to adjust it made no difference. I clearly did not realize the enormity of my sins. The keys clicked relentlessly, the pads covered irregularly, the action was sluggish, the springs responded with uneven tension, pins were too loosely anchored, and water gurgled helplessly in tone holes. Now I stood before W. Hans Moennig and expected him to repair the damage!

When he learned that I had even managed to play the famous solo from *Boléro* on a brand-new instrument, untouched by his hand, he stared in disbelief, for a very long time, as if I were mad. Then the first words he uttered to me were: "You should have come here!"

He motioned to me to take the instrument out, and I played a few scales, not realizing that I was, in effect, auditioning for him. In those few moments he was deciding whether he would assume the lifelong responsibility of keeping #9174 in good condition. I handed the instrument to him, and he held it over his work counter as a sacrificial lamb at the altar. "Just because they have their name everywhere, they expect their instruments to play," he muttered, referring to the Heckel logo that appeared on every joint of the instrument. "They don't know how to put the simplest pad in place. Impossible tension!" With that, W. Hans Moennig had used his quota of words for the day. Instead of talking, he set his mind and his surgeon's hands to making sure that the instrument would finally do justice to the player in whose hands it was due to reside.

With absolute glee, in a form of ecstasy and fervour that I saw only when he was attacking an unredeemed instrument, he took that precious virgin instrument to pieces, screw by screw, key by key, ring by ring, spring by spring. Such was the baptism to which each new instrument was subjected in order to receive Hans's benediction.

After a while he appeared mollified. Perhaps he liked the distinctive black stain of the instrument. Maybe he felt a momentary pang of sympathy for this green youngster who knew so little about the bassoon world. Maybe he even accepted the reality that I had not been able to afford the time or the airfare to come to Philadelphia. Always a man of few words, his second sentence to me was, "Anyhow, at least you left it for me."

His clients generally were wise enough not to interfere as he worked on their instruments. Sometimes, one of them would be assigned the role of operating room assistant. "Screwdriver, file . . . no, not that one, idiot . . . over there . . . the other one . . . pliers, please. That piece of wire . . ." Mostly, though, we would creep into the workshop and lean over his shoulder to mutter a word of admiration for the tightening of a screw, the setting of a spring, the drilling of a new hole. In some ways it was like watching a tennis match: "Splendid shot . . . advantage Hans." Hans Moennig never lost the advantage.

Inevitably, he would pass the instrument back to the unsuspecting custodian with an innocent query, "How is it?" In that question lay a minefield of potential wrong answers. To reply (with alacrity) "It's great!" would usually bring nothing but disdain, and the chance that Hans—thus offended—would simply put the instrument together again and assume the player knew no better than to accept a half-done job. On the other hand, to suggest that the repair (to that moment) was anything less than perfect was to court disaster for inexcusable insult to his skill. Who, after all, could tell when it was safe to say to Hans, "Yes, I think it is good now. I can play again."

Usually that cathartic moment arrived with about twenty minutes to spare before the last train departed from the Market Street station. To Hans, rail was the only acceptable form of long-distance travel, and he had memorized the timetables for all the express trains north to New York, Boston and Montreal; south to Baltimore and Washington; west to Chicago and San Francisco. Uncannily, his internal clock allowed him to hand over the instrument for testing (and a mandatory twenty or thirty minutes of final adjustment) before each player rushed to the station.

How well I recall the exalted feeling of handling my instrument after one of Hans's day-long ministrations. Much of it may have been psychological, but it always seemed as if the key clicks were softened, the action was smoother, the tone more responsive. Convinced of another trouble-free playing year ahead, I would happily run the five city blocks to the railway station, clutching my bassoon in one hand and my ticket in the other, and barely catch the northbound 7:21.

Latterly, when I travelled by air, I would take overnight flights from the West Coast to Philadelphia. I would be waiting downstairs at Hans's door when he arrived punctually at 9 a.m.

Nobody ever turned up at W. Hans Moennig's establishment without an appointment, but even to such an ironclad rule there were two exceptions. Sol Schoenbach, principal bassoonist of the Philadelphia Orchestra, could come when he wished, and Hans would drop everything to attend to his needs. The other exception was made for the nuns from the nearby parochial school. Hans's Catholic upbringing snapped him to an inner attention the minute one of the Sisters entered the workshop. And they came often, usually with decrepit and broken school clarinets that needed immense overhauls. When this happened, the principal oboe of the San Francisco Symphony, the bassoonist of the Berlin Philharmonic and even the clarinetist of the New York Philharmonic could wait, and wait, and wait some more.

While we waited we might study the walls of the workshop, covered with photographs from a myriad of our distinguished colleagues, fondly inscribed "To Hans—who made it possible to play . . . again!" Or we might wander into the anteroom, once an office, where there was a dusty counter beneath which was a cabinet full of instrument accessories. I never saw it open, and I suspect Hans had lost the key many years earlier. Or we silently observed Casimir, Hans's apprentice, who after seventeen years of apparent indenture still deferentially referred to Hans as "Meister" and was quite content to spend his entire life reseating clarinet pads.

The workshop was filled with the permanent sound of Philadelphia's classical music radio station. Well, not quite permanent. Mozart, Beethoven, Richard Strauss, even Wagner would accompany Hans as he worked away on some daunting adjustment. If the music changed to something even mildly contemporary, perhaps Debussy or Ravel, he would suddenly shout, "Turn off that modern music!" literally holding his breath and his screwdriver in mid-air until one of the visiting clients rushed to the radio and turned down the offending cacophony.

And then came lunch. At twelve thirty on the dot, every day of his working life, Hans put down whichever portion of whatever instrument he was working on, folded his apron over his lap and reached across his workbench to light his pipe with the Bunsen burner normally used to heat and mould keys. He then unwrapped a liverwurst sandwich, identical to every other liverwurst sandwich consumed at each of his daily noon-hour breaks. "No music at lunch," shouted Hans to those who had the temerity to stay and try their instruments. "Is there no peace?" he lamented. The rest of us filed out for our own lunches on Philadelphia's nearby streets.

Precisely thirty minutes later, he swivelled around at his workbench, relit the Bunsen and picked up the same instrument and the same screw on which he had been working. The afternoon continued, a blur of pads, keys, springs and tone holes, until Hans was prepared to announce "Game, Set" and close shop for the afternoon.

And now, for a moment, let me return to the Pacific Islands, because this, too, is related to W. Hans Moennig.

As part of a lengthy southern hemisphere tour, which had proudly included a performance of the Mozart bassoon concerto in one of the halls of the recently completed Sydney Opera House, I played a concert in Nouméa, New Caledonia, where the temperature in non-air-conditioned facilities reached a shocking 42 degrees Celsius (107 Fahrenheit). At one point the shellac that held one of the larger pads in place on the instrument melted in this gruelling sunshine. The pad was, quite literally, swimming out of place in its socket. Of course, it was causing unspeakable performance problems.

You can, perhaps, imagine how many expert bassoon repairmen resided in Nouméa, New Caledonia. I approached the Hotel Royal concierge, an urbane hotelier who, in keeping with his immaculate Swiss training, could be presumed to know exactly how to deal with every conceivable guest problem. He listened while I described the difficulty. He looked at the offending pad. Once inside the air-conditioned hotel the shellac had coagulated, seating the pad in a useless position. He replaced his specs on his nose (he saw better without them) and as if he had been dealing with leaky bassoon pads all his life, he directed me to an amazing craftsman in the hotel basement. (Did he live there permanently, a troglodyte of the concierge's imagination?) "I suggest you see the gentleman who 'fixes' the slot machines in the casino," he said. (I suspect the term "fix" was used in both its literal and colloquial sense.)

Downstairs, the slot machine fixer took a tool of his trade, a jeweller's loupe, and peered intensely at the offending pad. But he could suggest no cure. From the basement I was shunted to the sub-basement, where an old and wizened Dutch auto mechanic resided. No delicacy of a jeweller's loupe for him. He summed up the situation in a moment and reached for a pot of a foul-smelling treacle-like substance that was boiling nearby. This was a Dutch product, manufactured under the anglicized name of "Make-a-gasket." Without asking, he smeared a liberal quantity around the bottom of the instrument. It was stark white against the black stain of the instrument's original varnish. "It will set in a minute," he warned, so I quickly adjusted the offending pad as best I could and waited to see what happened next.

What happened next was that the instrument was so severely glued at all points that it would not disassemble that night, or for many nights afterward, without two sets of strong hands to pry loose the wing joint from its newly connected base. Incidentally, the offending pad had sealed magnificently. If the Dutch manufacturers of "Make-a-gasket" want a testimonial, I will hereby state that their product is utterly splendid for improvised bassoon repairs in especially hot climates. Sixty years later, when I sold my bassoon, the white stain left by this underground operation was still visible.

On my return to North America, I made my annual pilgrimage to Philadelphia. Not only could Hans Moennig see what had happened to the bassoon; he could smell it. "What have you done to my bassoon?" he lamented.

"Hans," I stuttered, "I was seventeen thousand kilometres away. I had to play at the Sydney Opera House the very next week . . ."

He looked long and slowly. He pried loose the base of the boot and sniffed loudly to make sure I knew just how much he disapproved. He then looked up at me and said once again the very words with which he had greeted me fifteen years earlier: "You should have come here."

Reflections in a Moscow Mirror

If you are a careful reader, you may have noted that in the litany of those worldwide travels there is very sparse mention of my numerous journeys to the Soviet Union. This was certainly not an oversight, since I visited there eight times between 1971 and 1992. I have kept these tours separate in my narrative for a good reason. My time in Russia was a reflection of those years when I was both virtuoso and impresario. On each of my trips to the Soviet Union I was forever changing hats as I switched between performing artist and concert planner.

∾ GOSCONCERT

During the Soviet regime the only way to bring Canadian artists to the Soviet Union, and soloists and groups from the numerous republics of the Soviet Union to Canada, was through the state concert agency, Gosconcert. Their method of organizing these tours was to work with a single impresario in each country with which they chose to conduct business. In the 1970s, their man in Canada was Nicholas Koudriavtsev. He was based in Montreal, from where he successfully organized major Russian orchestral, choral, ballet and celebrity recitals for all the larger Canadian cities from coast to coast.

I first met Koudriavtsev at a New York booking conference hosted by the legendary American impresario Sol Hurok. Nicholas sat at the head table with Hurok and the other entrepreneurs who could count on large enough audiences in their cities to fill huge theatres for the spectacular attractions Hurok was bringing from the Soviet Union. I had little hope of finding affordable artists or groups on the Hurok roster, and when I confided to

George, third from left, with members of the Moscow Philharmonic Orchestra.

Nicholas—the only other Canadian present at that gathering—that I was looking for attractions for my small community network, he blithely offered me a chance to join with him on some of the major Soviet attractions that he hoped to present in Canada.

With their limited populations, it was clear that these small towns could not possibly guarantee the massive fees required for such attractions. There were simple physical restrictions, too. Schools and community halls were not equipped for massive touring attractions. Professional stagehands were unlikely to be available in smaller centres. Even finding sufficient parking space for an eighteen-wheel tractor-trailer rig adjacent to the concert venue might prove an insurmountable problem.

Koudriavtsev reluctantly accepted the reality that such groups as the wildly popular Moiseyev State Academic Folk Dance Ensemble, the Red Army Chorus or the Bolshoi Ballet—the latter with seventy-five dancers, an orchestra of forty-two and a crew of twelve technicians—would never be able to appear in Hay River, NWT.

At one point in my conversation with Koudriavtsev, I asked him to enquire whether the Russians would be willing to consider something as unprecedented as a bassoon soloist on tour. His initial reaction was predictable. "Gosconcert," he said, "would think it a preposterous suggestion. The bassoon has never before been presented as a solo instrument in the Soviet Union." He shook his head, sadly. "The instrument is unknown. You are unknown."

But even as he spoke, it was apparent that he was considering the other side of the equation. He was intrigued to contemplate the existence of my network of small Canadian concert societies. If he had hardly known of its existence, he was sure that his Russian partners knew absolutely nothing of its potential. He determined to introduce me to Gosconcert as a new kind of impresario who could offer them access to an untapped market of small communities across Canada. At the same time, although he didn't think it would have much success, he would present me to the Russians as a soloist on an unusual instrument.

When Koudriavtsev next headed to the USSR, he took with him two vinyl LP discs of my new Vox recording of the Mozart and Weber concertos. Even before he returned to Canada, I received an astonishing telegram inviting me to perform in Moscow and Leningrad, as well as to meet with Gosconcert bureaucrats to discuss possible tours of Soviet artists to Canada. They offered a round-trip Montreal–Moscow airfare on the state airline, Aeroflot, and they would provide a hotel wherever I was in the Soviet Union. Strangely, there was no mention of a concert fee. No matter! I was sure it was a clerical error.

So it was that my first invitation to visit the Soviet Union came with a simple unspoken caveat. In exchange for my own performance opportunity I would be expected to bring Soviet artists to the smaller towns of Canada. It was sheer bribery, but not so unusual in the concert world. This was an exciting offer that I could not refuse! I would play in the two great musical centres of the Soviet Union, and at the same time I would be accepted as an impresario partner in their artistic exchanges.

Even though I feared a devil's bargain, I began to see benefits for everyone. Our smaller Canadian communities would suddenly find themselves enjoying Soviet artists, while Canadian artists would discover new touring opportunities in the many republics of the Soviet Union. As I planned my first trip to the USSR, I realized that I was about to create a Soviet mirror of my Canadian double existence. I had to be properly prepared. I purchased a *ushanka*—a Cossack fur hat.

∼ 15 NEGLINNAYA STREET

Gosconcert maintained offices just one block behind the Bolshoi Theatre, in a faded old building at #15 Neglinnaya Street. When I arrived, Moscow was at the height of a raging blizzard. I pushed through the wooden exterior doors of #15 and shook the snow from my coat. The lobby was flanked by an old-fashioned steam radiator that in turn led toward an impressive carpeted stairway. There was a comforting damp smell of the warm indoors.

The entire marble floor at the foot of the staircase was buried under dozens of soaking-wet pairs of galoshes, each dripping the last remnants of the blizzard's fresh snow and emitting plumes of steam whenever they came in contact with the creaky radiator. Taking coats from each new arrival were two elderly ladies dressed entirely in black, headscarves dutifully tied beneath their chins. They were the celebrated Gosconcert "Babushkas" who, I was told, enjoyed a city-wide reputation for their uncanny ability to return the correct set of footwear and coat to each person departing from #15.

Leaving the semi-tropical musk of the downstairs radiator, I climbed to the head of the staircase to meet my Soviet counterparts.

I suppose my earliest meetings at Gosconcert could be compared to an unequal chess match between Soviet grandmasters and a Canadian novice. I knew barely enough to avoid the impresario's equivalent of the Fool's Mate. However, I was prepared to believe that the men and women at Gosconcert were, for the most part, very much like us. They were dealing in the same human commodity. Certainly at the practical level of day-to-day planning they were engaged in the same mysterious equation of bringing together performers and audiences.

I was pleasantly surprised to sense that our discussions were on a parallel path. The artists they proposed were not yet established celebrities. I could accept that. After all, the towns to which I would try to send them were equally unknown. They peered at a map of Canada on which I had marked—in appropriate red—all of the towns to which I might be able to send their artists. They had never heard of most of these communities, but they recognized immediately that there were lots of them.

Since one of Gosconcert's primary tasks was to earn foreign currency for the state, somebody in the upper echelons of the organization must have recognized the potential and rightly calculated that a few Soviet engagements for an unknown Canadian soloist was a small price to pay to open up a valuable new Canadian market for their own artists.

I was aware that Soviet artists who came to Canada would receive only enough dollars to cover their expenses on the road. The largest portion of any contracted fees would go directly to Gosconcert.

I think they understood that the fees I could offer for their artists reflected the limited resources of small Canadian concert societies that depended on subscriptions rather than ticket sales to establish their budgets. At first my offers must have struck them as ludicrous, but gradually Gosconcert began to realize that enough of these small-town engagements put together into one tour could yield as much as a single appearance of a great orchestra, ballet company or celebrity soloist in a large city.

Then we turned to the other side of our exchange. I had come prepared to offer an array of Canadian soloists and small ensembles to follow me on tour to the various regions of the USSR. Of course, I explained to my Gosconcert hosts, I would have to pay them each a modest fee and—by the way—this seemed like a good time to bring up the unresolved question of my own fee for the Moscow and Leningrad concerts. What did they have in mind to offer?

The answer was prompt, and blunt, and brought home the economic reality. I was negotiating with the Soviet state's foreign currency collection machine. The omission in their contract offer was not an oversight. The Russians were not prepared to offer any hard currency fee to me, or to any of the other artists I was proposing for tours of the USSR. They would be very generous with roubles, but those could only be spent on limited commodities while in the Soviet Union and could not be taken out of the country.

Although we now had agreement on Soviet artists to come to Canada, there was absolutely no way Canadian artists could come to the USSR without hard currency fees. I made a suggestion to my new-found Gosconcert colleagues. "We'll take the dollars from the fees we pay for your artists, and pay some of them to the Canadian artists who are going to tour in the USSR." I then added generously, "You can have all of our roubles from any concerts we play for you. It's a win-win for everyone!"

Of course I knew they would reject the proposal, but I also knew that I could not ask other Canadian artists to visit the Soviet Union without a transferable fee. Throughout the ongoing negotiations, details of a compromise were tortuously hammered out. In the end, I paid more dollars for their artists. They agreed to pay a small percentage of hard currency to the visiting Canadians. In effect, they had accepted my compromise proposal.

By insisting on a percentage of the fee for visiting Canadians in hard currency, I had successfully broken the long-standing obstacle to continued worthwhile artistic exchanges. I thought it was a fair exchange for Gosconcert's unstinting willingness to invite me to perform in their two largest musical centres and their ongoing plans to bring other Canadians to the USSR.

Our first agreement was signed and celebrated with a traditional vodka toast. Then I was led back down the great marble staircase. One of the Babushkas wordlessly handed me my galoshes and coat, and—back to being a virtuoso on tour—I was on my way to catch the night train to Leningrad. I needed to change hats again. I was putting my *ushanka* to work.

Over the course of the subsequent twenty years of association with Gosconcert, the toggle switch of earlier days shifted constantly between virtuoso and impresario. The following stories recall some of my own experiences in Russia as well as some of the memorable visits to small-town Canada of a distinguished array of Soviet soloists and ensembles. I invite you to join me switching hats again on this journey through the looking glass.

∾ VIRTUOSO: THE FIRST BASSOON SOLOIST IN THE USSR

On the train to Leningrad (this was still several years before the city reverted to its earlier name of St. Petersburg) I learned that I was to play in the Glinka Hall of the Philharmonic. By unexpected coincidence, I was planning to play the Glinka bassoon sonata on my program that evening.

I strode out on stage for my opening work, and to my surprise, the entire audience rose as one in a standing ovation. I had not been warned of one of the city's musical traditions. If an artist played the works of Glinka in the hall so lovingly named after that patriarch of Russian national music, the audience would rise in silent tribute the minute the artist entered the hall. This was certainly the first and only time I had ever enjoyed a standing ovation without playing a single note. It was a fine beginning for my first Soviet concert! Two nights later in Moscow, over two hundred people turned up at the House of Scientists when they announced a bassoon recital by an unknown Canadian virtuoso. The standing ovation came at the conclusion of the concert. Just before I played an encore, I addressed the audience through my translator and asked if they had any questions, or whether there was anything they would like to know about the bassoon. She turned very pale and whispered in my ear, "I do not think you wish to ask such questions of this audience."

"Why not?" I whispered back. "There is so much they may want to ask. The bassoon isn't seen that often as a solo instrument."

"Nyet, nyet . . . no, no," she repeated. "Not here!" The urgency in her voice betrayed some horrible secret of which I was clearly oblivious. "You do not understand," she persisted. "Of two hundred and six people here this afternoon, one hundred and ninety-four play the bassoon!"

Regardless, I took their questions, and we found far more common ground than disagreement. Clearly, my Moscow colleagues shared my view that the bassoon could hold its own on stage as an honoured soloist. What my translator did not know was that the remaining twelve non-bassoon-playing members of the audience were my Russian aunt and several of my Moscow cousins!

A report on both concerts rapidly reached Gosconcert. I think they were as surprised as I was by the favourable response in both their major musical centres. Quick to recognize the success as well as the potential of this tour, they proudly proclaimed me the first solo bassoonist ever invited to perform in the Soviet Union.

I was flattered to enjoy that honour, although I could never have guessed that they were already making plans to send me to other capital cities in distant republics of the USSR, and that this would be just the first of eight equally successful Soviet tours that would be offered to me in the coming years. Before I left the Soviet Union, I already had an invitation to return the following season.

∼ IMPRESARIO: WINGED HARPS, TERRESTRIAL HARPISTS

One of the Soviet ensembles that I brought to Canada was a remarkable quartet of virtuoso harpists, *Chitiri Arfi* (Four Harps). We equipped a van with an elaborate system of hanging seat belts. The harps were nested in two pairs, and travelled thousands of kilometres suspended by the belts, never touching each other or the floor of the vehicle. Chitiri Arfi proved to be one of the most successful small ensembles that Gosconcert ever sent from the Soviet Union. In four separate tours they performed for seventy-four communities across Canada. The group had an unabashed appeal, both musical and visual, to community audiences everywhere.

On one of their tours they arrived at Regina, Saskatchewan, after a day-long trip from Antigonish, Nova Scotia. The station manager handed them a telex message from the airline cargo department:

> Regret shipment not loaded at Halifax. Current priority
> all flights from Atlantic cities, lobster shipments to Montreal.
> Will forward your equipment on earliest flight on space
> available basis.

This cryptic message was delivered to Svetlana, leader and translator of the group, on the night before a scheduled concert at Swift Current, 245 kilometres west of Regina on the Trans-Canada Highway. On receipt of the message, Svetlana let out a howl of distress. The off-loaded "shipment" just happened to consist of their four precious instruments.

Russian women are trained from childhood in the effective tools for battles with bureaucracy. Versed in Soviet ways, the harpists were thoroughly accustomed to dealing with indifferent state-run shops where customer service was non-existent. Chitiri Arfi put this experience to work with a tirade of rapid-fire Russian—a language that often sounds far more furious than the actual meaning of its words. The Regina airport had never before heard such shouts and screams as those emanating from the four women of the quartet. Was it possible that in Canada lobsters were more important than harps or harpists?

It didn't take long for the news to reach me in Vancouver. In rapid succession I received calls from the stage manager, "What do we do now? We have some pretty distressed ladies on our hands"; from Svetlana, "Call the prime minister"; from the three other harpists "*Gdye arfi*?" (Where are our harps?); and from the airline station manager, "We'll do our best but Halifax says the lobsters can't sit around." I sympathized profoundly with the hungry diners at Montreal's finest restaurants, but I was deeply perplexed: where on the Canadian prairie would we find four concert harps in the next twenty-four hours?

By now it was too late to call the airline in Halifax. That would have to wait until they opened in the morning, which would be 3 a.m. Vancouver time. Meantime, perhaps the challenge could be met. There were four major cities in the provinces of Alberta and Saskatchewan. There would surely be a harpist and a harp or two in Regina, Saskatoon, Edmonton and Calgary. Four cities, four harps. We weren't asking for much. However, not just any harp would do. This called for top-of-the-line concert instruments on which the Russian artists could successfully perform their amazing repertoire. From the tight little family of Vancouver harpists, I quickly learned the names of key players in the prairie cities and began phoning. One by one I left messages, late into the evening, describing a harp emergency of unprecedented magnitude.

The orchestral colleagues responded unstintingly.

Within an hour of my call to Regina, the principal harpist of the symphony was sitting with the Russians in their hotel room, drowning collective sorrows in suitable quantities of vodka. Of course her instrument was available and, in a spirit of splendid international harp solidarity, she would drive it to Swift Current herself!

Players in Saskatoon, Edmonton and Calgary readily made their instruments available. All we had to do was come and get them! Our stage manager, with the help of a hastily recruited second driver, would take the quartet to Swift Current and then drive our specially equipped Harpmobile through the night to pick up the instruments. It would constitute a trip of 1,200 kilometres—and eighteen hours of steady driving. To our eternal good fortune, the roads were bare, the driving fast and steady.

As a precaution, I arose early and placed a call to the airline in Halifax. I felt as if I were enquiring at a hospital about a friend's condition following surgery. Yes, the harps spent a comfortable night in the warehouse. Yes, the building is well heated, and their temperature is normal. Visiting hours are any time. (I had spoken with a Halifax harpist and asked her to look in on the patients.) When will they be discharged? The reply from the agent was unchanged: "The lobsters have to go first before the whole shed-full is spoiled! Other freight goes whenever space is available."

Meantime, the harp cavalcade continued its relentless drive toward Swift Current. On the morning of the concert we had one harp already in Swift Current with three more wending their way toward the destination. Svetlana called again, "Did you speak to the prime minister? There is still only one harp." I told her that the three others were on their way from the final stop in Calgary and would be in Swift Current approximately one hour before concert time.

Two hours later, over the phone, I heard a cascade of glissandi. Tchaikovsky's *Waltz of the Flowers* had never sounded so good. The harps had obviously arrived. The artists were on stage, tuning and warming up. For the first time that day I allowed myself to relax.

Less than ten minutes later the stage manager called again. It was five minutes before concert time. He was laughing hysterically.

"What's up?"

"You won't believe this."

"Try me."

"A FedEx truck has just arrived from Regina with four Russian harps . . ."

Now there were eight harps on stage, and it was not a mirage. I hoped there were also hordes of contented diners enjoying lobster thermidor in Montreal. I spoke to the artists. "Which instruments will you play tonight?" I asked Svetlana.

"Is proper occasion to celebrate Soviet-Canadian friendship and international harp solidarity," she declared. "We play Canadian harps in first half, Russian harps after intermission. Please thank the prime minister."

⌇ VIRTUOSO: THE DVARIONAS DVARIATIONS

My Soviet tours all took place in post-Stalin times, but much of the rigid regime control of the earlier times remained in place. In the 1970s and 1980s the Soviet Union was still a land caught up in the firm grip and suspicions of the previous decades.

It was all reflected on arrival at Moscow's Sheremetyevo Airport, where the ambience was both dreary and foreboding. The arrival hall, drab and low-ceilinged, was dimly lit, shabbily furnished and belligerently staffed.

Immigration inspectors looked down on arriving passengers from narrow windows set in raised cubicles. Passports were taken, inspected, sometimes passed to unseen associates, held for a needlessly lengthy time, and then—for the lucky ones—stamped and silently returned. In the customs hall, inspection was selective and wordless. Snarling Doberman pinschers, severely muzzled, pulled relentlessly on leashes as they patrolled the baggage zone. Wallets were arbitrarily searched in the hunt for undeclared hard currency. Visas were re-examined at a secondary inspection point. It was a cheerless arrival.

I tried not to be intimidated by this quasi-inquisition when I arrived on my third Soviet tour. Clutching my bassoon, and hauling my suitcase behind me, I threaded my way through the crowd until I was finally released into the chaotic waiting area outside the customs hall. I tried to locate my "handler" among the throngs awaiting the disgorgement of the planeload of newly arrived travellers.

Nobody rushed over in instant recognition of a bassoon case, so I scoured a panoply of name signs being waved by a small army of official greeters. I finally caught sight of a placard emblazoned with a Canadian flag and happily surrendered myself to the machinery of Soviet bureaucracy. Nadja, my interpreter from the first tour, would be with me again for the next nine days. She marched me to a waiting taxi.

As we headed to the city I had many questions. Where will I be playing? Which hotel am I at? Am I playing with orchestras? Who is my pianist? When do I rehearse? When do I travel? When is my meeting with Gosconcert? Hard as it may be to believe, none of these essential points had been discussed. My contract, scrutinized so carefully for details by the immigration officers at the airport, stated simply that I was to give five concerts for Gosconcert within a designated time period.

Answers came slowly, almost reluctantly. On this tour we would be going to the Baltic states and Byelorussia (now Belarus). I would play with piano in Tallinn, Vilnius, Kaunas, and Riga, but first with the symphony orchestra in Minsk. We would leave the following afternoon from the Moscow Belorusskaya Station. I could hardly believe my good fortune. My mother's hometown was a tiny village not far from Minsk. My father's birthplace was near Vilna—now known as Vilnius. Was it possible that I would be able to visit the birthplace of either of my parents? I put the question to Nadja. Both were answered with an enigmatic *Mozhet byt* (maybe).

Other questions were answered with the single word *Potom* (later). We arrived at the Minsk hotel, a notoriously shabby and older property, and there I was handed a typewritten itinerary and an envelope containing a supply of roubles for immediate expenses. While I signed a receipt for the cash advance I quietly hummed the melody of "Nobody knows the roubles I've seen." Probably just as well that Nadja did not recognize the bad musical pun. "*Potom*," she said. "I will try to have more answers for you tomorrow." With that she bade me goodnight, and I was left to sample the meagre offerings of the late-night buffet at the hotel.

By the time we met the following afternoon to head to the railway station, *mozhet byt* had turned into a full-blown *nyet*. The litany of excuses was unnecessary but impressive: there is no time to go; there is no transport available; it is an unsafe area to visit; and anyhow, there is nothing to see there.

Already on my earlier tours I had learned the simple lesson that there are three ways to say "no" in a Soviet interpreter's lexicon: *nyet* simply means "no"; *mozhet byt* means "maybe" and is conveniently used to delay negative decisions; *nye vozmozhno* means "not possible" and implies that somebody—other than the translator—has a good reason for saying "no." Used interchangeably, they all ultimately turn out to mean precisely the same: "no."

The reply to my Vilnius request was more complex. *Mozhet byt* still meant "no," but they could not claim that we did not have time available, since we were already going to be in the city. They had a much grimmer excuse for not visiting my father's neighbourhood. The Jewish part of the city had been completely destroyed by the Nazis.

Musically my visit to Vilnius was far more rewarding. Backstage at the concert I was visited by Balys Dvarionas. I had not known of him, but Nadja made sure to let me know that he was the director of the Vilnius Conservatory and renowned as composer, conductor, pianist, teacher, and administrator. We chatted briefly in bad German, and as he was about to leave he took a folio of music from his briefcase and offered it to me. "Perhaps you will enjoy to play this one day." I looked at the title of the work, Theme and Variations for bassoon and piano. I thanked him profusely and tucked the work away in one of the several zipper pockets that encompassed my bassoon case.

It was an immensely busy touring season, and although I had glanced briefly at the Variations, I did not appreciate its value at the time and did not immediately set about preparing the piece for performance. It was eighteen months later when I finally studied the work more closely and was enchanted by its haunting melody and its immense suitability for the bassoon. I nicknamed my new-found treasure the *Dvarionas Dvariations*, and from that time on it became a featured work on many of my programs. It proved to be an exciting bassoon discovery.

Two years after receiving the work in Vilnius, I came home from a lengthy tour and decided to write to the composer to thank him again and to let him know that I was including the Variations as a major work in numerous recitals. I told him that I particularly appreciated the Lithuanian folk melody on which his variations were based—in part because, although I had not been able to visit the house where my father had lived, perhaps I was now playing a melody that he had once heard or even sang.

Two months later I received a letter back from Kaunas. Dvarionas's nephew, who had been with him at the time of my concert, wrote to thank me for the letter to his uncle. Sadly, he reported, Balys Dvarionas had fallen ill in the previous year and died shortly before my letter arrived. At countless concerts after that, when I featured the *Dvarionas Dvariations* on my program, I thought of the generosity with which he had given me his score, and how much the bassoon world owed to this unlikely contributor to the bassoon repertoire.

≈ IMPRESARIO: WHEN THE EAGLES LANDED

My final trip to Russia did not begin auspiciously. When the flight from Rome arrived at Sheremetyevo Airport late at night in February 1991, there was, surprisingly, no Gosconcert representative at the airport. I took a taxi to the Metropol Hotel, and there was no hotel reservation in my name. I marked it all down to the political confusion of the day.

Gosconcert was still there at #15 Neglinnaya, where little seemed to have changed. I handed my overcoat to the Babushka. I added my galoshes to the mountainous pile, secretly wondering how they would ever identify them for my departure. I climbed the stairway to the conference rooms.

Upstairs there was embarrassment and confusion as I encountered two Gosconcert bureaucrats, both of whom I had met on previous tours. "Didn't you receive our telex?" one of them enquired. "Of course!" I replied and reached into my briefcase to produce their latest message. It was my contract to perform in Moscow, Kaliningrad, Smolensk. Dates and fees were confirmed. The telex included an invitation to discuss future Canadian tours for their artists. It was signed by a deputy director. My visa would not have been approved without this document.

Heads shook sadly. "Sergei Nikolaevich is no longer with us," said one of the officials. "He had no authority to invite you. We sent you another message. Unfortunately your concerts are not possible at this time. *Nye vozmozhno.*" Perhaps their telex was still chasing me from hotel to hotel in England, Spain and Italy. There was no point in asking to see a copy. Clearly my contracted concerts in Russia had been peremptorily cancelled.

I was determined to make good use of my time in Moscow. On a previous trip I had initiated discussions about a children's choir from the Siberian city of Krasnoyarsk. "I still think we could organize a very good Canadian tour for them. Can you arrange for me to visit them?" I asked.

One of the two officials interjected: "We have fine children's choir in Moscow." The other added, "It is so much easier, so much less expensive than travelling so far." I demurred. There was something alluring about the once-forbidden reaches of Siberia. I insisted: "A choir from such a distant region would have an instant appeal for our audiences."

They persisted. "We have a video to show you from Krasnoyarsk." That sounded hopeful, so I followed them into a small theatre. The video began with a display of the distant city, followed by the program. Lovely costumes, brilliant choreography, but it was a dance company, not a choir.

"We spoke about a children's choir," I reminded them. "I am not interested in a ballet."

"But they are from Siberia, the same city. They are prepared to tour." Apparently the expense of travel from Siberia was no longer an issue.

I remonstrated, "Dance is impossible for our small cities. The theatres are not suitable. We are wasting everybody's time."

And with that I thought my hopes of going to Siberia (and coming back again) were dashed. It was a sad moment. We had worked together for eighteen seasons, but now, apparently, there would be no more Russian tours to small-town Canada. I closed my briefcase, shook hands politely and trudged back to the Metropol. I wondered who would pay for the hotel after the first night. Perhaps I would finally have time to visit comfortably with my Moscow cousins, maybe even see a little more of the city. On all of my previous trips, I had never even had time to visit the Pushkin museum!

One hour later I was summoned to the front desk. One of the Gosconcert translators stood there clutching a large manila envelope. "You are going to Krasnoyarsk tomorrow morning! You will meet the youth choir. I have the tickets," she announced, waving the manila envelope. "I will call for you at 6 a.m."

I was headed to a place that few enough Russians ever get to visit, let alone a Canadian impresario.

At Moscow's domestic terminal we were herded across the tarmac to an aircraft that had once been a military bomber, its glass nose instantly ready for conversion. Men, women, children, ducks, chickens, even a docile sheep, boarded. There were safety belts strung across the seats but nobody instructed the passengers to fasten them. The two stewardesses were smoking in the galley. Everyone clutched the parcels and carry-on baggage in their laps as the plane lurched forward and took off toward Siberia.

Five hours later we landed on a darkened runway at Krasnoyarsk, halfway between Novosibirsk and the Gulag! We Canadians come from a vast nation ourselves and often marvel at the 7,500-kilometre distance between Victoria and St. John's. The trip to Krasnoyarsk may have only been 4,200 kilometres, but as we crossed the steppes, the taiga, the dried-out seabed of Lake Aral and the vast Ural Mountains, there was no escaping the reality of Siberia's remoteness, isolation and barren immensity.

By daylight, Krasnoyarsk turned out to be a modern, relatively busy metropolis. It is an unprepossessing city of high-rise apartment blocks, institutional government buildings and—unexpected surprise—a magnificent theatre and opera house! I remember being equally surprised that there was no visible military or police patrol. But then, why should there be? I was falling prey to the stereotypical view of Siberia.

Krasnoyarsk is located at the junction of two great northern rivers, the Yenisei and the Kacha, both of which flow, like our Mackenzie River, to the Arctic Ocean. At that time the city had three major industries: aluminum, hydro power and chocolates. The confectionary industry catered to the Muskovite sweet tooth by manufacturing the finest chocolates anywhere in Russia.

My guidebook also told me that Krasnoyarsk had a population of 995,000. It was actually larger than that, but an arcane Soviet law decreed that cities over a million were required to build an underground metro line. Krasnoyarsk, loosely translated, means "red clay," and engineers had long concluded that it would be impossible to dig a subway through such soil. The population remained, officially, under a million.

The skyline of Krasnoyarsk was dominated by two major structures that characterized the economic difficulties of the Soviet Union at that time. The first was an incomplete office tower designed to house a major ministry of the central Soviet government. It had been under construction for seven years; there was no visible sign of work at the site. The second, overlooking the junction of the two rivers, was a splendid piece of Finnish architecture, an innovatively designed fifteen-floor tourist hotel, half-built and presumably also half paid for by a joint venture with Germany. The big mystery that everyone in Krasnoyarsk was trying to solve was where were the tourists, and why, particularly, would they flock there in large enough numbers to justify the investment in a luxury hotel?

Things may well have changed since then, but at that time Krasnoyarsk was simply not a part of tourist-land. Until the late 1980s it had been a closed military territory, and although it lay on the route of the Trans-Siberian Railway, visitors would have had little reason to stop there. The last major influx of tourists was probably back in the sixteenth century, when the original Cossack fortification was valiantly defended against invading Tartar hordes.

Shortly after my arrival, I finally heard and was deeply enchanted by the Krasnoyarsk Children's Choir, soon to be renamed the Little Eagles of Siberia. They were magnificent. Their discipline and musicality matched that of the world-renowned Vienna Boys' Choir. I had judged correctly that a Siberian choir would welcome touring opportunities in western Canada.

Russia was about to be represented on the world stage by a dazzling ensemble from Siberia. I was smitten and returned to the hotel to prepare for a night flight back to Moscow, where I would negotiate terms with whoever remained at Gosconcert.

At the Krasnoyarsk airport I was surprised that the Moscow flight was actually called ahead of departure time. We were guided to a bus that took us to a distant area of the airport where half a dozen Aeroflot planes were silently lined up. Only one, presumably our Moscow flight, was being serviced.

The outside temperature was well below zero. The bus was unheated. Many passengers were standing and all were huddled together in the extreme cold. The only person to hear the complaints was the bus driver, who was just as cold as everybody else. Suddenly he pulled a lever, and the door of the bus creaked open. Even more cold swept in, and with it came an Aeroflot pilot. His impassioned announcement in Russian was greeted by groans of dismay from those who understood what he had said.

He repeated it, in broken English. "We have problem, dear friends," he declared. "Airport not willing accept credit from Aeroflot." English groans were now added to the earlier Russian ones. "They say only U.S. dollars now possible for gasoline for flight to Moscow. We need . . ." He consulted a notepad. ". . . three thousand four hundred eighty-four dollars." A further pause. "Then we take off," he stated, and for our benefit added, "with passengers." He paused again, then made a final comment. "Okay to take credit cards, but not American Express." It struck me, then, that they had been practising this collection routine with numerous earlier flights. He made his way down the aisle, accepting handouts of U.S. dollars.

I contributed $120 in cash. Many others contributed far more handsomely. It was still not enough. I saw the pilot consulting with one American, also a German businessman. They followed him off the plane to a small baggage jitney, then disappeared into the terminal, presumably to charge a sufficient sum to their credit card accounts. As they came back, we saw the fuel truck, pulling up next to our aircraft, hoses ready, fuel streaming into the tanks. Thirty minutes later we boarded and, marginally warmer, took off through the vast night, over the taiga, across the Ural Mountains, over the Aral Sea and the steppes of central Russia, landing in Moscow five hours and twenty minutes later.

On my last day at Gosconcert, somebody offered me a Krasnoyarsk hazelnut chocolate. Delicious. It set the tone for easy negotiations for the North American debut of the Little Eagles of Siberia. The choir was destined to become the most successful of all my Russian tours. Six months later, the Eagles began their first Canadian tour. They returned on six more occasions, eventually negotiating their contracts without the help of Gosconcert. On their final tour of North America, I was even able to organize a massive forty-four-concert itinerary in the western United States.

It ended on the west coast. Aeroflot had instituted a new flight from Seattle to Khabarovsk via Anchorage, Alaska. It was a daring route and saved thousands of kilometres' travel for the passengers. However, in taking advantage of this new service, the Little Eagles had not counted on Aeroflot's inexorable search for every possible source of hard currency. The airline was greedily eyeing all potential excess baggage revenue. How could the Little Eagles possibly pay all the excess charges on the new clothing they had acquired in their two-month shopping spree with U.S. and Canadian dollars?

The answer was simple. Most of the choir members arrived at the Seattle airport wearing two pairs of underwear, two sweaters, a cardigan, a jacket and an overcoat. No matter that the temperature in the Pacific Northwest in early June was in the low 30s (90°F). Sweltering in the heat, the choir members lined up to place their baggage on the Aeroflot scales. They were still vastly overweight, and they needed to check in twenty-five extra cases over the basic allowance of one suitcase per passenger. Predictably, none of the choir members had any dollars left to pay excess baggage charges.

Alex was one of four young boys in the choir—their voices had not yet broken. He was an inventive and fearless youngster, and when confronted with a bill of over $300 for his additional baggage, he knew he had to take action. In desperation, he asked the Aeroflot agent what would happen if two suitcases were tied together. The agent was a sympathetic soul, a Siberian from Novosibirsk. Alex might just as well have been his own son! He winced at the question, but answered truthfully. Yes, if they were bound together properly, he would count them as one bag.

It was Sunday afternoon. Most of the shops in the Seattle airport were closed. Alex started hunting for string. Departure time was nearing. After twenty minutes he came back clutching five rolls of dental floss. "It was all I could find," he shouted joyously to his companions. They busily tied their bags together with floss and reloaded them on the scales. Aeroflot flew to Khabarovsk that afternoon with minimum baggage revenue from the Little Eagles.

I looked back at my years of collaboration with Gosconcert. In retrospect it seemed to be as insubstantial—but at the same time as practically useful—as that dental floss. I had brought pleasure to many Canadian audiences with the groups that came from the Soviet Union. Numerous Russian ensembles and artists had experienced the warmth of Canadian audiences. I had given musical satisfaction to a number of Canadian artists and ensembles who were able to add the glamour of Soviet touring to their biographies. I certainly benefited musically from the performance opportunities that Gosconcert created for me. Perhaps we even opened some windows into the Western world for Soviet audiences. But in the end it was like the dental floss the Little Eagles offered to Aeroflot. It may have served an immediate purpose, but it was clearly never destined to last forever.

The Hunt for New Repertoire

On a visit to a Saskatoon elementary school sometime in the 1970s, I had demonstrated the bassoon and told the youngsters much fascinating information about its history, its construction, its uses and its amazing range. I told them how long I had been playing the instrument, how old I was when I started, who my first teacher was, where I played my first concert, and my favourite music. They were intrigued, and afterward some of them drew fanciful pictures of the bassoon and the bassoonist. One child added a memorable comment. He wrote: "Dear Mr. Zukerman, If you have really been playing the bassoon for thirty years, how come you aren't sick and tired of it?"

How could I ever become tired of the bassoon? For seventy-five years the instrument was an inherent part of my life, a fundamental feature of my existence.

In 1959, still some years before I had truly embarked on my solo career, the conductor Bruno Walter was in Vancouver for an appearance at the second Vancouver International Festival. I had the courage (and temerity) to ask his advice about becoming a bassoon soloist. There was a conspicuous passage for me in the orchestral repertoire at that festival event. I had apparently played it to his considerable satisfaction and public praise. Yet his reply to me was not what I had hoped to hear. "But my dear," he admonished, "it doesn't really matter how well you play. There is so little repertoire."

So it would seem. Early editions of music encyclopaedias listed bassoon concertos by Mozart and Weber, with a passing reference to Vivaldi's propensity to write for every known instrument in his eighteenth-century band. Even the non-scholarly Schwann record catalogue added no more than a few concerti by Johann Christian Bach, Johann Nepomuk Hummel, Carl Stamitz and, from the early twentieth century, a solitary recording of the opulently orchestrated *Romance* by Sir Edward Elgar.

I was determined not to be disheartened by Bruno Walter's pessimism. I would search wherever I could for repertoire for my instrument. Once I stepped outside the ranks of an orchestra, I had no choice but to seek out a repertoire to play. This became my lifelong challenge.

I had no idea how to go about creating a viable bassoon repertoire. While I knew that I had to approach composers, I lacked any funds to commission new compositions. I could hardly expect the composers to start approaching me. Yet, in effect, that is exactly what had happened in late 1959 when the Canadian composer Murray Adaskin presented me with his newly composed bassoon concerto, apparently in thanks for my stepping in to perform in the premiere of his *Prairie Suite* (described in "A Gift to Be Simple").

Shortly after the surprise arrival and premiere of the Adaskin bassoon work, John Weinzweig, considered by many to be the dean of twentieth-century Canadian composers, penned a divertimento for bassoon and strings as part of a series of solo pieces for each instrument in the orchestra. It was wonderfully written. The slow part, reflecting John's instinct for jazz styles, was meant to sound like the blues, sung by a cool saxophone. The finale was based on a pure twelve-tone row, but it still bounced along with infectious jazzy rhythms.

Armed with endearing works by these two major Canadian composers, I somehow expected the requests to flood in for orchestral appearances both at home and abroad. Of course, I was wrong. While the composers were both eminently distinguished Canadians, outside Canada they were barely known. At the same time, here at home in the late 1950s and 1960s, there was a prodigious reluctance to program contemporary works.

It was clear to me that there were two ways I could expand the repertoire for my instrument. I could either hope for new works, whether by commission or good fortune, or I could start searching the archives for lost and neglected manuscripts from earlier centuries.

Each route posed its own problems. I had already discovered that commissioning was an expensive proposition, and at that stage of my career I had no immediate source of money to support new composers in their creativity. On the other hand, I soon recognized that the search for solo repertoire for the bassoon was much like gold panning. With luck a few flakes of pure gold might emerge along with the immense quantities of pyrite and quartz.

⟲ PARADISE LOST

I turned my thoughts to the great titans of twentieth-century composition, all of whom wrote so superbly for the bassoon in their orchestral works. Why had they never produced a sonata or a concerto? With unbounded enthusiasm, I approached them all. Yet one by one they declined for different (and probably valid) reasons. Let me recount a litany of my recurring disappointment.

COPLAND—I last met Aaron Copland at Banff one summer in the early 1980s. The Alzheimer's that finally conquered him had not yet appeared,

and he was giving a number of spirited lectures. I remember playing the bassoon passages from his *El Salón México* for him. "My God, Aaron, if you can write a short orchestral passage like that for the bassoon . . . imagine what a concerto or even a sonata would be like." He smiled enigmatically, then shook his head. "I don't think I am going to be able to write anything more," he said. He stopped, looked up at me and said, "Why don't you take the flute sonata and make it into a bassoon piece." I

George with Aaron Copland.

never followed his advice, but I gladly refer this memory to anyone who feels inclined to accept the composer's authority as sufficient grounds to embark on a transcription. Who knows? There could be a Copland bassoon piece about to be revealed.

BRITTEN—In 1959 the CBC acquired an old garage on Georgia Street in Vancouver and converted it into the broadcaster's first television studio. Initially they had no cameras, and they borrowed equipment from a private TV station in nearby Bellingham, Washington. Once that small problem was overcome, the CBC was able to fulfill the contract between the public broadcaster and the musicians' union, which called for a guaranteed annual expenditure on televised live music. The former garage became an active production centre for numerous musical telecasts.

When Benjamin Britten and tenor Peter Pears came to Vancouver in 1960, they were invited to televise the composer's 1958 song cycle, *Nocturne*. It was imaginatively scored for tenor soloist, string orchestra and seven obbligato instruments. I was one of the lucky seven. My musical task was to portray the Kraken, an ancient sea monster from Norse mythology, while Pears sang Tennyson's poetic version of the creature's ancient sleep "below the thunders of the upper deep." Under Britten's baton we were treated as musical equals, sharing the exaltation as the work came to life.

Apparently Britten liked my interpretation of the Kraken's dreamless, un-invaded sleep. Otherwise, I doubt I would ever have had the courage to ask if he would consider writing a solo work for the bassoon. He didn't respond immediately, but I knew that a composer of his stature would have many commissions on hand, and I would have to wait patiently for an answer.

The reply came much more quickly than I expected. The telephone rang very early the following morning. It was an unprecedented call from CBC Radio headquarters in Ottawa. (They tended to forget little matters like time differences.) "We understand you are recording with Benjamin Britten today." I confirmed that this was indeed the case. "Mr. Britten tells us that you have requested that he write a work for you." Well, if Britten had told them, I could hardly deny it, so I concurred. CBC headquarters continued, "Yes, quite. Well, hmm ... yes, this is all rather difficult. We would like to ask you to withdraw your request." I was mystified. "May I ask why?" "Well, yes, you see, the CBC is commissioning a major chamber orchestra work from Mr. Britten, and we feel that it is only possible at this time to allow one request from Vancouver. We hope you understand." By then, even though it was still only 6:45 in the morning, I understood, all too clearly.

At rehearsal that morning, Britten invited me to join him in the conductor's room, one of the former lubrication bays of the garage, where the CBC had installed a sagging used sofa, a small upright piano and a coffee table. I was surprised to see my colleague the harpist, another of the seven soloists in *Nocturne*, seated on the derelict sofa. Britten apologetically explained that a network commission came with the imprimatur of national government. And then, finally, I understood why my harpist colleague was there. She, too, had approached Benjamin Britten for a new work, and she, too, had been awakened by an early morning call from Ottawa. Britten, unfailingly polite, sadly confirmed that he had to decline both our requests.

STRAVINSKY—With Igor Stravinsky, I muffed what should have been a perfect opportunity. He was in Vancouver for the International Festival in 1965. The program included his *Le Sacre du printemps*, a work that opens with a solo passage for the principal bassoonist. It is a moment of exquisite psychological tension. The conductor points at the player, who, before a hushed audience of three thousand, starts the work, completely unaccompanied, with one of the highest notes on the instrument, and then, still playing entirely alone, proceeds even higher! The bassoon in the extremity of its upper register has to conjure up an otherworldly soundscape. Stravinsky was due to conduct, but, frail in health, he passed the task to his amanuensis, Robert Craft. So, on top of everything else, the composer was sitting there in the front row!

I remember little of my playing of that celebrated opening, but I suppose it must have gone passably well. At intermission I spoke with Stravinsky backstage. He reminisced nostalgically about the bassoonists in the Paris orchestra for whom *Le Sacre du printemps* was originally written fifty years earlier. "They played the French-style bassoons," he mused. "They could reach more easily into the stratosphere."

He was right, of course. The French instruments were designed to play high notes with great technical ease. But the players of 1911 in Paris were no less challenged by Stravinsky's musical demands than we were in 1962.

I was awestruck that the composer had deigned to talk to a mere bassoonist, and I recalled briefly the apocryphal story of the work's world premiere. It was widely reported that the Parisian public had pelted the composer with tomatoes. I remember thinking that the tomatoes might well have come from the opposite direction. In that case it would have been the bassoon section that was sending the squishy message of disapproval, not the audience.

I was consumed with this irreverent thought, and Robert Craft was standing by to rescue his Maestro. Thus I missed the moment when I could have asked the incomparable Igor Stravinsky to write a solo bassoon work.

SHOSTAKOVICH—How many concertos equals a plate of grilled sardines? This curious metaphysical question may have no answer. Its validity, however, was put to the test in the latter years of the Soviet Union.

I had always been haunted by the dream of persuading the great Russian composer Dmitri Shostakovich to write a solo work for the bassoon. It was a heady musical thought. Shostakovich's writing for the bassoon was masterful. In each of his great symphonies there were major solo passages that hinted vividly at the possibility of a significant solo work. Here was a composer who understood the potential and the nature of the instrument.

In the rigid post-Stalinist days when I first visited Moscow, everything was controlled by the multi-tentacled concert booking organization Gosconcert. I had little choice but to reveal my dream of a Shostakovich bassoon concerto to Gosconcert in one of our meetings. Then followed a series of letters and telexes in which I outlined the possibility of commissioning such a concerto. I had accumulated funds and had the offer of a supporting grant.

Gosconcert finally made its move and arranged an appointment for me to meet Shostakovich when I was next on tour in the Soviet Union. I had sent him a cassette tape of the cadenza of his Ninth Symphony which so prominently featured the bassoon. My Russian colleagues had told him of my efforts to launch an international solo career. It would be up to me to persuade him to create a work that featured the bassoon as soloist.

On the morning of the scheduled meeting, my hotel phone rang. Mr. Shostakovich was not well. Our meeting was rescheduled for the next day. Gosconcert, lured by the temptation of a hard currency commission, the major portion of which would go straight to its coffers rather than to the composer, easily made the necessary changes to my flight home to Canada. On the next day, and again on the following day, I was told that Mr. Shostakovich was still unwell and unable to meet with me.

On the fourth day of postponement I was summoned to the Canadian embassy. In the "bubble" (a soundproof, bug-proof plastic dome) the ambassador broke the news. Mr. Shostakovich's illness was purely political. Negotiations over fishing rights on the Grand Banks had broken down. By way of retaliation, the Soviet side had cancelled all discussions of proposed cultural exchanges. Sardines won out over bassoon concertos. Two years later, when I next returned to Moscow, international fishing was restored, but Dmitri Shostakovich was dead.

POULENC—Finally, consider the case of Francis Poulenc. Unfortunately, he died in 1963, and I never had the good fortune to meet him. However, ten years later in Paris I encountered his lifetime collaborator, baritone Pierre Bernac, at an embassy reception. I jokingly asked Bernac why Poulenc never wrote a bassoon sonata. Bernac carefully put his martini on a nearby mantelpiece and looked at me seriously. "But, my friend, he did, of course he did!"

The air in the room stood still. "Not possible! Are you sure? Nobody ever knew! What a discovery! Where is it?" I exclaimed.

The excitement was palpable as well as audible. From the other end of the room, the ambassador looked up, sensing an international incident that he would need to report to his superiors.

Bernac continued, "Mais oui! Vraiment, il a écrit une sonate pour le basson." He reverted to English. "You must be familiar with the trio for oboe, bassoon and piano?" I nodded. "Well, there you have it. Poulenc, he was lazy. The trio he viewed as two sonatas, one for the oboe, one for the bassoon. Instead of writing them separately, he wrapped them up in a single package! Voila! Your bassoon sonata!"

I had arrived on the scene too late. I may have been too young, too green, too inexperienced to persuade these masters. I realized then that neither the bassoon nor I would achieve recognition riding on their coattails. In fact, the result was exactly the opposite. Over the succeeding years I introduced some of our finest Canadian composers to the world stage that had previously been reserved exclusively for the established international celebrities.

So it was that Adaskin was heard in Australia, the Soviet Union and the U.K., and Weinzweig was performed in the Soviet Union, China, Singapore, New Zealand and the Netherlands.

In so doing, world records were established. Along with Murray Adaskin and John Weinzweig, two other composers stand out, not only for their significant contribution to the bassoon repertoire, but also for the opportunity they provided me to give multiple performances of their works. In 1979, Elliot Weisgarber wrote an evocative three-minute solo piece, "Thoughts on an Ancient Japanese Melody." It was performed, if my poorly kept record book is any guide, on 491 occasions in twenty-three countries around the world. Jean Coulthard wrote "Lyric Sonatina" for me in 1973. It also enjoyed multiple performances, 113 times for which I have records. But the true significance of that work is that it is now part of the curriculum for Royal Conservatory bassoon exams, a tribute to Jean's uncanny ability to capture the essential quality of the instrument in each of its three contrasting movements.

There are many more, too, and I must apologize to those of my composer friends I have not mentioned specifically. In the end I always return to the earliest works written for me. These were jazz transcriptions created in the mid-1950s for CBC broadcast by the gifted composer, arranger and trombonist Dave Robbins. The bassoon had not been much used in jazz arrangements since the days of the *Chamber Music Society of Lower Basin Street*—the innovative NBC wartime radio program that served as a launch pad to fame for the singer Dinah Shore. Dave treated the bassoon like a true vocal soloist and allowed the instrument to sing out in a sexy version of "All the Things You Are" and in two original compositions, appropriately entitled "Heckel, the Hipster" and "The Broken Reed Blues." The first was a tribute to my relatively new bassoon; the second a plaintive lament common to most woodwind players. His arrangements, buried somewhere deep in the CBC archives, exploited the many varied tonal colours and the lyrical potential of the bassoon. If Bruno Walter had heard those arrangements, he might have found grounds to reconsider his views on the bassoon as a viable solo instrument.

～ THE CUFFLINK CAMERA

Economically, the search for existing but neglected repertoire was the only course I could pursue when I was starting out, so whenever I travelled to Europe I scoured libraries, museums, *Schlosses* and private estates. By dig-

ging through countless uncatalogued boxes of barely decipherable manuscripts, I hoped to find hidden treasures. I accumulated hundreds of film
canisters, often obtained from nations that viewed microfilm as a weapon
of espionage rather than a tool of musical research. At the Royal Library of
the Royal Palace of Madrid, even after the demise of the Franco regime, requests for microfilm were summarily rejected. As if to emphasize the point,
my cufflinks were confiscated lest they contain hidden cameras. Only then
was I grudgingly permitted to copy by hand, from the library's immense
collection, a set of six quintets by Gaetano Brunetti. For hours I sat under
the constant watchful scrutiny of two members of the Guardia Civil, suitably armed with automatic weapons pointed threateningly in my direction.
Granted, I had my cufflinks returned when I left the library.

Composers in the seventeenth and eighteenth centuries would deliberately publish their sonatas and concerti in collections of six. Bach, Handel,
Corelli, Veracini, LeClair all abided by this unwritten rule. The number
six, being twice the Trinity, assumed divine properties. Some believed so
fervently in its unerring and pantheistic significance that they devoutly exceeded their publishers' expectations with extraordinary multiples of the
sacred number. Among the more than 170 works that I discovered and
transferred to film, or wrote out laboriously by hand, there are eighteen
quartets for bassoon and string trio by Georg Schneider and—exceeding all
records—forty-eight bassoon sonatas by Joseph Bodin de Boismortier, who
surely vindicated his name with eloquent proof that bassoon music was not
written by or for "dead wood."

The German-born French composer Johann Ernst Galliard, the Franco-
English Luigi Merci, along with the Italian Brunetti, were among the many
who stuck more modestly to sets of six at a time. When a composer couldn't
come up with the required number of works, ingenuity was required. The
Englishman Capel Bond wrote only four sonatas for the violin. Nobody
would publish them. He completed the required number by adding a concerto each for the bassoon and the trumpet. His publisher was happy. Bassoonists and trumpeters were elated. The Trinity took no offence.

Were there, perhaps, good reasons that many of these works remained
buried for so long? I wondered, on more than one occasion, whether

perhaps I had been sentenced by some cabalistic court to a form of musical purgatory that involved the endless performance of works created by this army of lesser-known artisans.

~ THE GREAT MOZART HUNT

The challenge of finding new works to play, whether from contemporary composers or dusty European library archives, was never far from my mind. One discovery launched a drastic change in my playing career when a microfilm from the depths of an East Berlin library led inexorably to the Great Mozart Hunt of 1991.

Most people would lay the blame squarely on the shoulders of the publishing house of Breitkopf and Härtel. If they had not listed an F major bassoon concerto, complete with passable Mozartian themes, in their 1812 catalogue, and attributed it to Wolfgang Amadeus Mozart, there probably would never have been a Great Mozart Hunt.

By the time Ludwig Alois Friedrich von Köchel compiled his first catalogue of the works of Mozart, nobody could find the work in question. Köchel, always a trusting sort, took the Breitkopf catalogue listing at face value. He assigned the work the number 230 and parenthetically suggested that the work was probably lost. He included the orchestral opening and the solo entrance themes as shown in that early Breitkopf catalogue. On the same page, Köchel listed the one known concerto that Mozart wrote at age eighteen, possibly for his bassoon-playing patron, the Count Thaddäus Freiherr von Dürnitz. There is no question about the provenance of that work, assigned the number K. 191.

And so it was for many years. A bassoonist who wanted to play a Mozart concerto happily made do with K. 191. And why not, after all? It was a cheerful, youthful work, exquisitely fashioned for the bassoon of Mozart's day. Not surprisingly it has been widely recorded. Archie Camden, the British bassoonist who played in most of the major London orchestras between 1920 and 1940, made one of the earliest known recordings under the baton of Sir Hamilton Harty. Fernand Oubradous, a legendary twentieth-century French soloist and arranger, recorded it on a 78 rpm shellac disk in 1936 with Eugène Bigot conducting. German soloist and chamber musician Klaus Thunemann recorded the work under the baton of Herbert von Karajan in the late 1960s. I recorded it in 1974 with Jörg Faerber and the Württemberg Chamber Orchestra. Somehow this disc (latterly re-mastered onto a CD in 20-bit technology) has found its way, semi-permanently, onto major European "best-seller" lists.

Many of my orchestral colleagues have also taken a crack at this work, including my marvellous teacher Leonard Sharrow, who, while he was a member of the NBC Symphony Orchestra, recorded the concerto at Toscanini's breakneck tempi. At one time, the now defunct Schwann catalogue listed seventeen recorded versions of K. 191. Well, what else can you do when there is just one known Mozart bassoon concerto?

Learned musicologists have been pondering the question of the missing Mozart bassoon concerti for years. A pervasive rumour suggests that von Dürnitz actually commissioned four such works. Equally prevalent is the counter thought that the patron was slow to pay his musical bills, and Mozart's father discouraged Wolfgang from submitting the finished work, or accepting any further commissions, until he had been paid. In either case, Mozart hunters could not be faulted for believing that K. 230 was worth tracking down.

Armed with such a tantalizing suggestion, it is no surprise that generations of bassoonists from around the world have embarked on the Great Mozart Hunt. I joined the hunt as a student and continued it through my decades of European touring. I quickly learned to depend on the memories of a host of librarians who guarded their collections with severe custodial pride. Much music in obscure archives and in family collections was not routinely catalogued. Since I had no idea what I might find, I could hardly ask for specific composers. Instead, I asked whether the librarians knew of anything in their collections for the bassoon as soloist.

This unschooled research technique finally proved wonderfully successful in Berlin in 1967. After being guided up dimly lit stairwells and through musty corridors to the fourth floor of the east wing "stacks" at one of the many state libraries, I was shown a folio containing a roughly copied set of parts for an F major bassoon concerto. My elderly guide spoke in staccato phrases. "Received this in 1932. No scores in those days," he said. "Parts

George working on a score.

probably copied for a Berlin performance. No name on the piece. Publishers liked that. They could pass the piece off under any name they chose. Didn't quite know where to put it. Haven't been up here since then. Is it of any interest?"

It was twenty years before I answered his question. In 1967, had I looked carefully at the Berlin folio, even from the second horn part (which was the first to be revealed after the dust had been blown away) I would have been able to tell that the opening theme was identical to that listed in the Breitkopf catalogue for the supposedly missing K. 230. As it was, I didn't pay much attention to the manuscript until the late 1980s. When I examined more closely the microfilms the Berlin librarian had given me, my heart rate jumped. The excitement was palpable. Had I really discovered some missing Mozart? It was just three years before the worldwide commemoration of the two-hundredth anniversary of the composer's untimely death, and I immediately began the laborious process of recreating a score from this hard-to-read set of orchestral parts.

I thought back to the laconic comment of the Berlin librarian. Of any interest? What a question!

I was on the international touring treadmill that season, and I enjoyed glorious opportunities to play this newly resurrected F major concerto in Perth, Hobart, Glasgow, Bloemfontein and even Dnipropetrovsk. At home the piece was heard in Kelowna and Prince George. Much as I hoped that I had unearthed another genuine Mozart manuscript, the work was dismissed at most of these early performances as little more than an intriguing musical curiosity.

The breakthrough occurred in Mozart Year, 1991. For the occasion I wrote a script and created *The Great Mozart Hunt* as a "dramatized concert in two acts," featuring both the "new" F major concerto and the one known genuine Mozart bassoon work, K. 191. A part was created for a costumed actor to join me on stage. Ron Halder, recently returned to Vancouver from stints at Neptune Theatre in Halifax and Citadel Theatre in Edmonton, helped create the multiple roles of Mozart, his archrival Salieri, the publisher Breitkopf (and his partner Härtel), Mozart's early patron Count Thaddäus von Dürnitz, an impresario, an eminent musicologist, the statistician Ludwig Köchel and a splendidly seedy Mickey Spillane–era private eye whose task it is to track down missing manuscripts. With thespian virtuosity and multiple quick costume changes, Ron dazzled the audience as he switched between all nine parts. We made one commitment to ourselves: we could have as much fun and irreverent good humour as possible, but we would avoid inflicting bodily harm on the essential music.

As promised, the music prevailed. The show opens with the gumshoe checking police files to see whether I have a record. "You bet he's got a record," he tells the audience, "dozens of them . . . CDs, DVDs . . . European best-sellers . . ."

The concert was rounded out with other anonymous works that might, or might not, prove to be lost Mozartian snippets. There was some real Mozart—an early string divertimento written for von Dürnitz, and a movement of the *Musical Joke* to highlight Mozart's rapier-like attack on the poor composition that he witnessed all around him. We soothed Salieri's wounded ego by including a movement of his gentle and charming double concerto for flute and oboe. We inserted the *Impresario Overture* to open the second half of the program and to introduce another of Ron's splendid Mozart-era characters.

Finally, just before K. 191 is heard in its entirety, there is an actor's cadenza for all nine characters that allows the private eye to admit his musical shortcomings. "Bassoon concertos ain't exactly my line of work," he says, "but when you feast your ears on this one, you'll know why it's worth waiting a couple of hundred years to find another Mozart concerto!"

The Great Mozart Hunt was seen and heard from coast to coast. With the assistance of Petro-Canada and the Canada Council, Ron and I headed across Canada for a twenty-one-concert tour with an orchestra of seventeen. It was led from his concertmaster's seat by the indomitable Arthur Polson, who so splendidly captured the spirit of the hunt that he affably argued each night with Mozart (and Salieri, when he had the chance).

That first tour culminated in Vancouver on December 5, 1991, two hundred years since Mozart's death. We had surely satisfied our prime sponsor by spending a substantial portion of our grants on gasoline. The reviews were effusive and gratifying: "Tributes to Mozart tickle audience"; "Musical whodunit intriguing"; and "Mozart Mystery unique adventure delights appreciative audience." That was just what we had hoped for, and indeed, the fun, mystery and intrigue continued for many seasons and many tours.

The reputation of *The Great Mozart Hunt* spread to the United States, and then in 1996 overseas to the Queen's Festival in Belfast, where a slightly tipsy Sean Fitzgerald in his *Festival Diary* declared, "A funny thing happened on the way to the bassoonist . . . delectable, delightful, delicious."

There was a total of eighty-three performances. Did we ever prove convincingly that the F major concerto was truly by Mozart? I would have to say it is unlikely, although we have conducted a good and noble hunt. Late in the script I admonish Mozart with a bassoonist's favourite line: "One bassoon concerto just isn't enough!" He laughs (straight out of *Amadeus*) with a glint in his eye that suggests that, after all, there may be one or two others around. Teasing, indeed.

Just after our 2007 tour, something very strange occurred. An email turned up, quite mysteriously dated. It was so curious that I take the liberty of reproducing it in its entirety:

1 January 1802

Lieber Georg Zukerman!

I understand from my friend Franzl Süssmayr that you have been looking for a Fagotkonzert by the sel. Mozart.

Just to let you know that for 20 ducats my brother Ludwig, now considered one of the most important composers in Wien, recently author of the ballet Prometheus, would be prepared to write you a piece of that description, which according to usual business practice here in Wien, you would have exclusive world rights to for a year. After that I would take charge of publication, and collect what I can on behalf of my brother from the dedicatee.

You can write to me at the Rote Igel Bierhaus in Wien. We're talking gold ducats...

With greetings from my brother, who has often admired your playing on CBC rebroadcasts,

Karl von Beethoven

Without evidence, I suspect this creation came from the pen of my distinguished brother, Beethoven authority, scholar, dean of American musicologists, Joseph Kerman. (He dropped the "Zu" a long time ago when encountering anti-Semitism at post-war Princeton University.) I thought of replying to the email and trying to arrange a rendezvous at the Bierhaus, but I had read enough le Carré to be aware of the potential for manifold duplicity even among my closest colleagues. In any case, it would have been nearly impossible to find that many gold ducats. Beethoven's ephemeral email address had been cancelled before I could click on "reply all," and for all I know, the Red Hedgehog is no longer there. Vienna, which was in any case never particularly renowned for its beer, has presumably changed a little since the time of that 1802 email.

Nonetheless, deferring to true musicology, I am willing to believe that, but for twenty gold ducats, there might have been a Beethoven bassoon concerto somewhere out there. Maybe it's time to close shop and start the Great Beethoven Hunt.

IV: RECAPITULATION

The Music Bridge

Distance Is in the Eye of the Beholder

I suppose that by 1998, at age seventy-one, I should have been thinking about retirement. Instead, that was when I embarked on a plan to take music to every remote and isolated community in northern Canada.

The north has different meanings for different people. To our neighbours in the United States, all of Canada is "north." If you live in Vancouver, you might think Port Hardy, at the tip of Vancouver Island, is far north. To a Torontonian, Edmonton qualifies, but to a resident of Yellowknife, in the Northwest Territories, Edmonton and most of the rest of the nation is part of "southern Canada." From Yellowknife you need to look toward Tuktoyaktuk and the other scattered villages of the Beaufort Delta to discover the "true North."

This was not my first venture to the remote north. From the very beginning of Overture Concerts I had determined to include the north. By 1960, Port Hardy and Fort Nelson in British Columbia, Fort McMurray and Cold Lake in Alberta, Uranium City in Saskatchewan, and Flin Flon and Churchill in Manitoba had all formed concert societies. Overture was also active in the larger centres of the Northwest Territories. Everywhere—at least in what I then considered "the North"—a network of concert groups was successfully meeting the needs and interests of transplanted southern audiences.

A decade later I organized an extraordinary orchestral tour of the eastern Arctic. In planning the itinerary I realized that along with the single city of Iqaluit—still known as Frobisher Bay at that time—there were many small villages and settlements scattered throughout an unbelievably vast region of a thinly populated land. I instinctively knew that once we were travelling that far north with an orchestra, it would be unforgivable not to include every community that lay along the route, regardless of the audience potential. That tour may have celebrated a determination to confront the daunting logistics of remote touring, but it is not hard to see why it encountered disappointingly sparse turnout along the way.

The obvious reason, of course, was that orchestral tours were designed for adults who had moved north, and in the eastern Arctic there weren't many of them around. I soon recognized that I was offering a program that was primarily of interest to the southerners living and working in the single large population centre of Iqaluit. The smaller communities along the route did not have any sizeable transplanted adult audiences. If I ever hoped to include the smaller en-route villages in future itineraries across the north, I would need to change my entire view of remote touring.

And that was when I had my musical epiphany.

The answer was dazzlingly simple. I would reverse the approach and plan the tours around the school visits, with the adult events only added when possible. I would also start looking at smaller ensembles, which were obviously easier to move around. Orchestras were spectacular but also expensive.

In most of these villages the school served as a community centre. A program may well have been planned and announced as a school event, but it was not unusual for our original audience of students and teachers to be augmented by throngs of adults from the community at large. Sometimes they came with their own musical instruments: a fiddle, an accordion, the ubiquitous drums. Sometimes they played with us. On one occasion they came up and challenged us to a throat-singing competition. We lost! No matter. We had successfully turned our recreation of southern city life into a true northern musical event, fit for any Indigenous settlement.

Overnight, it seemed I had solved the two greatest problems of northern concert touring. I now had educational justification as well as a practical possibility of visiting even the smallest settlement.

This was the birth of Remote Tours Canada.

We took small ensembles to the Northwest Territories, Yukon, and the three spread-out regions of Nunavut (Kitikmeot, Kivalliq and Qikiqtaaluk), to Nunavik, Quebec, and to Nunatsiavut, Labrador, as well as to the vast northern areas of each of the provinces except PEI, which—although it undoubtedly has remote and isolated areas—could never quite convince me that it belonged to the northland. In the course of those tours we played, at one time or another, for just about every school child in the remote north who wasn't home sick with the flu.

Since so many of the northern communities were accessible only by air, and scheduled flights were few and far between, much of our travel was by chartered aircraft: Cessna, Piper Navajo, Grumman Mallard or Goose and de Havilland Beaver. We landed on floats, on skis, on frozen ground, and sometimes, when the weather turned against us, we did not land at all at our chosen destination. In blizzard conditions, aircraft would land at the nearest safe location. That often determined where we presented our next performance.

Even when there was access by road or water, it was a daunting challenge to organize the necessary travel. Along the Quebec and Labrador coastlines we travelled on the *Nordik Express*, a freighter that linked the outports on its weekly schedule down the St. Lawrence River. I had heard of vessels locked in ice jams and stranded interminably, and I feared that we might become a musical Franklin Expedition. In my grant application for that particular tour, I judiciously requested an allowance for six months of per diem. This was summarily rejected. Fortunately, we completed the tour within the allowable eleven days.

Elsewhere we arrived by war canoe, by Bombardier Ski-Doo and by dogsled. Guided by oil cans along the side of ice roads, we avoided driving out into the frozen wasteland of the Arctic Ocean. Beneath the beauty of the northern lights, we found our way across frozen lakes to the next remote village. Elementary schools, covering all the grades, were sometimes occupied by no more than fifteen to twenty students and a single teacher. Total population of some of the smaller communities was as little as 250.

Few communities in the north owned pianos. Most of the time we carried a portable keyboard, a guitar or an accordion. We created unlikely instrumental combinations such as violin, trumpet, bassoon and accordion, or flute, cello, bassoon and keyboard. On one occasion we worked with a remarkable Quebec soprano who doubled on saxophone. We added bassoon,

George and his bassoon in the Arctic.

violin and guitar. Mozart didn't write anything for that strange combination, but we somehow managed an aria from *The Marriage of Figaro*. Our
arrangers' nibs were constantly in the ink pot.

I will never know if we actually met our goal of visiting every village, but
we came close. The statistics speak for themselves. Over thirteen seasons of
constant and rugged travel, Remote Tours Canada organized thirty-seven
tours. I played for twenty-seven of them. We visited 318 different communities in nine provinces and three territories. We played for 92,440 students
and operated on a total budget of $936,000. In the course of those thirteen
seasons we played 759 concerts.

Except they weren't really concerts at all.

Yes, we played musical works, Mozart or Verdi, Gershwin, the Beatles or
the theme song from some popular television show; and yes, there was an
audience that joined us in the room.

But there the similarity with a conventional concert ended. Very often
we abandoned the stage and sat on the floor of a school gym, surrounded
by the listeners. We played our instruments. We invited students to take a
crack at making sounds on them. We tried to relate our music-making to

familiar activities so that our presence didn't come across as yet another outside imposition. Our sessions became links between societies that had not always communicated very well with each other.

Music was a bridge that could join us in common understanding, friendship and mutual appreciation. In contrast, so much of what was being sent north, even to the schools, was patronizingly instructive, if not politically destructive. Canadians from outside the north so often presumed to tell Indigenous populations exactly how to conduct their lives. Visits by government deputies, by planning agencies, by problem-solving experts, by learned legal authorities, by earnest scientific researchers turned out all too often to be confrontational. The glory of music was that it did not impose a preconceived order on the audience. It was theirs to listen to, to marvel at, to emulate, to enjoy or—equally—to reject. It was non-confrontational.

It didn't take long in the north to discover that daily life in many of the communities we visited was dominated by a seemingly endless wait for improvement projects from the outside, whether clean drinking water, adequate (and sufficient) housing, a new access road, a medical centre or a cleanup of a nearby river. These projects, promised year after year, so often seemed to remain unachieved mirages. The villages could not always rely on their own resources for such necessary and costly infrastructure. In the end the neglect experienced by these remote communities left them little choice but to develop a fierce self-sufficiency.

Against that background, music could not possibly be an instant salve, but it made a difference. If the youngsters left the hall humming a familiar tune, we had made contact. If they returned to their classrooms with an appreciation that a musician was a fairly normal human being, we had begun to break down barriers. If they welcomed an hour with southern visitors who spoke to them as equals, we had established a link on which future commissions of enquiry would do well to build. The students, the teachers, the residents and even administrators seemed to understand the uniqueness of these musical visits. None of us ever felt hostility or resentment during those moments of ephemeral involvement with northern life.

It was almost by default that I found myself acting as the CEO of a million-dollar operation. That is not a huge amount these days, but for a relatively obscure project involving schools in remote regions of Canada, it was a monumental task to raise and administer that much money. The schools contributed, sometimes from school board budgets, but very often from carefully guarded discretionary funds that each school was allowed to disburse. There were also grants from provincial arts agencies, municipalities, foundations and corporations, and even a few private donations. However, the two major contributors were the Music Performance Trust Fund and the Canada Council for the Arts.

The Trust Fund, known generally as the MPTF, was a little-known organization established in 1948 by contract between the American Federation of Musicians and the recording industries. The agreement called for a tiny percentage of all record sales to be set aside for distribution through the various locals of the union for free public concerts by professional union-member musicians. Recording was in its heyday when the fund was launched, and the industry, on the threshold of switching over to LPs and then to CDs, was profiting handsomely from huge record sales. As a result, the Trust Fund thrived, and from its annual revenue I was able to funnel a small sum for the needs of Remote Tours Canada.

The MPTF's regular contributions were matched by the Canada Council for the Arts. This was surprisingly good fortune, because the Council, as a federal agency, did not normally support educational activity, which was considered the jurisdiction of the provinces. The Council may have hoped that Remote Tours Canada would ultimately lead to regular adult programming in these same communities, but I remained skeptical about that happening or even being necessary. The population was pitifully small, the costs mercilessly high, the traditions not yet, if ever, relevant. Perhaps it would be another case of outside imposition. What worked in Swift Current would not necessarily come to life with an adult audience in Igloolik.

There are occasions when I experience a profound yearning to travel to the north again, but I find myself wondering whether I could even claim the right to return without useful purpose. I shall miss the villages of Qikiqtarjuaq, Pangnirtung, Kuujjuaq, Kangiqsujuaq and Kangiqsualujjuaq. It took me ages to learn to pronounce them all! Now, as more settlements discard the names given to them by explorers, missionaries and traders, I would have to add such names as Iqaluktuuttiaq, Mittimatalik and Kanngiqtugaapik to my list of magnificently difficult-to-pronounce places.

I fondly remember the simple excitement of those years of northern touring. Capricious weather constantly frustrated the most carefully prepared travel plans. Circumstances of normal daily community life sometimes took precedence over our concert arrangements. The touring routine constantly had to be adjusted as we travelled. It was as wonderfully close as anyone could come to an improvised cadenza.

Northern Improvisations

~ THE ALASKA MUSIC TRAIL

Whitehorse, the thriving capital city of the Yukon, had enjoyed classical concerts during the early 1950s when the pianist Maxim Shapiro formed the Alaska Music Trail. He wanted to take concerts to all the scattered communities of Alaska, from the panhandle to the far-off Aleutian Islands. He included Whitehorse because it lay directly on an air route to Fairbanks and Anchorage.

Even though the newly completed Alaska Highway ran down the spine of the Yukon, directly to the city, Shapiro did not use the highway to bring his concerts to Whitehorse. The narrow, winding and mainly unpaved roadway had been hastily (some say too hastily) constructed by U.S. Army Engineers in 1942 mainly as a military link between the forty-eight contiguous states and the isolated Alaska Territory. The highway stretched 1,400 miles (2,300 kilometres) from the B.C./Alberta border to the heart of Alaska. The pavement ended at Fort St. John and began again close to Fairbanks. The artists on the Alaska Music Trail depended on air connections to reach their northern destinations.

Shapiro died tragically in 1958 in the middle of a performance of a Mozart piano concerto, and the innovative Alaska Music Trail faded with his untimely demise. Whitehorse, however, continued with an active concert society. I played for the society as an artist on tour. Ben Heppner sang there. In the years that have passed since the days of the Alaska Music Trail many other artists and groups, touring elsewhere in the north, have added

Whitehorse engagements. As far as I know, they all flew in. Few dared to drive such a vast distance for a single concert.

There was a prominent "Mile Zero" signpost at the start of the highway at Dawson Creek. I often looked longingly at the ribbon of gravel that flowed north beyond the signpost, but I reluctantly accepted the common view that concert tours could not practically venture very far on such a precarious and lengthy roadway.

I once stood with a colleague outside a Dawson Creek hotel, within sight of the Alaska Highway "Mile Zero" marker. I must have commented to him on the perceived difficulty of sending concerts to the Yukon. As if to assure me of some future possibility, my friend strode resolutely twenty-five metres along the highway, past the Mile Zero signpost. There, despite the bitter cold, he removed his gloves and played five plaintive notes on his oboe. He then returned and proudly proclaimed that he had just completed the first Canadian concert tour on the Alaska Highway. He had, indeed, travelled the fabled route in both directions!

Maybe it was this incident that spurred me to launch an ambitious plan to take John Avison's radio orchestra to Alaska. The ensemble already had a growing reputation as "the little band that could," and here was a touring project for a Canadian orchestra that would include a neglected northern Canadian territory.

I decided that while Anchorage and Fairbanks would follow Maxim Shapiro's Alaska Trail formula and depend on air connections, I would make Canadian musical history by organizing the first orchestra tour to travel to Whitehorse on the Alaska Highway. Partly it was a matter of cost, but equally it was a challenge that needed to be confronted. There was a highway to Whitehorse, and at last we were going to use it! Those five notes on my colleague's oboe simply weren't enough.

On Thursday, March 26, 1964, I flew to Anchorage to discuss a plan to bring the orchestra to Alaska's largest city and commercial centre. I am not usually so precise with dates, but this one I shall always remember. The following day was Good Friday 1964, and that was the date of the Alaska Earthquake, magnitude 9.2 on the Richter scale. It devastated much of downtown Anchorage.

The night before the quake I slept well in the old wing of a distinguished Anchorage hotel. My meetings completed, I was due to return home via Seattle at noon on Friday. The morning was without incident, and along with sixty-seven other passengers I boarded my flight for a normal on-time departure.

In those days, planes bound for Seattle made a fuel stop at a military airport on Annette Island, just offshore from the city of Ketchikan. The airport terminal there consisted of a single Quonset hut, with a coffee and gift counter that operated whenever a commercial flight arrived. We were not allowed to stay on board while the plane refuelled, and all sixty-eight passengers crowded into the tiny terminal area.

As I stood there, I realized that I had left my pajamas behind at the hotel. I purchased a postcard and a stamp at the gift shop and scribbled a note to the hotel's lost and found. "Dear Sirs," I wrote, "I stayed last night in room 303 and left my pajamas behind. If convenient, would you please forward them to my Vancouver address?"

By the time we arrived at Seattle, the earthquake had struck. The pilot had chosen not to panic the mainly Alaskan passengers and held the news of the disaster until we were securely on the ground. There, surrounded by reporters with microphones and newsreel cameras at the arrivals gate, we learned that much of the downtown business section of Anchorage was in ruins. It was appalling news. There was nothing I could do by remaining in Seattle, so I escaped the crowd and found my connecting flight to Vancouver. Later that night I watched the full report of the Anchorage catastrophe on the nightly TV newscast. Seeing the massive damage inflicted by the quake, lost pajamas were soon forgotten.

Weeks later I received a message from the hotel in Anchorage. "Dear Sir," it read (reciprocating the formal courtesy with which I had addressed their lost and found department). "With regard to your postcard from Annette Island, we regret we could not find your pajamas. Furthermore, we could not find room 303. Sincerely..." There followed a scrawled signature and the name and proud logo of the hotel chain, with a picture of the decimated old wing, completely flattened, its parking lot resting at a precarious angle to the hotel's remaining sixteen-storey tower.

Given the circumstances, it was not a surprise when Anchorage withdrew from the planned tour. I determined, however, to carry on with the concerts in Whitehorse and Fairbanks, and I was even able to add performances in Fort St. John, Dawson Creek and Fort Nelson. They were the only other towns along the highway with sufficient population to support a concert series, and they had each been recently organized by Overture Concerts. As threatened, the orchestra drove the Alaska Highway.

⌇ WRONG TURN AT JAKE'S CORNER

You would think there would be few chances to get lost on the Alaska Highway, as the road pursues its relentless route through northern British Columbia and the Yukon. But we did manage to do this as we headed to Whitehorse from Mile Zero. Let me set the scene.

The bus carrying the orchestra to Whitehorse stopped at Jake's Corner, one of the few rest stops/gas stations along the way. While the musicians enjoyed a coffee break, the bus was filled with diesel fuel. Everyone quickly came back on board, and the bus swung in a wide arc out of the parking lot to follow the road. About an hour later the orchestra arrived in a village that did not appear on any map of the Alaska Highway.

The driver had inadvertently taken the only turning off the main road. We found ourselves in the village of Carcross.

To justify driving the vast distances on the highway, we had arranged to play for schools in some of the communities that lay along the travel route. (That early orchestral venture on the Alaska Highway foreshadowed the future accomplishments of Remote Tours Canada.) According to our itinerary, we were not due in Carcross until the next day.

Still, we stopped at the school, and I found my way to the office. The principal was sick that day, but I met the harried vice-principal at a classroom break. "We're supposed to be here tomorrow," I told her.

"You're a bit early, aren't you?" she replied.

"Yes, but our driver brought us here today ..."

"Ah," said the vice-principal wisely, "another one confused by the exit road at Jake's."

I pressed the point: "Shall we return tomorrow?"

There was a quick reply, "Oh, hell, no ... you're here now!"

She sounded a school bell and made an announcement on the public address system: "All classes, all classes, attention please. Proceed to the gym. A concert will be starting in less than ten minutes."

I heard the rumbling of school chairs in rooms up and down the single corridor of Carcross Elementary, and I dashed back to the bus to tell my colleagues that we should unload, set up and be ready for an immediate concert. Within minutes our indomitable orchestra contractor, Judith Fraser, had organized chairs and music stands on the floor of the school activities room. While the last class was arriving for the concert, she wheeled in our two tympani. As the musicians took their places, Judith—also acting as librarian—set out the music folios, and in a single sweeping action handed Maestro Avison his baton as he walked "on stage" to greet the Carcross student audience.

The driver sat at the back of the hall, musing at how he could possibly have taken the one and only wrong turn. We urged him to contemplate his navigational skills and plan our onward route. There was a back road to Whitehorse. We didn't even have to return to Jake's Corner. Bus tours are always landmarked by coffee breaks and meals, and we could still make it to our original destination in time for a celebratory dinner that night.

So it was that the school concert in the tiny village of Carcross on Tuesday afternoon turned out to be the perfect dress rehearsal for the Wednesday night symphony concert in Whitehorse.

Next day we headed to the airport for the flight to Fairbanks. As we cleared our last suitcase from the bus, we wished our driver a safe return journey and, probably unnecessarily, reminded him to avoid all turns, either left or right, until he reached Dawson Creek and safe and secure highway markers.

~ ZUKERMAN'S FOLLY

I probably should have learned a severe lesson from the immense cost and the parallel logistical nightmare of the Yukon–Alaska orchestral tour, but the excitement of bringing an orchestra to remote and distant parts never left me. Ten years later I decided to take Avison's orchestra to the eastern Arctic.

The region was still a part of the Northwest Territories at that time. Its major centre was Frobisher Bay (now Iqaluit). The distances involved were vast, and I planned the tour to include concerts in several tiny hamlets along the route. André Fortier, director of the Canada Council at the time, accompanied the tour. Given the limited audience at some of the smaller locations, he fondly referred to that Council-funded project as "Zukerman's folly."

In one of the settlements along the way, M. Fortier purchased a large and truly magnificent soapstone sculpture, which later adorned the Ottawa offices of the Canada Council. His plan was to transport his acquisition south aboard our workhorse Convair 600 aircraft. A truck was found to transport the sculpture to the airport. On a precariously balanced forklift, it was raised to the rear freight door of the aircraft only to descend (equally precariously) five minutes later. "It won't fit through the door," reported the young man at the controls of the forklift.

"Can we remove the door?" enquired M. Fortier.

None of us wished to frustrate the Council. They were, after all, footing the bill for our tour. How long does it take to remove an aircraft freight door? Nobody knew for sure, but Conductor Avison agreed that a delay of an hour or so would not disrupt our performance schedule later that evening in Frobisher Bay. Pilot and ground crew consulted. More workmen arrived, and, miraculously, the door was relieved of its hinges and gently lowered to the ground.

The sculpture was raised again, and this time, with 1.5 centimetres to spare, it was edged into the rear freight area of the plane. There were great cheers from the assembled musicians of the orchestra who had been watching events unfold from planeside. Then the ground crew eased the door back onto its hinges, and the pilot headed to his cabin to prepare for takeoff.

Two minutes later he returned with a worried look on his face. "I'm sorry, folks," he said, addressing nobody in particular. "We are over our allowable weight. We simply cannot take off. If the sculpture goes with us to Frobisher Bay, we have to leave four passengers behind."

Conductor Avison exercised artistic prerogative, the door was unhinged a second time, and the sculpture off-loaded, to be sent south by barge. It reached Ottawa eight months later. Perhaps, in the end, that grand orchestral tour of the eastern Arctic might equally have been known as "Fortier's folly."

~ FIDDLER ON THE ROOF IN TUKTOYAKTUK

The orchestra had scheduled a school concert in the village of Tuktoyaktuk. Set on the edge of the Arctic Ocean, "Tuk" was still a very small settlement. There was an airstrip, but no terminal building. The runway, just two hundred metres away from the centre of town, was frozen solid for many months of the year, and gumbo mud for the rest. We arrived just before the muddy time. It was still cold, and the ground was frozen.

Downtown Tuk boasted a Hudson's Bay outlet, a power station, a school, a post office, a Northern Store, a six-room guest house and an RCMP office, along with a scattering of houses and huts set apparently without design along the waterfront. Nobody could have imagined that this tiny cluster of homes on the edge of the Beaufort Delta would experience a vast economic, physical and social change in the closing decades of the twentieth century. Today Tuk has become a transportation and government centre and a base for extensive oil and natural gas exploration with a year-round highway connection from Inuvik, but fifty years ago the village was yet to experience the boom.

A symphony orchestra arriving in such a small centre might have been expected to draw some public attention, but the village appeared strangely deserted. Not a soul in the post office. Nobody in the RCMP office. The school empty, silent, but warm and heated. Had we come on the wrong day? To the wrong town? Was the delta so confusing that the pilot landed by mistake in Aklavik—160 kilometres in the other direction?

And then, humanity. The janitor appeared, sweeping the school gym floor.

"We're here for the concert..."

"Right," he said. "Eleven o'clock!" The school clock showed 10:50. "They'll be here. They're all out fishing. I'll dig up some chairs," he added loquaciously. Which he proceeded to do.

Our conductor, John Avison, had an idea. "You," he pointed to our concertmaster, "become the first fiddler on the roof in Tuk! Go outside and climb on the roof of the post office, take your fiddle with you... and *play*!"

The concertmaster climbed on the roof, gingerly removed his violin from its case (fearing it would crack in the cold) and, for the first time in

Fiddler on the roof in Tuktoyaktuk.

his career, began a performance without tuning. The opening melody sang out, and the sound was amplified across the ice. The vibrato stemmed much more from the sheer cold than from any emotion. He shivered his way through the phrase made famous by Isaac Stern in the movie *Fiddler on the Roof*. And it worked!

Suddenly on the ice we saw movement. They had heard the call to the concert! From their ice holes they raised their heads, downed their fishing gear and streamed toward the townsite. Men, women, children, dogs, who knows, maybe cats, chickens, even an Arctic char or two converged on the Tuktoyaktuk school. By the time we started (admittedly late, at 11:09) there were 342 people packed into the gym. Close to 80 percent of the total population of the village.

At 12:30, after a lunch of—yes—smoked Arctic char, we headed back to the airstrip. Our plane followed the ice road back to Inuvik. The pilot swooped low over a vast herd of caribou heading for their northern calving grounds. Oblivious to the whirling propellers, they moved at a sedate migratory pace as we started our descent, at airspeed, to the metropolis of the Beaufort Delta.

∽ THIS TELEPHONE IS OUT OF ORDER

Northern touring was full of unexpected moments of improvisation.

On a late winter afternoon I arrived with three colleagues at an apparently deserted airstrip. We were on a school tour of fly-in communities in far northern Ontario. The pilot promptly turned his aircraft around and took off for his next destination. His parting words: "I'll pick you up tomorrow at noon."

On the ground there were no vehicles to be seen. Nobody was there to meet us. A single set of footsteps in the snow hinted at some recent visitation, and we followed them to the front door of a building two hundred metres from the silent landing spot. Under the weight of our baggage and instruments, we sank deeper into the snow with each laborious footstep.

Finally we pushed open a heavy wooden door and were met with welcome light and warmth. Still, not a single person came to greet us. On a desk by the front door there was a typewritten notice. It read:

HOTEL INSTRUCTIONS:
(1) Keys are available in the right-hand drawer.
(2) Be prepared to share your room if unexpected flights arrive.
(3) Bathroom and shower are unisex.
(4) The freezer is well stocked. Help yourselves for dinner.
(5) Make sure to turn down heat on Microwave and Ring burners in kitchen before retiring. Please clean dishes after use.
(6) Do not smoke in bed.
(7) Telephone only for local calls.
(8) Please pay in the morning. Leave payment in left-hand drawer.

In pencil somebody had added, "Telephone is out of order."

The freezer was indeed well stocked. We could have been stranded for a month and we would not have starved. But we were effectively disconnected from the outside world, and we could not be sure that anyone in the community knew we had arrived. The next morning, as we finished rinsing our breakfast coffee mugs, an overwhelming wave of relief swept over us as the school bus pulled up to the front door.

⌁ FAILED DELIVERY

More improvisations. Our chartered aircraft, a Cessna 182, arrived at an isolated runway situated at the confluence of two great rivers in northern Ontario. Over the noise of the whirling propeller, our pilot shouted, "There's no fuel here. I'm going to the next village to gas up. I'll pick you up in an hour or so." He was right. There was no fuel, no gas pump, no facility of any kind, and, worse yet, not a single human being anywhere in sight. We watched him depart and went inside the dilapidated shed that served as the terminal building. There was a solitary pay phone but it was clearly out of order, its wires ripped from its base. Torn airline posters clung precariously to the wall. On the desk, which once served as a check-in counter, were faded travel posters for the Spanish Riviera and a typewritten page of stern instructions about proper hygienic disposal of sickness bags. There were also Thunder Bay telephone numbers to call in case of emergency. We stood around wondering how we would contact anyone in the community, let alone Thunder Bay, to tell them that we were there for the school concert.

We need not have worried. Our arrival had been duly heard and instantly noted. The single-engine aircraft is the transport of choice for drug drops. Charging at full speed down the airport access road, with whirling red and blue lights, came the local RCMP. A young constable emerged from the car, her hand on her holster. She looked quizzically at the three musicians, clutching instrument cases and music stands, clustered on the deserted airport runway.

"Where's your plane?" she demanded.

"Off for fuel," we replied.

"Nothing unloaded?" she asked.

We assured her that nothing had been left behind except us and our instruments. Her trained suspicious eye focused on our instrument cases. Her task was to seize any drug shipment before it was cut up and sold in the community. One by one our cases were inspected, and one by one it became clear that there were no drugs anywhere. Assured of our relative innocence (at least of drug-running), our saviour then offered to serve as airport limo, and, this time without the flashing red and blue lights, drove us sedately into town and to the school.

The concert? Sadly, it had been usurped by a community funeral. Best to move on. Our pilot returned in forty-five minutes as promised. Our limo driver politely checked the aircraft and then, before authorizing our takeoff, radioed to her colleague in the community with the gas pump to make sure the day's drug shipment had not, by some nefarious design, been off-loaded there.

∼ HOLD THE MUSIC

At northern airfields, medical evacuation flights have priority over regular scheduled service. Passengers often endure long delays while waiting for emergency aircraft to arrive, or take off, with the injured and sick. In crowded, barely furnished waiting areas of single-room airport terminals, dozens of passengers mill around aimlessly. A travelling musician might be forgiven for taking out a saxophone and playing an impromptu airport concert for anyone who wishes to listen. Halfway through a lonesome blues, the passenger agent (who is also tower control radio operator) charges into the waiting area from his office behind the counter. With earphones hanging around his neck he shouts, "Cut the d____ noise. I'm trying to talk the medevac flight down and all we can hear is you. The pilot wants to know what the tune is that you're playing, but after that, would you please shut up for a few minutes while I bring the plane in?"

∼ KANGIQSUALUJJUAQ

When you fly north from Kuujjuaq at the southern tip of Nunavik, it's a good idea to make sure your pilot knows whether you are headed to Kangiqsualujjuaq or Kangiqsujuaq. The two villages are 325 kilometres apart. Kangiqsujuaq, which lies on Hudson's Strait at the northern end of the Ungava Peninsula, translates as "The Large Bay." Kangiqsualujjuaq, situated on the east coast of Ungava Bay, has two extra syllables in its name and also picks up an adverb in its English-language version. It proudly translates as "A Very Large Bay."

We were travelling on a cloudless but bitterly cold (35 degrees below zero) day across a vast area of frozen seascape between Kuujjuaq and Kangiqsualujjuaq. At seven thousand feet, the sunshine was so brilliant that the pilot wore sunglasses. The sea below was dotted with icebergs. The tiny shadow of our Cessna 182 followed us across the endless snow and ice. Northern flying was not always this good.

We could see the village clearly from twenty kilometres away. And there it was, the very large bay, around which the houses of this tiny hamlet were scattered, as if dropped from above by some haphazard celestial hand. Soon the runway stretched before us, between houses and the school on one side and the bay on the other. It was perfect weather for an easy landing. Wings were tipped in the salute of the bush pilot, and we circled, so close to the ground that it was almost possible to count the number of people staring up at our plane. An unscheduled flight was a major event in Kangiqsualujjuaq. School kids had been told we were coming to play for them, and they waved excitedly to us. Still we did not land.

The pilot circled the village and made another loop around the gravel runway. We shouted over the noise of the motors, "Why aren't we landing? Is there anything wrong?"

"Nothing wrong," our pilot replied. "I just have to make sure you guys can pronounce the name of this place. Then I'll land."

The gauntlet thus tossed, we practised all seven syllables: *Kang-iq-su-al-u-jju-aq*, and one by one we pronounced the name while the plane continued to circle the village. Kangiqsualujjuaq, Kangiqsualujjuaq, Kangiqsualujjuaq, Kangiqsualujjuaq.

"You all pass," our pilot announced as he banked the plane toward the runway for a perfect three-point landing. We pulled up to the single hut, which served as control tower, passenger waiting room, baggage and freight storage area. The former name of the town still showed on the sign: "Welcome to George River."

⌣ THE MOTEL 6 HOOSEGOW

Hotel facilities in small northern communities were indeed unique—when they existed at all. In one village a shipping container, once used for delivery of major electrical equipment, had been furnished as a three-bed guest house. With limited ventilation and infrequent use, it provided musty (but warm) accommodation when needed.

When we arrived for an orchestral concert in one northern fly-in community, we learned that the only hotel in town had burnt to the ground the previous evening. Undaunted, the community had arranged private accommodation for the thirty-two visitors. This was the north, where nobody stays without a bed for the night. At the airstrip a fleet of snowmobiles was lined up to take the musicians and flight crew to the various homes.

The pilot and I planned to be the last to head into the village, but there were still two violinists without billets and without transportation. We could not all fit on the single remaining snowmobile. Suddenly, bouncing across the frozen ridges of ice at the edge of the airstrip, came one last vehicle. It was emblazoned with the badge of the RCMP. The officer, resplendent in his dress uniform, sprang from the vehicle, saluted smartly and, pointing to the two violinists, commanded: "You two, come with me!"

Before the concert, we compared notes on our temporary residences. One was staying with the Catholic priest, another with the hamlet administrator and yet another with the high school principal. Three were at the nurses' residence, two were put up in the back of the Northern Store, while others were scattered around the community in an assortment of private homes. The constable brought the two young violinists to the hall, where they proudly announced that they were spending the night in jail. But what a jail!

The prison was completely unoccupied. At a recent town meeting the village had voted unanimously to ban liquor. There were many dry communities in the north, but in this case the decision had also included an agreement by the non-Indigenous administrators and service employees to refrain for six months from bringing any alcohol into the community. In the short term, it was working. The cells were vacant and unlocked. The musician residents enjoyed free access to the outside world, and their uniformed host had even prepared a gourmet dinner for his guests.

⁓ FLYING PIANOS

The German word for a grand piano is *der Flügel* (the wing). No reason, therefore, that the piano shouldn't occasionally fly. I do recall one classic example when the Vancouver Symphony Orchestra used a helicopter to hoist a piano to the top of a nearby ski hill for a summer pops concert. And in northern Saskatchewan, the Eldorado mining company flew not one but *two* grand pianos to their mine site at Uranium City.

A little background. One of the earliest and most successful ensembles that I ever toured was the American duo-piano team of Melvin Stecher and Norman Horowitz. They carved a unique slice of musical history across North America in the 1950s and 1960s, touring to every corner of the United States and Canada, presenting duo-piano recitals to audiences that had, in most cases, never enjoyed even a single piano in concert. They were part of a grand touring tradition that grew up in the post–World War II era in North America. Along with Stecher and Horowitz were the following celebrated duos: Vronsky and Babin; Nelson and Neal (who wrote a delightful book of touring memoirs entitled *Wave as You Pass*); Eden and Tamir; Bouchard and Morisset; Robin and Winifred Wood (we called them "Two by Four"); Parsons and Poole; the Medleys; the Roman Sisters; the Marlowe Brothers; the Kohnops. There are others, too, and I beg forgiveness if I have neglected to mention some who toured for me. It is no surprise that in the twenty-first century we see duos such as Elizabeth and Marcel Bergmann touring with their two pianos to perform in a myriad of small and isolated communities. They are taking a leaf out of the past century's touring history.

Most of these pianists also qualified as expert truck drivers, furniture movers and piano tuners with the same degree of excellence that they lavished on their nightly performances.

As far as I know, the only time Stecher and Horowitz ever missed a concert was on the way to the town of Bralorne, in a remote mountainous section of British Columbia. They were turned back from their destination by a uniformed Mountie, who had parked his vehicle across the road to prevent them from continuing their journey. With a flexible tape he carefully measured their Ford 1.5-ton truck from headlight to headlight, and then declared, quite apologetically, "Gentlemen, you'll have to back down over the road you have just navigated. There's no place to turn around. Your truck measures six foot five inches across the front. Up ahead, the road is only five foot four inches wide. Your choices are clearly limited."

216 / George Zukerman

Having no road at all was not quite as bad as finding one too narrow to accommodate their truck. That was the problem confronting Stecher and Horowitz when they agreed to play a concert in Uranium City. The tiny mining town, which lies on the border between Saskatchewan and the Northwest Territories, boasted a flourishing concert society. In a frenzy of enthusiasm following a highly successful membership drive, the society insisted on booking a concert by the duo-piano team—but there was no road to Uranium City.

In the spirit of good community citizenship, and as a pioneer in imaginative community relations among northern mining companies, Eldorado arranged for its aviation division to assume the role of aerial piano movers. The two instruments would travel to Uranium City on an old but extremely reliable propeller aircraft, a DC-4 that rattled and shook each day as it shuttled back and forth between Uranium City and Edmonton's industrial airport, carrying yellowcake, partially refined uranium ore, from the mine.

On a stormy April morning, two nine-foot Steinway pianos were brought to the far end of the Edmonton airport. There a forklift hoisted them, one by one, to the side of the plane, where they swayed and shuddered precariously with each violent gust of wind until the loading crew finally managed to twist and turn each instrument through the freight door into the bare belly of the DC-4. Two hours later, at Uranium City, the pianos were transported by a backhoe earthmover from airstrip to school. That evening the audience streamed into the hall to hear an extraordinary concert and to marvel at the sight of the two concert grands, weighing heavily on the shaky floorboards of a school gym. Next day the Eldorado aviation division repeated its magic and successfully returned the pianos to Edmonton and the waiting truck. When the artists performed later that week in Lethbridge, Alberta, 450 kilometres farther south, their instruments were still lightly dusted with yellowcake powder.

The arrival of the two artists in Uranium City was quite another story. This was the first year that Stecher and Horowitz had decided to engage a driver-technician to accompany them throughout the tour. They would have help on the road with the driving, tuning and adjustments, and even with the mandatory consumption of peanut butter and banana sandwiches at post-concert receptions.

At the time of this caper, there was a bitter licensing dispute raging between the commercial airline that served Uranium City and Eldorado's privately owned and operated aviation division.

"There will be no passengers on the Eldorado plane," proclaimed the spokesman for the airline. A logical compromise was reached. The two pianos would fly on the company freighter to await the arrival of the artists and their piano tuner on the commercial flight. Accordingly, flight reservations were made for Stecher, for Horowitz and, well, who was the tuner? "Name unknown" would have to suffice, since he had not yet been engaged. The teletype chattered the message across the mountains to the airline's reservations department in Edmonton.

Once the decision had been made to go north, a new set of questions arose for the intrepid duo. How cold would it be? What might happen to the pianos on the flight? What if they were damaged in the loading and off-loading of the plane? Perhaps, it was suggested, the tuner could travel with the pianos on the Eldorado plane in order to work on the instruments at the hall before the artists arrived?

It seemed a reasonable request, and indeed, six weeks later the Air Transport Board, which had jurisdiction over such matters, telegraphed authority for the piano tuner to accompany the two irreplaceable Steinways on the Eldorado flight. There was no objection from the commercial airline. The piano tuner's seat on the regularly scheduled flight (still listed under "name unknown") was cancelled.

On concert day, as the flying pianos, accompanied by the tuner-technician, winged their way north, the soloists dutifully checked in for their flight, which would leave later that morning. A smiling reservation agent checked the list for their names (there were no computers, just a teletyped list) and politely informed them that while there was, indeed, a seat confirmed for a Mr. Horowitz, there was none to be seen for anyone by the name of Stecher. "The flight is full. I can book you on the Friday flight, if you wish."

Duo piano recitals seldom work when one artist is sitting eight hundred kilometres away from the other. There was a great deal of shouting and hammering on the counter until someone blinked and a space was somehow opened up for Mr. Stecher.

It was a precarious situation, only resolved at the last minute, and the airline was just as anxious to find out why this had occurred as I was. Today's travellers, accustomed to computerization of every phase of the booking process, will find it hard to realize that at that time all flight information was kept on handwritten file cards containing reservations, changes, cancellations, payment records, no-shows. A passenger's entire flight history could be extracted from these records.

The airline located the reservation card. It had been completed quite properly, and the correct messages had been relayed to Edmonton. However, in the process a small typographical error had crept onto the card. Melvin Stecher's last name received an extra letter—an unwanted "r." His name emerged as "Strecher." An agent in Edmonton received the message and read it several times. He reached three important conclusions: (1) his colleagues at the Vancouver office couldn't spell very well; (2) there was no need for a capital letter for a stretcher; and (3) a certain Mr. Horowitz was apparently accompanying a stretcher case (so severely wounded that he could not be identified, hence "name unknown") on the flight to Uranium City. The agent went into the terminal, where he carefully measured a stretcher that was wedged between the main check-in counter and a bulkhead. He concluded that it would require three seats in the aircraft. He then returned to his desk, recorded the required seat for Mr. Horowitz, erased the capital "S" in Mr. Stecher's name, and set aside three spaces for the stretcher.

Events followed with unerring and inevitable logic. Once the Air Transport Board had authorized the tuner to travel with the Eldorado plane, a subsequent message was sent to the airline in Edmonton, cancelling the space for "name unknown." The same agent read it and thought to himself: "Ah, how very sad. The poor chap has succumbed to his injuries," and promptly released the three seats that were being held for the stretcher. Mr. Horowitz's space remained as valid as ever.

Fortunately, Uranium City's first event with grand pianos ended happily, and the opening concert of the town's twenty years of subsequent musical history was an unqualified success. The two artists, ultimate urbane gentlemen of the keyboard, looking as freshly polished as if they had stepped from a formal-wear rental store window, played their hearts out for 310 people jammed into the hall for the concert. That was 9 percent of the city's population, rivalling the best attendance figures at major events in most of the world's metropolitan music centres. It was proof, if any were needed, that organized audience subscription plans can produce miraculous results when a community is ready and a committee is determined to make it happen.

∼ NO PIANO, NO CONCERT

It took a visit by tenor Luigi Infantino to galvanize the Uranium City audience into piano-purchasing frenzy.

Infantino was a giant of a man, a pre-Pavarotti prototype of all Italian tenors. He had a wondrous flair for the most romantic of tenor arias, and for his own superb Neapolitan arrangements. In the 1950s, he had boasted one of the great voices on the Italian opera stage, and still in the 1960s, Infantino retained stage magic and charisma. In 1967 he undertook an arduous western Canadian tour that, among other venues, included Uranium City.

A cable arrived from the artist's management one morning. "Where is Uranium City? No airlines indicate service. Please clarify." A facetious reply urged him not to worry: "Uranium City north of Edmonton. Motorized Geiger counters fly in daily." The sophomoric joke fell on unreceptive ears. "Will not take risks," read the cabled reply. "Request conventional, repeat, conventional transportation, or it will be impossible to fulfill contract."

Fortunately there were alternatives, and Infantino finally accepted a space on the thrice-weekly commercial flight. The airline guide showed Beaverlodge (YBE) as the airport terminus. How was an artists' agent in Palermo, Italy, to know that this destination served Uranium City?

Infantino's anxiety about aircraft was replaced by apprehension for caloric survival. "What shall I do in your cold and dark country?" he moaned one day in Vancouver before heading north. "Will there be anything to eat?" Assured that uranium miners required sustenance akin to the food intake of mountain climbers facing Everest, or tenors about to sing *Tristan und Isolde*, Infantino grudgingly resolved that his only remaining concerns should be musical. He did not yet know anything about the piano that would confront him on arrival.

On the day of the concert, the flight from Edmonton was delayed several hours and arrived less than an hour before concert time. From the airport, the artists were taken straight to the hall, where the audience was already seated. There was no time for even the briefest of rehearsals.

Uranium City had not seen a grand piano since that opening concert when the Eldorado company flew instruments north for a performance by Stecher and Horowitz. Most of the pianos in use in schools on the northern prairies in the 1960s were small spinet-style uprights, which had been purchased in bulk by school administrations throughout the western provinces. The instrument available for Infantino's Uranium City concert had been sadly neglected during its years in the elementary school's all-purpose room. It had probably not been tuned since its acquisition ten years earlier. For the arrival of such a distinguished artist, the instrument had been dusted off after being wheeled to centre stage.

In the 1960s, most concerts in smaller communities still began with a stirring rendition of "God Save the Queen," joined by the audience in a lusty and patriotic singalong. Infantino's pianist strode out on stage, sat down at the piano and played what he thought was the national anthem. Because the audience knew what was expected to emerge from the instrument, they sang the right words to the anticipated melody.

But Infantino, listening from the wings, was appalled at what he heard. Not only was the instrument atrociously out of tune; there were several notes that simply did not sound at all. A resident mouse had chewed through the hammer felts. The conclusion of the anthem was Infantino's cue to emerge, and with the shuffling of chairs as everyone sat down, emerge he did, resplendent in white tie and tails. He stood a moment, looking first at the pianist, then at the piano, then at the audience and then back in horror at the piano.

"I cannot sing with this piano," he declared to the assembled crowd.

The audience shuffled restlessly, not quite certain what to do. Should they believe him? Should they leave? They were concert society members. They were entitled to their concert. Was this madman from Sicily (possibly *mafioso*) really going to refuse to perform? What was wrong with the piano, after all? Hadn't the local drama society used it just three weeks before for their version of *Paint Your Wagon*? Committee members hurried on stage and tried to reason with Mr. Infantino. The pianist tried to subdue the unrest with a background rendition of what he later declared was the "Blue Danube Waltz."

Eventually the prolonged onstage negotiations were resolved, and Infantino returned. Hand in hand with the chairwoman of the society, he stood at the edge of the stage. He eyed his antagonists (for surely the audience that demanded his performance with this monstrosity of a non-piano was an enemy), and finally he spoke. "I cannot sing with this piano." Again, sounds of distress from the audience. "However . . ." Ah! Relief. "I have travelled all this way to your cold and dark country. The plane was delayed. I have not eaten since breakfast." All of his complaints came pouring out at once. "Nonetheless, I will sing for you." Relief again. "But first you have to agree to buy a good piano for this town!" Stunned silence. A piano? In 1967 that meant at least $7,000. Uranium City had full employment to be sure, but who was to purchase such an instrument, and for what use? How many occasions a year? Infantino must have sensed disbelief at his ultimatum.

"I am not joking," he continued. "You agree to buy a piano. I agree to sing the concert." And with that he opened his wallet and threw a twenty-dollar bill on the stage floor. It fluttered off the edge of the stage, and a six-year-old picked it up and held it high for everyone to see.

"We start the piano fund!" Silence.

"Overture Concerts contributes their commission," shouted the tenor, risking his vocal cords for the evening yet to come. The Maestro was carried away at his fundraising success. "We have $320!"

And then it happened. From all corners of the hall, like lost souls finding God at a Baptist revival meeting, they streamed forward and laid their offerings on the stage, whether a dollar or ten or twenty. Infantino and the pianist, on all fours, counted a grand total of $847.50.

Nobody remembers much about the concert. It must have been a success. Infantino himself embellished the story in future years as one of the crowning events of his career. The tale of Uranium City was recounted to willing listeners backstage at opera houses, large and small, throughout Italy.

Several months later the local concert committee purchased a six-foot grand, and by the end of the year the "Luigi Infantino" piano was in place, inaugurated by the Viennese American pianist Walter Hautzig at the opening concert of the 1967–1968 season. Community pride grew as a stream of visiting artists marvelled at the availability of such a relatively fine piano in so isolated a community, and in 1969 a tuner began regular visits to adjust the instrument. Before leaving town, his calling card could be found on the panelling above the keyboard of a dozen assorted instruments in church halls, schools and private homes. Infantino's influence in matters musical spread throughout the community.

By 1982 the Eldorado mine had almost depleted its ore body. A worldwide drop in metal demand and prices sealed Uranium City's fate. The condemned town began the slow and painful task of closing down. The mine shafts were sealed. The workforce slowly began to drift away to seek jobs elsewhere. Stores closed. Houses were boarded up. Schools completed their annual cycle of registration and graduation for one last time.

During that last winter, nearly a thousand people remained in isolation to perform the rites of closure. Slowly, as the town's economy entered its death throes, an idea sprang to life. Uranium City should go out with a musical bang! A committee was formed to schedule an "end-of-the-world concert series." To those who remained, it was a logical move. They still had social, communal and artistic needs. Perhaps the usual frenetic community activity was heightened by the awareness of the town's fate. Uranium City, in that last year of its existence, boasted seventy-three different clubs and social organizations designed for everything from birdwatching to concerts, from curling to amateur drama, from cross-country skiing to shortwave radio communication.

The dilemma of the new concert society was threefold. First, all but one stalwart of the earlier committee had already left town. Second, even allowing for modest attendance and a pre-subscription sale of memberships, could they pay properly for a full series of touring events? Third, Eldorado was no longer operating regular air service, and by January the only transportation would be with Buffalo Air (surely as reliable as the 1963 motorized Geiger counters!). Artists would not only require fees; they would have heavier than usual travel costs.

In the end, the spirit of Luigi Infantino's 1967 concert guided the committee. Who, after all, it was reasoned, owned the piano? What on earth would be done with it when the last resident of the town finally left? If it did not leave Uranium City on one of the flights south, it would disintegrate into waste with the boarded-up homes and the sealed mine shafts. The decision was reached to save the piano from the wrecking ball. It would be exchanged for a final series of concerts in the dying town.

And so, sometime in June 1983, a 737 jet belonging to the aviation division of the Gunnar-Nesbitt mining company left Uranium City on a flight to Edmonton, 680 kilometres to the south. The gleaming new 737 had replaced the creaky DC-4 but still served the same multi-purpose needs of the mining company. Instead of yellowcake ore, this particular aircraft carried an ebony-black Yamaha grand piano, which for nearly twenty years had been at the heart of Uranium City's musical life. The piano was unloaded and extensively overhauled at Edmonton, then shipped down to White Rock, where Erika and I enjoy playing it in our home. It was reported as a taxable benefit received in lieu of artists' fees for the last season of public concerts ever held in that most northern of Saskatchewan communities.

Overture Concerts, which had initiated the birth of the concert series in 1963, celebrated an elegant, even joyous final season with Uranium City's dwindling concert audience. The only problem was to find a concert series that no longer needed a piano. Perhaps that explains why so many harps, guitars and even a brass quintet helped brighten up that last winter in the north.

⌣ MARY HAD A LITTLE LAMB IN NORTHERN MANITOBA

There is a little village in northern Manitoba that can only be reached by water from its nearest neighbouring community. There is no airport, and no runway for landing wheeled aircraft. The only stretch of open land long enough for an airstrip is also a traditional burial site.

In order to play our promised school concert, we needed to appeal to Manitoba Hydro. They came to the rescue and agreed to rent their helicopter. It was a ten-minute flight.

When we landed on the school playing field, it looked strangely deserted. We proceeded to the school, which lay at the far end of the playground, and explored the building, corridor after corridor, room after room. There was absolutely nobody there. Yet the building was heated. The lights were on. The clocks all showed 10:55 a.m. I checked our calendar. It was the right day, the right time.

We headed back, past the helicopter, which sat with its rotor turning idly, its meter presumably clicking steadily. On the far side of the field we found the Band Council offices. Somewhere deep in the building we heard the sound of activity. Clouds of cigarette smoke wafted over us as we climbed the stairway toward the voices.

"Is that your helicopter?" somebody enquired through the smoky haze. "Did you bring the order from the Northern Store?"

"Wrong delivery," I replied. "No pizza, either. We're here for the school concert," I added, in case our instruments and music stands didn't reveal our purpose. "Where are the kids? Where do they want us to set up?"

A head came into view through the smoke. "School's gone for the day. They're all out on the land—field trip, annual event—back tomorrow morning." The gentleman emerged more fully and inspected our group. "What you got there? Instruments?" I acknowledged our profession. "Why don't you hang around, stay over. We'll find some rooms for you. While you're at it, play us a tune."

It was the birth of an idea. "Is there a community radio station?" I asked. The reply was instant. "Sure there is. Just walk back, past the school."

"Can you call them and say that we're on the way?" I asked. "We'll play for anyone who is listening!"

Another instant reply. "No point calling. Dennis is the only one there. If he answers the phone, he goes off the air."

The band councillor crossed to a nearby table and turned on a small portable radio. Dennis had already seen our helicopter. "I see the Hydro chopper has just landed. Does anyone know who's on it? Anyone need a lift to the mainland? Call here and we'll see if there's space when they head back. Meantime, let's play another song." Community radio was broadcasting to every household in the village.

I led my trio across the playing field again, musical instruments and music stands at the ready, and we entered the single room of the community radio station just as Dennis started to talk again. "That was [here he mentioned the name and performing artist on the disc]. Now to find out more about that helicopter. I sure would like to know who was on it."

At that point he realized he had company. "We have visitors," he announced to his audience. "Are you the guys from the chopper?" He thrust the solitary microphone into my hands. "Introduce yourselves," he said and went off to a corner to light a cigarette.

While my colleagues took their instruments out of their cases and set up some chairs and the stands, I told our story. "We're here to play for the school. I gather the kids are all away, but we would be delighted to play for you." We set the microphone on a table and urged Dennis to turn a few knobs on his control panel. We were on the air. After our first piece we looked curiously toward Dennis, sitting comfortably at his controls. "Do you think anyone is listening?" I asked.

"Sure," he replied. "Everyone's listening. Play some more." I decided to ask the listeners what they might like to hear. From house No. 15 came a request for "Mary Had a Little Lamb."

We quickly improvised the tune. The caller's name was Mary, so we appropriately dedicated the performance to her. When we finished, the phone rang again. Dennis spoke rapidly with whoever was calling and seemed to agree with whatever he was being told. "I'll let them know," he said. Turning to us he relayed the message. "You bet they are listening to you. But you've got a problem. There are seven other Marys in this village. You better play the piece again for all of them." Every word we spoke was on the air and was probably heard in every household in the village. So we played the request again, and then for forty-five minutes more we played assorted music, from Mozart to the theme song of *The Simpsons*.

Later that afternoon we skimmed back over the water to the mainland, and the Hydro helicopter went back to fixing downed power lines. At hundreds of dollars for each quarter-hour, waiting time included, our budget was splendidly shattered, but we had made some kind of broadcasting history.

⌁ GRAND BANKS, GRAND OPERA

The airport for Happy Valley–Goose Bay was the aviation hub for Labrador and the Inuit region of Nunatsiavut, with its scattered coastal villages. As always in the north, the weather was the ultimate arbiter of arrivals and departures, and even though sophisticated radar made it possible to land the largest passenger aircraft under extreme conditions, neither jumbo jet nor Piper Cub could count on taking off when fog shrouded Goose Bay's two extra-long runways.

Along with three colleagues from the Newfoundland Symphony Orchestra, I had flown into Goose Bay from Wabush, on the Quebec border. We were on a tightly booked school concert tour and were headed to the "outports"—those tiny isolated villages along the coast of Labrador, most of which were accessible only by air. Our chartered plane was supposed to leave at first sunlight, but relentless fog swirled around the airport as we arrived. Obviously nobody was flying anywhere.

The tarmac outside the terminal building was jammed with aircraft of all sizes. There was an Air Canada 737 jet, four de Havilland Beavers, one Grumman Goose on wheels, two DC-3 freighters, half a dozen private Cessna 182s, and three Piper Navajos, one of which was our charter aircraft for the day.

Inside the terminal, eighty-four stranded passengers moved restlessly from airline counter to coffee shop, from coffee shop to restrooms, from restrooms to the pay phones, from pay phones to the "viewing lounge." Some viewing lounge! They could barely see their parked aircraft, let alone the panorama of Happy Valley. The fog thickened and, predictably, the message from the control tower remained unchanged: "The ceiling is too low for takeoff."

The tiny coffee shop ran out of doughnuts and coffee. The restrooms ran out of toilet paper. The waiting passengers ran out of small change for the airport's three overworked pay phones. Airline staff ran out of patience answering the same repeated questions, while announcements of one delay after another echoed through the cavernous converted hangar.

Our instrument cases were suddenly noticed. "Play us a tune," someone urged. A little music would presumably be more cheerful than endless announcements of delayed flights. Why not an impromptu concert? At least we would have a captive audience.

We cleared a space in front of the solitary car rental counter, found four armless chairs in the now-empty coffee shop, unfolded our portable music stands, tuned up as best we could and began to perform. This was no ordinary ensemble. It consisted of an accordion, a violin, a clarinet and a bassoon. The music included a Mozart serenade, a Strauss waltz, an aria from one of Verdi's operas, the "Carnival of Venice," music from *The Pink Panther* and even our guaranteed crowd-pleaser finale, a snappy version of the theme song from *The Simpsons*. All of it had been specially arranged for our peculiar instrumental combination.

The restless crowd gathered around, no longer quite so restless. Some sat on the floor, some used their suitcases as chairs. As far as I can recall, there were no noticeable complaints about faulty intonation as we played our entire school concert repertoire. Halfway through the concert, "La donna è mobile" from the opera *Rigoletto* was interrupted by an announcement of a further delay of Eastern Provincial's Flight 181. An airport commissionaire rushed hastily to the tower to invite the air traffic controllers to join the audience. I'm not sure if they actually came, but at least the PA system remained silent for the rest of our concert.

We finished playing and I took my place in the line at the pay phones. I had held on to one last dime, and I called through to the school. Of course they knew about the fog, if not by phone, by instinct. "Don't worry," they told me. "You'll play if and when you get here."

Meantime, some of our morning audience had strayed back to the viewing lounge. It seemed a little brighter outside the terminal building. Was that the power of music? Perhaps the fog was really lifting? Suddenly a voice exclaimed excitedly, "It's clearing! We can see the runway." At the same moment our pilot came dashing down the corridor. "We're cleared to go," he shouted. "Grab your gear. If we can take off in the next ten minutes we'll be on our way." Passengers on the larger commercial flights looked on enviously.

We packed our instruments and hurriedly followed the pilot onto the tarmac. "Where are we going?" I shouted over the din of the Navajo's twin motors, already whirring at takeoff speed.

"I don't know yet," the pilot shouted back. "We'll get off the ground, and then we'll find out what's open."

And that is precisely what happened. At 3,500 feet the sun was shining and the town of Goose Bay lay under a thick blanket of snowy altocumulus. It was 10:40 a.m. Our pilot turned his craft due east (more or less toward Greenland) and was on the radio to nearby airports. After a few moments he raised his thumbs in a sign of victory. "Black Tickle is open. Let's start there!" He radioed ahead and sent a message to the school: "On the ground at 11:35. Pick us up. Delay lunch. Over and out." We were three hours late, but at least we would be able to rescue one of the three concerts scheduled for that day.

The tiny village of Black Tickle (population was then just 220) is about as far out in the Atlantic Ocean as one can possibly travel and still remain in Canada. Located on the Island of Ponds, off the coast of mainland Labrador, the community is subjected to fierce Atlantic storms, as well as endless fog from the nearby Grand Banks. The village is nearer to Qaanaaq, Greenland, than it is to Ottawa. As the crow flies (and as we flew that day) from Goose Bay, it was only 270 kilometres.

We landed beneath an ominously low ceiling. A school bus drew up alongside the plane as the motors were stilled. In twenty minutes we were in the school, set up and ready to play. All twenty-two students (grades 1 to 12) were there that day, and a sizeable number of the town's adult population joined us.

As we played, our pilot stood at the back of the room. Every few moments he disappeared to the principal's office to check the weather conditions. But he didn't need the telephone. He could see the front moving in. We were in the middle of a slow waltz-like section when he started waving his arms furiously, gesturing first to the door, then to his watch, then helplessly at the approaching clouds. As we came to an early stop, he pre-empted the balance of the concert. "Sorry, folks," he called out. "If we don't get off the ground in the next twenty minutes, you'll have house guests for a week!"

The teachers nodded sympathetically, helped us dismantle our music stands, thrust a huge bag of sandwiches into our hands and piled us back into the school bus. Fifteen minutes later we were airborne. The fog buried Black Tickle five minutes after we left. The ocean surrounding the Island of Ponds was no longer visible. All we could see, emerging magically from the clouds, was the gleaming, translucent peak of an offshore iceberg.

As we climbed above Black Tickle, the sun shone brilliantly above the cloud blanket. We turned toward Cartwright, a mere seventy kilometres inland, but in minutes our pilot reported that the airport there was socked in. "We have just enough gas to make it to Rigolet." He paused, then added, "With luck they'll have fuel there for the trip home!"

We lunched on Black Tickle sandwiches. As we were landing, we could see the school bus waiting for us. It crossed our mind that by this time, given that our pilot had contacted at least eight airports and schools, there must be a school bus standing by on every remote airstrip in Nunatsiavut in case we turned up at that particular village for a possible concert. At the Rigolet school we once again played our repertoire, this time complete and without interruption. As in each of our other school performances, we concluded with an aria from Verdi's *Rigoletto*.

Our pilot, meantime, had successfully found enough aviation fuel for the Navajo's twin tanks, and when the school bus brought us back we all breathed a collective sigh of relief that the Rigolet airfield had remained open for our final takeoff that day.

That night, back in Goose Bay, we contemplated whether we could re-schedule Cartwright for the next day as our charter headed to Nain and Natuashish. Meantime, I wrote my report to the funding agencies. I described the day as best I could and concluded that they could take great satisfaction in the fulfillment of most of the program. Despite the most daunting weather, we had successfully played two out of our three scheduled concerts. A justly proud pronouncement.

But, in the end, we had one that was even better. Who else in the world could possibly claim to have played *Rigoletto* in Rigolet?

CODA

A Gentle Close

Why Coda?

You may have noticed that this book is in sonata form, with introduction, exposition, development, recapitulation and coda. Codas, to my mind, are quiet, reflective musical moments. Sometimes old themes reappear, sometimes new material creeps in, but always a coda allows for a gentle unwinding and a release from the tension of exposition, development, modulation and recapitulation.

There were occasions while writing this book when I was convinced that I would never be able to complete the story. Sometimes I despaired because there was too much material. Sometimes memory failed me and I could no longer recall some incident that seemed essential to the narrative. At the height of my despair (disguised as writer's block) I found myself wondering whether *any* of these recollections were really worth recounting. Was anyone going to be interested? At such times I subjected Erika and a few close friends to ruthless (and probably tedious) previews. In spite of that, they encouraged me relentlessly. Together we kept the spark alight.

Inevitably there were some odds and ends left over that did not seem to fit anywhere in the flow of my story. The coda turned out to be the ideal home for some of these curious items.

⁓ NAMES

Let me begin with an interlude of names that harks back to the very beginning. I shall take the opportunity to reveal (and explain) my peculiar lifelong antipathy to my given name: George. To do this, I will eventually introduce you to Edward C. Delaney who, without ever knowing me, exercised a disproportionate influence on my life.

My parents held American citizenship and were living in England when I was born on February 22, 1927. With uncharacteristically patriotic zeal, they named me after America's first president, George Washington. It is pointless to complain now, but I may as well say it: I have never felt entirely comfortable in the skin of a George. I know that the name derives from a Greek god of crops and the harvest, and while I have an immense respect for the dedicated men and women who produce the food on which we all depend, I cannot visualize myself as a farmer.

My parents did better when they added a second name to my birth certificate. They chose the name Benedict to commemorate the life of the seventeenth-century philosopher Spinoza. Benedict Spinoza actually died on February 21, not the 22nd, but that was the kind of incidental detail my father brushed away as irrelevant.

My birth was duly and properly registered at Somerset House, that grand repository of all British records. There I was, George Benedict Zukerman, aged less than two months, about to be brought up in middle-class London suburbia bearing a first name with which I would never be pleased. Indeed, it soon became clear that I did not like to be called George or, even worse, its diminutive, Georgie.

Uncomfortable with my given name, I took matters into my own hands and, with the help of a dramatic tantrum, insisted that I should henceforth be known as Dick. Why this peculiarly un-Jewish name? Family tales abound that try to justify, or at least explain, such an arbitrary choice. One theory claimed that I dropped the first syllable of my middle name and turned the remaining *Dict* into *Dick*. Another argued that I was a child of the 1930s, and even English children knew of Dick Tracy and his prescient radio watch. Is it possible that I wanted to be named after an American comic book detective-hero? A third view reasoned that I was familiar with the tale of Dick Whittington. The famous line "Turn again, Whittington, Lord Mayor of London" was stuck in my childhood memory, and perhaps I wanted to emulate Whittington's rags-to-riches accomplishment. This would certainly have been in keeping with my parents' determination to have my brother and me grow up more British than the little English boys around the corner!

In the end, each of these fanciful tales gives way to a reality of childhood. I have vague memories of my mother calling me "Dinky" and of feeling a terrible, uneasy embarrassment at hearing that name. And so it was that at five years of age I declared that I was quite grown up and would no longer be considered something so preciously small and adorable or, worse yet, be named after a die-cast toy car. Under threat of further tantrums, I persuaded everyone to drop the "n." In close family circles, even today, I am known as Dick.

The name George was successfully concealed until I made my first appearance at the High School of Music and Art on Convent Avenue in upper Manhattan. There I was caught up in the web created by Edward C. Delaney, a teacher at DeWitt Clinton High School in the Bronx. By the year 1940, his invention, the little-loved Delaney card, was in universal use in all New York City schools. This was a registration form that kept track of each student from the day they entered the system until graduation. Delaney cards were ubiquitous, they were permanent, and they required complete and precise information.

"What is your name?" demanded the formidable Miss Doran, my first classroom teacher.

I managed to squeak out a timid "Dick."

"No sir," she responded, "not Dick. This is a Delaney card." The room shook with the thunderous import of this pronouncement. "Delaney cards do not accept nicknames. Your real name, we suppose, is Richard? Is that so?" and she began to write.

"Oh no, please," I wept. "Not Richard. That has never been my name. Dick is what they call me, but," and here copious tears flowed, "my name is really George." Across the bridge, in the Bronx, Edward Delaney must have smiled. His card had triumphed, and from that moment forward I was stripped of my nickname, registered as George and introduced to an entire generation of schoolmates by a name that I barely recognized. Somebody called George was duly inscribed on a Delaney card and just as surely attended school, but what happened to him did not, for many years, really happen to me. It was a schizoid boyhood existence.

There began a lifetime, a career, a professional existence with the name assigned to me by my parents, and with the initials GBZ ritually confirmed by Mr. Delaney and his splendid system of file cards.

Many years later I pondered the curiosity of fate that dictated some degree of minor celebrity. How jealous I was of George Bernard Shaw, whose initials were so well known and respected that he was instantly recognized as GBS. No such luck for a wandering bassoon soloist! Those initials GBZ stand for many things: the IATA code for one of the three airstrips on New Zealand's Great Barrier Island; the centre for U.K. studies at Humboldt University in Berlin (*Großbritannien Zentrum*); a Dutch swimming club (*Groot Beverse Zwemclub*); the call sign for a British VLF radio transmitter that sends encrypted signals to submarines; medical identification for Guanabenz, a drug used to treat high blood pressure; vehicle registration for some licence plates in Gibraltar; and, from the latest Urban Dictionary, the seat in between two guys at the movie theatre, otherwise known as the "Gay Buffer Zone."

I thought of changing the name (and the initials), and had I moved early enough in my onstage life I might well have become equally or even better known as Baruch Zukerman or perhaps George Baruch. Both would have made fine stage names, but by the time I found myself longing for either, my career was already underway, and it seemed to be too late to change. In spite of all the obstacles imposed by such awkward initials, the career expanded, the name became marginally well known (at least among bassoonists!) and the faint possibility of ever changing the name and the initials disappeared in direct proportion to the marketing success of my several overseas managers. Even if only by default, Edward Delaney prevailed.

Fortunately Delaney cards had no room for middle names, since I wasn't particularly enamoured of Benedict either. It took me many years to appreciate that my middle name—a Latin version of the Hebrew *Baruch*, or *blessed* in English—opens most major prayers to an assortment of functioning deities.

I should also more readily have appreciated the significance of Benedict Spinoza to my parents. Spinoza was not just any philosopher. He was a rebel who suffered for his dissent. In his short mid-seventeenth-century life, he challenged the establishment and the political righteousness of the day by daring to question the authenticity of the Hebrew Bible. It was a dangerous position, which earned him excommunication from the Jewish community and ultimate burial in a Christian churchyard in his native Netherlands. The uncanny parallel with my father's resistance to orthodoxy throughout his lifetime sheds light on the decision to give me Spinoza's name as part of my nominal heritage. Despite my childhood reluctance to accept it, it is a name that now gives me a comforting sense of continuity with my father—a link that I failed to grasp, and sadly never felt, while he was still alive.

I had to wait until the late 1960s for another Bennedik (with slightly different spelling) to enter my life in a curiously unexpected way, and to assume major significance for me ever since. Erika, my partner for over fifty years, is a Bennedik, the second youngest of five siblings, children of a German Huguenot family with a father who was partly Jewish. Erika's father, Kurt Bennedik, who I remember as a gentle man of immense dignity,

Erika Bennedik and George Benedict Zukerman.

was confined to a wheelchair as a result of childhood botulism. His Jewish heritage was inherited from his grandfather, who had performed some extraordinary service for a ruling official and, when asked how he might be rewarded, had bargained for Christian safety for an increasingly vulnerable Jewish family.

One and a half generations later, a handicapped person who was partially Jewish could hardly anticipate an easy existence in Nazi Germany. But Kurt Bennedik was resourceful, and he was also a skilled engineer, whose services were needed by the state. A parade of minor officials managed to overlook his two great handicaps, and the family miraculously clung together throughout the war years.

I now have to risk boring you for just a moment longer with some observations surrounding the surname Zukerman. After all, I have now dealt with both my first and middle names. Why not the last name too? You will not be surprised if I tell you that the origins and spelling of the name Zukerman are not at all as simple as they might first appear.

Immigration authorities in the United States and Canada in the early part of the twentieth century accepted whatever spelling the new immigrant provided. New arrivals, unfamiliar with English spelling, sometimes shortened or simplified their names. When the officer on duty couldn't grasp the name at all, there were occasions where the space on the entry form remained empty. New names, including the family "Blank," emerged to take their place in the North American melting pot.

Some of my distant family members became Chuckermans, some Sugarmans, others an abbreviated Zucker. A few were fortunate enough to retain Zuckerman (with a letter "c"), while others (my father among them) began their American existence with a simpler version of Zukerman, without the letter "c." The two spellings were often treated as interchangeable.

I have devised a conceit to justify the difference. Those who now spell the name with a "c" (Zuckerman) must be remarkably sweet people, since the origin of this particular spelling comes from *Zucker*, the German word for *sugar*. Zukerman (without a c) might be pronounced as in the Hebrew "ch" and I'm inclined to suggest that this spelling comes from the German *zuchen*, that is *to seek*. I'll allow that those of us with only the letter "k" are not so sweet. But we are the seekers, the philosophers and, in my own case, uniquely and appropriately under the influence of Spinoza.

My colleague Pinchas Zukerman also belongs to the latter group. Various cousins have tried to find a close link between our direct ancestors, but without success. The musical Zukermen may both be "seekers," but they probably have to be content with a fifteenth or sixteenth cousinhood.

There you have it. Each of my three names (the G, the B, the Z) to which I have clung for over nine decades is surrounded by some kind of polemic. Certainly the ambiguity of my first name will haunt me forever, as countless cousins from my childhood continue to call me Dick, while Erika and the world at large forever know me as George.

It took my Russian aunt Pauline to devise some kind of resolution to this first-name dilemma. Like all of my mother's seven siblings, Pauline knew me as Dick in the family circle. But walking with me through snow-covered Moscow streets in the 1970s, she saw my name in large letters on concert billboards: *George Zukerman, Canada*. "What is this 'George'?" she wanted to know. I explained such things as birth certificates, passports and even Mr. Delaney.

She thought a while, and in that moment renamed me "Zgick." Perhaps Pauline had discovered the perfect compromise.

❧ MENAGERIE

Does music have charms to soothe the savage beast? English playwright William Congreve wrote that famous line in his 1697 play *The Mourning Bride*. He was concerned about the effect of music on the "savage *breast*." Popular usage has dropped the "r," and people today refer to the "savage beast," which is how I first learned the line. Early in my playing career I decided to test the effect of dulcet bassoon tones on any animal willing to stand still long enough to constitute an audience.

I never managed to play the bassoon for a rhinoceros, although I was close enough to one in Malawi. My concert at the university proceeded as scheduled, but the annual hang-gliding competition from the Zomba Plateau was precipitously cancelled because of rhinoceri grazing on the beach. I'm not at all sure how they might have responded to a bassoon

A Canadian bassoonist playing for an African trumpeter.

serenade. Wild creatures (and even some domesticated ones) have different reactions to modulated sound.

In Australia I discovered that crocodiles were remarkably uninterested. At home, when I played for a herd of cows, they were too busy chewing cud and attending to other overtly more important matters. This disappointed me gravely, since in the 1970s I had organized several tours for a saxophone quartet that had adopted the name "The Swinging Bovines." I would have expected warmer acknowledgment from their living namesakes.

In New Zealand, sheep could safely graze and displayed no signs of interest, even when I played Bach for them. Elephants, on the other hand, at least those I encountered in the Knysna region of South Africa, seemed to respond with gracious approval, even nodding their trunks in rhythmic accord. It was a gratifying and salubrious moment for a Canadian bassoonist to play for an African trumpeter.

At Gibraltar I tried to play for the famously thieving Barbary apes. They are not apes at all, but tail-less macaque monkeys—the only wild monkey population on the European continent. They are impervious to tourists and notorious for grasping shining objects such as watches, cameras, buckles on handbags and, presumably, silver-plated bassoon keys. I proceeded, cautiously, in the cable car to the top station. There, I was about to assemble the bassoon and play for a waiting simian family, when it started to rain furiously. My bassoon was certainly not waterproof, and I hastily packed it away. The monkeys scurried for shelter and I never found out how they would have reacted to "In the Hall of the Mountain King" or even "The Old Castle" from Mussorgsky's *Pictures at an Exhibition*.

Their cousins, the Cape baboons of the Kanonkop troop were not so easily dispersed. I ran into them on South Africa's Garden Route, which links Natal to Cape Province. It is a spectacular highway with magnificent views as it traverses the Indian Ocean coastline of the African continent. I stopped to pay the tariff at a toll booth. As I opened my side window to hand the coins to the attendant, a troop of baboons, residents of a nearby forest glade, hurled themselves across the road and took up positions on the pleasingly warm hood of my vehicle. Fifteen of these animals lying in front of the windshield made it impossible for me to see the road ahead.

I contemplated playing for them, but if they had liked the performance they might not have wanted to leave, and that would have delayed me even longer. Instead, I looked helplessly out of the driver's window at the agent who had just collected my payment. He was obviously familiar with this problem. In amused sign language, he raised the fingers of both hands, then five fingers of his right hand. The message was wordlessly clear. I handed over fifteen more rand (twice the toll cost). The attendant reached into his hut, and from there he tossed a large bunch of bananas over to the far side of the vehicle. The animals immediately jumped off the hood of my car and dashed after the fruit. I accelerated furiously and was quickly out of the toll gate, en route to Cape Town, sadly depriving the baboons of the opportunity to reassemble on the hood, where they could have enjoyed their banana feast in warmth and comfort.

⌣ BEGINNINGS AND ENDINGS

Sixty-nine years, two months and seventeen days elapsed between my first and final professional concerts. The two engagements span a lifetime and encompass my musical world. In New York City, 1944, as a newly sub-scribed union member, I played my first professional engagement under Leonard Bernstein. Neither of us knew what our respective futures held.

Fast-forward to 2013. I was taking part in a concert for elementary school children in the village of Fort Smith, NWT, as part of Remote Tours Canada. Our ensemble consisted of clarinet, bassoon and accordion, and we were playing a variety of music, ranging from a Mozart trio to a snappy version of "Pop Goes the Weasel" and the ever-popular theme song of *The Simpsons*. At the close of the concert I suddenly felt strangely ill. While my colleagues went to the hotel to enjoy lunch, I lay down at my temporary home.

There I spent a miserable day while my host and hostess did their best to provide some sort of first aid: Tylenol and hot tea, dry toast, a boiled egg—nothing seemed to help. The nausea worsened, the inflammation in-tensified, my right leg grew swollen and red. The malaise left me completely drained. Clearly I could not continue the tour.

In a town like Fort Smith—which is by no means the smallest or most isolated of the Northwest Territories' many communities—there is no hos-pital, no resident doctor, only a health centre staffed by a registered nurse. My hostess suggested that I should visit the clinic. "By the way," she added, "you're in luck. The locum arrived last night. I put you on the list. Go there early. Take a good book."

The monthly visits by the doctor were keenly anticipated by the entire village population. So at 10 a.m., when I staggered down the street to the Fort Smith medical centre, there were already forty-five residents signed up and waiting. I joined the crowd and waited . . . and waited.

Finally, late in the afternoon, a voice roused me from fitful dozing. "Dr. Finch will see you now." The name sounded vaguely familiar, but not enough to ring bells of instant recognition. I was led down a corridor and ushered into an examination room, where I waited some more. Finally the door opened and I looked up—and up and up—to the tallest doctor I have ever known. And then it dawned on me that I *did* know him! Dr. Finch. Of course. Chris Finch, former chairman of the Mission Concert Society, his daughter a bassoonist. I had been a guest at his home on several post-concert occasions.

I looked up and barely croaked, "What are you doing here?"

He peered down at me and echoed the same question. "What are *you* doing here?"

Chris proceeded to examine my swollen leg. "We should send you to Yellowknife, where they have better diagnostic tools. There's the danger of a blood clot." There were two planes a day north to the capital city of the Northwest Territories.

The coordinator of the tour was not happy at the prospect of having me in hospital in Yellowknife for days on end, and he shared my instinctive feeling that it would be better to get me home to medical care on my home ground. A local feeder airline operated small aircraft once a day to Edmonton, from where there were numerous connections to Vancouver. Dr. Finch telephoned my own doctor. At huge expense, two tickets were purchased so my leg could be constantly raised in case a clot was forming. I barely had time to hobble to my lodgings and pick up my suitcase and bassoon.

At the airport they were prepared for me. Over my years of travelling I have seen many instruments emerging from cargo holds, carefully labelled with conspicuous stickers: *Fragile* or *Handle With Care*. On that final journey with my bassoon from Fort Smith in the Northwest Territories to Edmonton, my instrument needed no labels since it stayed comfortably in my hands throughout the short flight. But the station manager decided to put his labels to work more effectively. Plastered over my parka were numerous warning stickers: *Fragile, Handle With Care, This Side Up* and *Do Not Refrigerate*. I arrived defrosted, right side up and handled with the utmost care.

At the comfortable and familiar Peace Arch Hospital I underwent all the necessary tests. Fortunately there was no blood clot. Regardless, we were profoundly grateful for Chris Finch's prudence.

I recovered quickly from whatever ailment had beset me in the north. Before long I had discarded the sticker that read *This Side Up* and was walking normally. The question of whether I should play again lay restless in my thoughts. Were illness and chance likely to conspire against my playing as well as I wished? Had the world, perhaps, exhausted practical use for an octogenarian bassoon soloist? I took a monumental step. I cancelled my few remaining engagements. Three months later I sold my precious instrument, companion for nearly sixty-five years. That was the necessary and gut-wrenching finale. Now that the circle was closed, there was no possible way I could be tempted to play again.

The virtuoso life was over. I embarked on a new wave of organizational activity. There was no further use for the toggle switch, and one of my hats was permanently hung in the hall closet.

Once Again from the Top!

Although I was no longer playing, I continued as artistic director of White Rock Concerts, which was one of our earliest organized concert societies. Since 1956, when I founded the organization with a local committee, we had presented an impressive array of international and Canadian celebrity artists to enthusiastic audiences. Living close to White Rock, I could see first-hand the success of the organized audience plan of subscription concerts, which allowed for no failure—only varying levels of success. The series was comfortably sold out, with a healthy waiting list of hopeful concertgoers ready to join whenever space became available. In an era when arts organizations so often incurred deficits, White Rock Concerts was entirely self-supporting and debt-free, grant-free and—as a result—artistically free. The COVID-19 pandemic created a two-year hiatus, but the organization has deep roots in the community and bounced back.

Curious to find out whether the organized audience plan could still work during the second decade of the new century, I set out to establish concert societies in three small communities not too far from Vancouver. They accepted White Rock as their model and offered subscriptions only, with no single tickets available to individual events. The results were astonishing. The old method still worked. I was reminded of those earlier days when we often organized three or four new societies each month. The new communities built predictably successful memberships, and as a result, each became an invaluable link in western touring itineraries.

Partly to meet their new program needs, I continued to organize tours of classical musicians, which were also eagerly accepted by many of the communities on our old touring circuit. In one splendid tour, I was able to organize an unusually lengthy itinerary for the Canadian Guitar Quartet. Just before they were due to set out, I received an urgent complaint from the ensemble. I was afraid they were about to tell me that I had not left sufficient free time in their schedule. On the contrary, I had allowed too much open time. Was there any way I could possibly fill the gaps? I did my best to oblige. They ended up playing, at their own request, twenty-nine concerts in twenty-seven days.

Equally extensive was a tour of the Bergmann piano duo. I sent Elizabeth and Marcel Bergmann off—like so many of their predecessors in the past century—with a truck, a tuning fork and two grand pianos in tow. It was a unique opportunity to deliver piano concerts to towns that did not have even a single good instrument available.

And here my touring plans and my long involvement with my hometown concert society overlapped. On their return, the Bergmanns took over responsibility for the artistic direction of White Rock Concerts. I could now step down from that tenure after fifty-nine seasons.

My impresario hat still had other uses, and it fit well when I began working with a savvy Viennese, Gery Valtiner of Special Travel International, to plan classical music programs for cruises on the great rivers of Europe. Valtiner gave me carte blanche and scrupulously avoided interference in musical matters. I reciprocated by not trying to steer the boats or meddling in the countless details of international travel. Mozart, Beethoven, Haydn and Schubert delighted passengers on the Danube. Ravel, Debussy, César Franck and Saint-Saëns created a genial ambience on the Rhône. Flamenco and fado joined Paganini, Gershwin and Respighi on the Douro. Bach, Handel and Buxtehude filled the days on the Elbe. Beethoven's 250th birthday was celebrated early in Bonn on a cruise on the Rhine. Many of the tales that I have recounted in the pages of this book were first given voice on these cruises. The extraordinary compatibility of passengers and crews, the spectacular wonders of history-steeped geography and the blended wines of Europe's river valleys probably served to incubate the brew of this book.

Of course, COVID-19 interfered here too. The travel industry and the music world shared honours for first place among those most severely struck by the pandemic. Classical music river cruises depended on both

George with duo pianists Elizabeth and Marcel Bergmann,
who took over artistic direction of White Rock Concerts.

those industries. But travel will undoubtedly recover, and music will always be there. Even before this book was published, another musical cruise on the Danube was being planned, and perhaps someone else will organize a music tour of the Volga from Moscow to St. Petersburg. No shortage there of great composers and superb artists.

Do you remember my mention of the booklet *How to Abandon Ship*, which was presented to me at the time of my 1944 enlistment in the navy? Somehow I doubt I shall have the pleasure of participating in another river cruise, so if that pamphlet comes to light in the twenty-first century, I cheerfully bequeath it to my river cruise successor. May he or she never have cause to use it.

COVID-19 frustrated another of my dreams. To celebrate the 250th anniversary of Beethoven's birth in 2020, I created *The Young Beethoven*, a show based on early Beethoven works, culminating with his Opus 20 septet. Using an ensemble of superb Vancouver-based colleagues, *The Young Beethoven* would present Beethoven minus the scowl!

My late brother Professor Joseph Kerman was renowned as a distinguished Beethoven authority. Although I could never hope to equal his erudition, I would try my best to pay tribute to his immense scholarship with a spoken commentary on Beethoven's youthful works, their origins and their influence on later periods of his creativity. The concert was booked by thirteen communities in and around Vancouver and Vancouver Island, but the pandemic descended on the concert world, and like so much else in the 2019–2020 season, the project was postponed.

Even though I was no longer organizing new towns for concert series, I was constantly thinking about tour possibilities for the network of small communities I had worked with for so much of my lifetime. I found myself musing theoretically: what is there that has never before been successfully exploited on the classical music touring circuit? Can I find a program that audiences will instantly recognize as "something new"?

Just before the pandemic struck, I found an answer in the world of percussion. By itself, percussion would probably not succeed if it were limited to the sheer display of bells, drums, cymbals, castanets, gongs and mallet instruments. It seemed to need more than that. With my friends the Bergmanns and percussionist Rod Squance, we created *Percussiano3*. Rod would travel with an array of thirty-eight different instruments—from bass drum to cowbells. The Bergmanns would perform, four hands at a single piano. In that way the program would retain a classical element, but the dazzling spectacle of the percussion instruments would still be allowed to shine.

Percussiano3 was ready to blaze across the concert horizon just as the pandemic closed down all touring activity. Of course, it too had to be delayed. Now, with the gradual reopening of the concert world, a myriad of small-town concert audiences across Canada are celebrating the arrival of that "something new," a glorious six-handed musical miracle—seven, if I allow that I had a hand in the program's success!

Future ideas must eventually shift from reality to memory. And there, too, I simply cannot stop planning, dreaming, imagining...and hoping that somebody will sense the excitement and the potential in such projects.

From today's repose I look back at the height of my playing and organizing careers, and a fond memory returns. Permit me one final restless flick of the toggle switch, one last time to change hats.

Let me set the scene for you. I have just played a concert in Montreal and have travelled on to New York to attend a number of meetings. I am there in my role of impresario, but the virtuoso is not far behind. In the evening I am invited to attend a concert at an elegant small theatre that specializes in chamber music and recitals. As I enter I see a notice posted conspicuously in the lobby. It reads, somewhat severely:

IF YOUR PHONE RINGS DURING THE CONCERT,
YOU WILL BE REQUIRED TO GO ON STAGE
AND PLAY THE BASSOON!

The impresario in me shudders at the thought of a disrupted performance. However—and here I hope you'll forgive the diabolic thought—for a split second, even though I don't own a cell phone, the virtuoso in me contemplates rushing out to the nearest tech shop to purchase one. What a way to secure another New York concert!

Let it ring, let it ring, let it ring!

AFTERWORD

This book has revealed some of what happens "behind the scenes" to bring music to you. Now a few words to give you a brief sketch of what happened behind the scenes to turn the stories George told to audiences into the book you just read.

There is always a history to everything we do. Even when we say "this led to that," there is always something that happened before "this." However, to make a story we have to choose a starting point. An obvious starting point for a life story is our birth, and thus George told of the circumstances of his entry into the world. From there he carried on with further stories that both revealed and entertained.

When George died on February 1, 2023, the manuscript was in rough form, and it has taken a small group of "co-conspirators" to bring this book to you, the reader. What follows is a brief overview of how their various connections with George and his music made this book possible. It's a further tribute to George to note how deeply he inspired them all to this volunteer work.

The most relevant, yet the most invisible story, is the ongoing encouragement, commentary and advice of George's long-time partner, Erika Bennedik. She was consistently his first reader as well as the strongest supporter of his travelling career, while she also had a musical career as a violin player.

George Laverock, an impresario himself, and a former CBC Radio music producer, has perhaps the longest history with George, as they played together in the Vancouver Symphony and the CBC Vancouver Orchestra in the 1960s. George remembers vividly that during every 30-minute break in the CBC recording studios, George Z. was across the street in the lobby of the Hotel Georgia, making calls on the public phone to book hundreds of concerts for his network of Overture Concerts! George L.'s background as trumpet player and concert producer gave him the necessary experience in the music community to check the accuracy of references in the book, as well as the connections to ensure the publication comes to the attention of concertgoers and others who knew George Zukerman.

Pille Bunnell, who loved to listen to Zukerman's DGG recording of bassoon concertos when she was a child, did not meet George in person till 2017, when he was the impresario for a musical tour on the Douro River. She was enchanted by his stories, and at one of the onboard informal dinners she suggested he write a book. Turned out she wasn't the first to make that suggestion, but she took it further and promised to help him with the conversion from stage to page. Pille and George worked closely on the book over the next two years. A few days before George died, she again promised to see the book to print, but she would not have been able to keep that promise without the others.

Bryan Atkins and his wife, Gail, decided their final major trip would be a small ship cruise from Prague to Berlin on the Elbe River, sponsored by Early Music Vancouver and marketed as a study of the Reformation and the Age of Enlightenment. Luckily the trip was more music than study, with the music part designed by Matthew White and George Zukerman. George took control of the dozen or so concerts, introducing each one with humorous tales of his adventures in music as both musician and impresario. It was then that, like Pille, Bryan mentioned these tales needed a book. George's reply: "It's almost done." Bryan's only regret is that there will not be a book tour. Like George L., Bryan called on his music, marketing and publishing connections to ensure the book reached its audience.

When Audrey McClellan heard George on CBC Radio's *This Is My Music* in July 2022, she had fond memories of a concert he gave in 1976, in her hometown in northern Alberta, as part of his Overture Concert series. He was wearing both his hats there, as virtuoso and as the impresario who organized the series. She wrote to thank him for the memories, and George, noticing from her email signature that she was an editor, asked if she could help with the book. Sadly, he died before she was able to work directly with him and Pille, but Audrey did give the manuscript its final edit. Through her connections in the publishing industry, she also found the perfect publisher for the book.

Wendy Atkinson had known Audrey for years through the B.C. book community. Shortly after Wendy acquired Ronsdale Press, Audrey approached her on behalf of the "co-conspirators" regarding publication of George's memoirs. From her previous work at the Chan Centre for the Performing Arts, Wendy knew George's reputation for organizing concerts and tours, but she was unaware of his extensive solo career and his impact beyond B.C. When she read the manuscript, she was amazed by the breadth of his professional career and captivated by his touring stories. She recognized that his anecdotes capture a vital period in Canada's musical history and are vivid reminders of the lengths musicians will go to tour our vast country. George's memoirs go beyond simply capturing a life. He expanded the cultural reach of classical music in Canada; no small feat and Canada is better for it. That is what inspired Wendy to publish his book.

INDEX

Page numbers for photographs are in bold.

IBM, 33
Idlewild Airport (New York), 43
Infantino, Luigi, 219–21
International Musician (magazine),
42
Iqaluit (Nunavut), 195, 196, 206–7
Israel, in 1950s, 51–53, 56–60, 65–66
Israel Philharmonic Orchestra, 18,
42–45, 53–55, 59–66

Jake's Corner (Yukon), 205
Jew in Revolt, The (Zukerman), 24
Jewish Daily Forward (newspaper), 18,
21–22
Jewish Newsletter (Zukerman), 24–25
Jewish Western Bulletin (newspaper),
40, 41
Johannesburg (South Africa), 147
Julius Caesar (Shakespeare), 123–24

Kálmán, Emmerich, 28–29
Kangiqsu1lujjuaq (Quebec), 200,
212–13
Kangiqsujuaq (Quebec), 200, 212
Karajan, Herbert von, 117, 187
Kaunas (Lithuania), 168
Kedmah (ship), 51–53
Kerman, Joseph, 191, 248. *See also*
Zukerman, Joseph Wilfred
(G.Z.'s brother)
Kessler, Susan, 87–88
Kleine Kammermusic für Bläserquintett
(Hindemith), 13–14
Köchel, Ludwig Alois Friedrich von,
186, 189
Koudriavtsev, Nicholas, 158–60
Kraken, 180
Krasnoyarsk (Siberia), 171, 172–75
Krasnoyarsk Children's Choir, 173,
175–76

Ksienski, Netta. *See* Zukerman, Netta
Ksienski (G.Z.'s first wife)
Kupferman, Meyer, 16–17
Kuujjuaq (Quebec), 200, 212–13

"La donna è mobile" (Verdi), 227
La Guardia, Fiorello, 11
Landy, John, 73
Laverock, George, 86
Le Sacre du printemps (Stravinsky),
117, 181
Leach, George, 72, 73
Leningrad (Soviet Union), 160, 163
Levin, Yitzhak-Meir, 59–60
Lithuania, 20, 170
Little Eagles of Siberia, 173, 175–76
Lord's Day Alliance, 75, 99
Lyric Sonatina (Coulthard), 184

macaque monkeys, 240–41
Malawi, 239
Mandela, Nelson, 145, 146
Manitoba Hydro, 223, 225
Mansbridge, Peter, 102
Marriage of Figaro (Mozart), 30, 198
Mauritius, 135
Merci, Luigi, 185
Minsk (Belarus), 168–69
"Miracle Mile," 73
Mission Concert Society, 242
Moennig, W. Hans, 151–55, 157
Morning Journal (newspaper), 18, 22,
24
Moscow (Soviet Union), 163–64
Moscow Philharmonic Orchestra, **159**
Motel 6, 36
Movshovitz, Miss, 8–9
Mozart (Saskatchewan), 90
Mozart, Wolfgang Amadeus, 30, 35,
147, 155, 160, 177, 186–90, 198

ABOUT THE AUTHOR

After a short stint with the Vancouver Symphony, George Zukerman's career as an international soloist took off. He was the first foreign bassoonist invited to perform as a soloist in the USSR, South Africa and China. Simultaneously, he was arranging concert tours across Canada and negotiating with the byzantine and secretive bureaucracy of the Soviet Union to bring USSR musicians to Canada at the height of the Cold War. Even in his nineties, George was setting up concert societies in small communities in B.C., booking cross-country tours and arranging concerts in his hometown of White Rock, B.C. George Zukerman died on February 1, 2023, just days before his ninety-sixth birthday.